KU-471-309

RUSSELL JAMES

THE PLAYING CARD KILLER

This is a FLAME TREE PRESS book

FLAME TREE PRESS
6 Melbray Mews, London, SW6 3NS, UK
flametreepress.com

Distribution and warehouse:
Marston Book Services Ltd
160 Eastern Avenue, Milton Park, Abingdon, Oxon, OX14 4SB
www.marston.co.uk

Publisher's Note: This is a work of fiction. Names, characters, places, and incidents are a product of the author's imagination. Locales and public names are sometimes used for atmospheric purposes. Any resemblance to actual people, living or dead, or to businesses, companies, events, institutions, or locales is completely coincidental.

Thanks to the Flame Tree Press team, including:
Taylor Bentley, Frances Bodiam, Federica Ciaravella, Don D'Auria, Chris Herbert, Matteo Middlemiss, Josie Mitchell, Mike Spender, Cat Taylor, Maria Tissot, Nick Wells, Gillian Whitaker.

The cover is created by Flame Tree Studio with
thanks to Nik Keevil and Shutterstock.com.
The font families in this book are Avenir and Bembo.

Flame Tree Press is an imprint of Flame Tree Publishing Ltd
flametreepublishing.com

A copy of the CIP data for this book is available from the British Library.

HB ISBN: 978-1-78758-124-1
PB ISBN: 978-1-78758-123-4
ebook ISBN: 978-1-78758-125-8
Also available in FLAME TREE AUDIO

Printed in the UK at Clays, Suffolk

RUSSELL JAMES

THE PLAYING CARD KILLER

FLAME TREE PRESS
London & New York

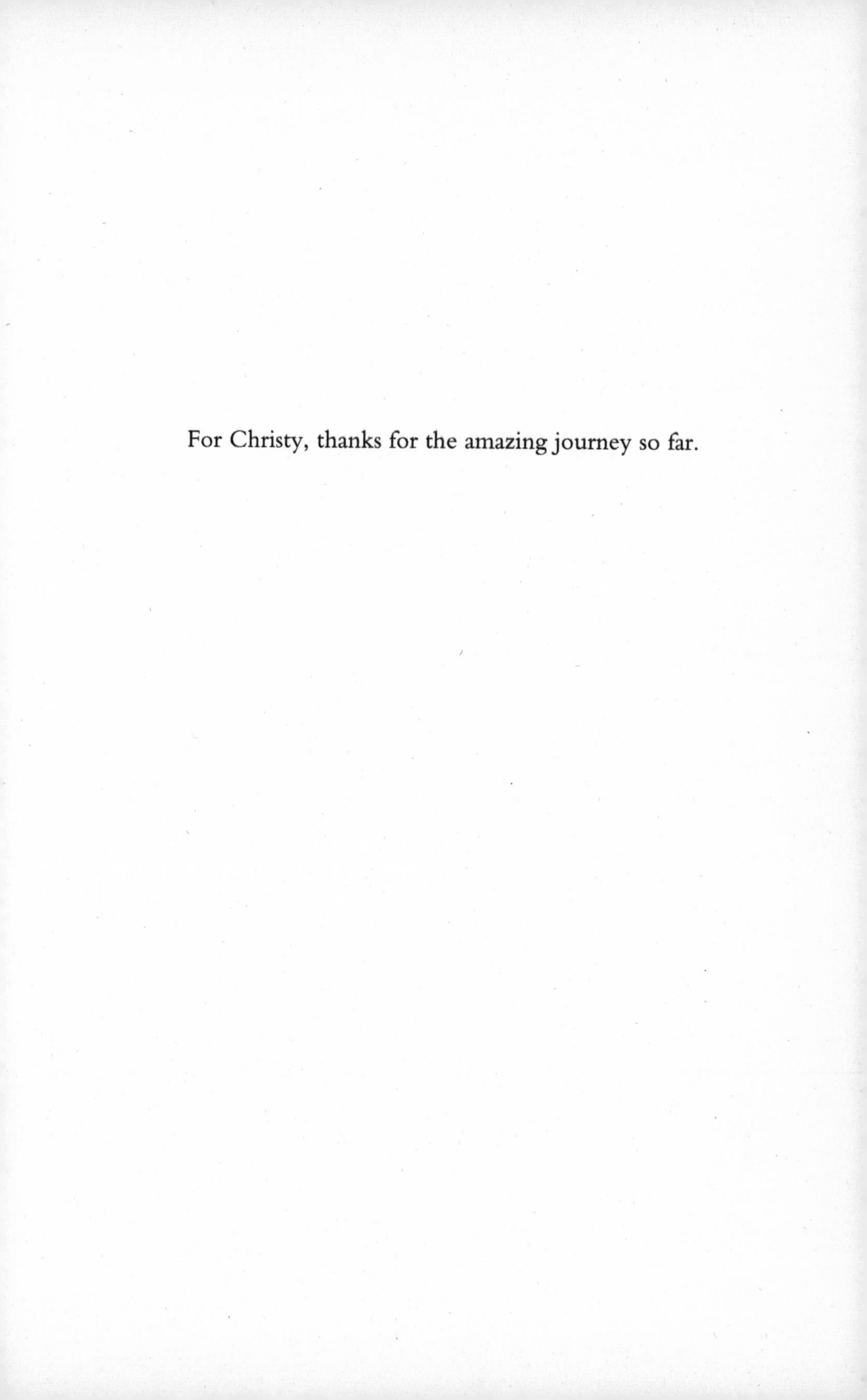

For Christy, thanks for the amazing journey so far.

CHAPTER ONE

Amidst aisles of cheerful childhood diversions, he shopped for the perfect killer's signature.

In the store's ultra-bright light, all the primary-coloured plastic toys shouted for attention. Skateboards' vibrant neon wheels screamed to touch pavement and race. Posters trumpeted video games that promised glossy escapes to amazing, undiscovered worlds. Bicycles' polished chrome offered assurances of long summer days under clear blue skies.

But he passed by all these distractions without a second glance. He stopped before a very simple display in the board games section, a tiny rack holding a half-dozen decks of playing cards. He stroked his chin, and fell deep into the decision-making process.

He discounted two of the six, the back design on one being cartoon flamingoes, and the other being a hippopotamus in a sailor outfit. Both seemed too juvenile, too lighthearted for the weighty task he had in mind. That only left four options.

Three of the remaining four were geometric designs: one a crosshatch of blue lines, one a set of green concentric circles like a bull's eye, and one that looked like a black-and-white Persian rug. But the fourth one caught his eye, and not just for its red colour.

A flourish-filled design swooped around and crisscrossed the outside third of the rectangle. A mermaid adorned each corner. In the white centre were two stacked red circles. Within the top circle stood the figure of a thin, smiling woman in a long, Greek-style toga, her feet near the centre of the card. Behind her rose a wide oak tree, branches full of leaves in springtime bloom. She held a flower in one hand.

In the bottom circle, an inverted figure of the same woman stood before the same tree, sole-to-sole with the other woman. Here, the tree's branches were bare, the oak locked in winter's

grip. Worry erased the smile on the woman's face. The flower in her hand was gone, replaced by a small skull, an oddly gruesome detail for the artwork.

He liked it.

Yes, the design spoke to him, spoke to the plan. He picked up the deck and flipped the box around so the winter woman, the harbinger of death, now stood upright. He smiled. Much better this way, with death ascendant, and the springtime woman now falling toward judgement day.

Using the deck's jokers would mock the solemnity of his task, but that still left fifty-two cards, fifty-two opportunities to set the world a little more upright, one snuffed life at a time.

He caressed the slick shrink-wrap that protected the pack, running a finger around the top's sharp edge. He raised the pack to his lips, the way another would coax a lover closer.

"What an adventure we are about to have," he whispered.

CHAPTER TWO

"Hell no! You are not going off your medications."

Daniela Schiavetta glared at him, adamant and furious, a combination Brian Sheridan didn't know she had in her. His cute, tiny, auburn-haired girlfriend had the nicest disposition in the world.

"I've been on them since I was a kid," Brian said. "I'm almost twenty-one. I think it's time to see if I still need them."

"Hell yeah, you do!" She paced the living room of his apartment like a caged tiger. She still wore a pair of oversized, dark blue scrubs from her shift at the veterinary clinic. They flapped like wings with each of her emphatic arm gestures. "Do you still have moments of extreme anxiety?"

Brian wouldn't call them moments as much as he would call them hours. "A few," he lied.

Anxiety and attention deficit issues had plagued him all his life, a gift from his birth mother, bestowed by the cocktail of drugs and alcohol ingested during her pregnancy. He'd called the onrush of an anxiety attack a 'visit from Mr. Jitters' when he was a child. But gallows humour made it no better, and the effects were usually devastating. It was true that meds had enabled him to navigate a bumpy course through middle and high school. But he was an adult now, with a job, no longer under his parents' roof.

"I'm a lot better than when I was a kid," he added.

"You're better because you're on meds," Daniela said. She stopped pacing and took a deep breath. She looked hard into his eyes. "We've been together nine months. I'm saying this as someone who cares about you. You need those medications."

"How do you know? How do I know? How does the doctor know, until I make a go without them?"

"Brian, you aren't one hundred percent even with them."

"I'm not one hundred percent *because* of them. They make me fuzzy, dull my senses, slow my brain. I can feel them holding me back."

"No, what you are feeling is called normalcy. That's what not having your brain race in three directions at once feels like."

"Maybe I can do better without them, get a better job, a real career." Brian worked as an evening-shift security guard, a position that catered to both his discomfort with crowds of people, and the insomnia his medications seemed to create. From his original goal of becoming a cop, security guard had been as close as he got.

"Look, Brian," Daniela said. "I spend the day mending broken animals. I don't want to spend the night fixing a broken person. You promise me you're going to stay on your meds, okay?"

Looking at her now practically made him sigh. With her pixie hairstyle she stood like a wingless Tinkerbell in the centre of his under-furnished apartment. Honestly, a day didn't go by where he didn't wonder what she was doing spreading her fairy dust in his life.

Her doe eyes searched his in anticipation, waiting for him to promise, to give the answer he knew he could only deliver as a lie.

"I'll stay on my meds," he said.

She gave him a hug, strong but angled just a bit off-centre. It perfectly summed up their relationship, one that hovered somewhere between friends and fiancés. Then she headed for the door, flashing him a mischievous smile on the way. "Have fun with Sidney tonight."

"Yeah, we'll party hearty." His voice dripped with sarcasm. Sidney, his evening-shift coworker, was a total ass.

She closed the door behind her. Brian's guilt rushed in and sucked all the air from the room. He wished he could make her understand, but he couldn't. No one who wasn't permanently medicated could comprehend what it was like.

He'd lost track of exactly what was in the pills he'd been taking all these years. The combinations shifted, but it was always a concoction of anti-anxiety meds and something to keep his ADHD at bay. He couldn't deny that they helped, but just as not taking them had mental side effects, so did taking them. They turned the world from colour to black and white. Sharp edges became indistinct.

A decade-plus of living in a dull haze was enough.

Adding insult to injury were the physical side effects. They'd stunted the development of his long bones, and he was inches shorter than he should have been, and very slight of build. The drugs also completely screwed with his appetite. He often forgot about meals until he passed out from not eating.

He knew those downsides would carry no weight with Daniela. She'd travelled this jagged road with her schizophrenic father. She hadn't said it explicitly, but he could hear it in her tone and between the words. The meds stayed or she went.

He'd be better without them. She'd see. Their relationship would be better. Once sobriety had stripped away the gauzy feeling that plagued him, he'd be so much more in touch with his emotions, so much better able to feel whatever it was the rest of the world seemed to feel when they were with someone special. She'd see, and their relationship would blast into a higher, more permanent orbit.

He entered the bathroom and opened the medicine cabinet. A pharmacy worth of pills lined one shelf, little yellow silos with white tops, filled to the brim with all that either kept him stable or kept him suppressed. He was about to find out which.

One by one, he poured the contents of each bottle into the open toilet, a stream of pills that pitter-pattered into the clear water. When he was done, he'd created a submerged pyramid, a monument not to some dead pharaoh, but to something worse, to the life he'd never lived. He pressed the toilet handle. A swirl of water spun the miniature edifice back into hundreds of tiny capsules, then sucked them down and left the bowl dry and empty.

He thought about how when that flush made it into nearby Tampa Bay, there would be some seriously stoned fish.

"No turning back now," he muttered to himself.

He knew it would take time before his body purged itself completely of the medications. But he already felt different.

He felt free.

CHAPTER THREE

One week later.

Terror fills her eyes, opened so wide that each iris becomes an island in a sea of white. Every grain of mascara, every stroke of eyeliner displays in perfect detail. Those dark accents, originally added to allure, now only highlight her horror.

This is all he sees, like some wide-screen close-up in an IMAX theatre, but in 1940s black and white. All is silent, yet somehow these eyes are shrieking.

While he sees the woman's panic, he feels the evil that hovers over her, senses the malevolence that reflects in her eyes. He knows he shouldn't be here, shouldn't be part of this experience.

The view zooms out a bit. Her glossy, sparkling lips pull back in a silent, oval scream. Bright white teeth frame her bouncing uvula. Under her perfect foundation, her cheeks flush. Tears roll from the corners of her eyes and down toward her ears.

The view zooms out some more. The woman lies on a cheap linoleum floor, scuff-marked and dirty. Two hands grip a thick, dark rope around her neck. The greyscale of the vision offers no colour, but he senses that the rope is red, a rich, vibrant shade of ruby. It appears softer than the usual nylon type.

The severed ends of surgical gloves cover the killer's fingertips. The assailant's knuckles whiten as he pulls the rope tighter.

His heart skips a beat. The woman is a stranger, but the hands are all too familiar. They are his. But worse, he can feel what they feel. He senses the power that surges through them, and shudders at the dark delight it inspires. He cannot control them. It is as if they control him.

The woman chokes, gasps. The hands pull the rope tighter.

Now he panics. He wants, he hopes, he begs for the power to stop the atrocity he is committing. But his hands keep pulling, powered by something stronger than his conscious self, something blacker than midnight.

The woman's eyes bulge to the point he fears they will burst. Then the light leaves them, and they go glassy.

★ ★ ★

Brian Sheridan snapped wide awake. His racing heart thudded against the mattress. The silent darkness of his bedroom seeped into and dissolved the memory of his nightmare. His pulse ramped down. The clock read 4:15 a.m.

He sighed. *Thank God.* Too early to get up for most people, way too early for someone like him who clocks in for work in the afternoon. He collapsed back into the pillow.

His throat felt like sandpaper. His mouth crackled, parched as an Arizona rest stop and reminded him why he'd just had that explicit nightmare. No meds. Two of the big withdrawal side effects were cottonmouth and strange dreams. Hallucinations and cold sweats were two more extreme impacts, but Brian hoped his symptoms wouldn't go that far.

"Damn it." He wasn't going to get back to sleep feeling like this. He headed to the kitchen for a drink. He didn't bother turning on a light.

The fridge door opened like a sunrise in the darkness. He flinched against the light, pulled out a bottle of water, and slammed the door shut. He downed half the container in an instant.

Back in his bedroom, he double-checked the cardboard wedged into the windows to block the sunlight. He tucked an errant edge back into the corner of the frame. He really needed to get back to sleep before the blazing Florida sun started to do its work, because then his body would decide to be up for the day. He was by nature a morning person, and each day he battled to stick to a sleep schedule matched to a job that kept him up until midnight.

He dropped back into bed, and managed to sleep until 8:00 a.m. Way better than he'd expected. He got up, started a pot of coffee, and retrieved two apples from his crisper drawer. Minimally processed food was one of the recommendations doctors had given his mother to alleviate Brian's mental issues. It probably didn't make any difference, but she'd stuck with it, and now Brian stuck with it out of habit.

He turned on his computer for a look at the world. The usual stream of distress popped up. War. Terror. Economic issues. A cyclone in Asia.

An ad popped up for a self-improvement course. 'Awaken the unknown you.' The known Brian was more than enough, thank you. He clicked on the Close button. The ad wavered, then went away.

He clicked over to his email. Two dozen spams clogged the page. But a message from Daniela caught his eye. He opened the email.

Still with Mom. She's recovering well, thanks for asking.

He winced. If there was such a thing as a sarcastic font, the last sentence would have been in it, and in bold. Daniela's mother lived in Gainesville and just had a knee replaced. Daniela was there supporting her recovery. The girl was born to heal things, people or animals.

Brian hadn't asked about her mother's progress. While Daniela was a dream, her mother was a bit of a bitch as far as Brian was concerned, and wishing her a speedy recovery wasn't on his to-do list.

The note's next line read: *You are still alive, right?*

That little dig hit home. He had barely spoken with or texted Daniela since she left a week ago, the day after he promised to stay on his meds.

That was why he'd stopped taking them after she left. By the time she got back, the worst of any withdrawal symptoms would be over. She'd be so thrilled with the new and improved Brian that she couldn't possibly be mad at him. He'd even be magnanimous and skip delivering the 'I told you so' that she'd so richly deserve.

But while he'd had some minor physical withdrawal symptoms, this early morning nightmare was the first of the promised psychological side effects. If those started kicking in now, their reign might not be over by the time Daniela returned. And he sure didn't want her to see him like this.

A feared, familiar twinge rippled through him, that mixture in his gut of dread, panic and adrenaline that presaged an anxiety attack. His brain screamed into a higher gear. His skin seemed to catch fire as neurons began to blast signals that made no sense.

If he didn't get a grip on this, he'd practically incapacitate himself. He'd done it before, but not for a decade. He hadn't fully danced with Mr. Jitters in a very long time, which only amplified his galloping terror.

Sweat prickled his forehead. His hands began to shake. The awful sensation of losing control came on like a runaway train. A hundred images of the hell that was ahead when Daniela returned flashed by him. She'd definitely walk out forever. He felt as helpless and terrified as he had when he was a child.

He realised he was hyperventilating, making everything worse. He focused on controlling his breaths, on slowing his sprinting heart.

In deep, out slow, he focused.

He calmed down a bit, pushed old Mr. Jitters further away. Brian needed to take action, positive action to address the anxiety's source. With shaking hands, he typed an answer to Daniela's note.

Doing fine, just very busy. Can't wait for you to come home.

He paused. Then with one finger, one slow letter at a time, he added:

My best to your mom.

He cringed and hit Send.

The worst of the panic subsided. The dread cooled down from white hot to warm red. He breathed as deeply as he could.

He turned away from the screen. It pinged that he had a new email. He sighed. Daniela must have been staring at her phone, ready to pounce on his reply. He turned back to his screen and checked the new message.

It's Your Time to Awaken read the title of the email from the Totally You Institute.

Half of him was thrilled it wasn't a terse, immediate rebuttal from Daniela. The other half of him was pissed that this new scam shop would be the spam generator of the week. He deleted the email and logged off.

He munched on one of the apples as disconnected images from his nightmare rose in his mind. They gave him a chill. He really wasn't happy his subconscious was capable of imagining himself as a killer.

His phone buzzed to distract him from his self-loathing. He had a text from his adoptive father, Derek.

It was a toss-up as to whether a message from Derek was better than one from the Totally You Institute about awakening his inner Brian. He opened the text.

Your mother wants you to join us for dinner day after tomorrow at 5.

Even in a text, the guy managed to sound imperious and distant. What a gift he had. Dinner with the ol' fam wasn't high on Brian's list of things to do. His parents and sister did not put the 'fun' in dysfunctional family.

Derek and his wife Camilla had started out with the best intentions, adopting him as a newborn when Camilla's doctor declared conception an impossibility. They had been assured he was a healthy baby coming from a good environment, right here in the old USA. The adoption records were closed and sealed, but the agency assured them their new son was perfect.

They soon found out otherwise. By the time he was a few years old, Brian's issues were apparent. Evidence quickly mounted that he had ADHD in spades and some serious anxiety issues. Their paediatrician gave the diagnosis of some kind of foetal poisoning. Drugs, alcohol, both. He'd need to interview the birth mother. But sealed records meant that wasn't going to happen. Brian didn't come with a money-back guarantee, so Camilla and Derek had to buckle in for the long haul.

And then, despite all assertions that she never could, Camilla got pregnant with the girl they'd really wanted. So Brian went from being a regrettable burden to be being an unnecessary, regrettable burden. Sister Ariana's birth sent Brian's life into eclipse. The adopted son became nearly invisible, his problems all his own.

He couldn't easily beg off from this text message invitation-cum-summons from his father. His parents knew his work schedule and that he'd have the day off. They also knew he didn't have a social life to speak of, so there went that excuse. The past legal woes his condition had spawned meant he couldn't just sever all ties and blow off his family, not until after he turned twenty-one in several months.

See you then, he sent back to Derek.

The day just kept getting better. And it wasn't even 10:00 a.m. yet.

CHAPTER FOUR

"Dude, you look like six pounds of shit."

Brian gave Sidney a weak smile. "I'm sure that you mean that in the best possible way."

"Ain't no good way to look like a heap of shit."

The two shared the Orange Star Trucking Terminal gatehouse. In contrast to Brian's para-police uniform, Sidney wore a dark blue coverall with the trucking logo on the back. He had it unzipped to the waist, which only made the tall, gaunt man look leaner. Sweat glistened like diamonds against his dark black skin. He wiped it away with a dirty rag from his pocket.

The narrow gatehouse building covered a slim island between the yard's inbound and outbound security gates. His first week there, Brian had managed to suppress his initial anxiety about having some truck barrel into the little shack in the middle of the night. The room was a tight fit for two. Sidney had to stand. But since it was the only air-conditioned space on the yard, he didn't complain.

Brian covered evening shift security at the terminal, from 2:00 p.m. to 10:00 p.m. Sidney, ten years Brian's senior, ran the crane. The terminal worked what were called combis, fifty-two foot commercial trucking containers. They got loaded on a rail car somewhere, and Sidney used the crane to unload them here and drop them on a set of wheels. Then a trucker would pick them up for their final destination. Train arrivals tended to be about as irregular as the digestive tract of the fibre-free, so the entire trucking schedule was in constant flux. The evening shift never had any supervision due to a lack of need. Sidney unloaded the combis, gave the train manifest to Brian, and Brian signed the loads out to arriving drivers. It was a hard job to screw up.

Working at Orange Star included a lot of waiting time. Cops sometimes describe their job as hours of boredom punctuated by minutes of sheer terror. Orange Star provided hours of boredom punctuated by minutes of mild activity. Brian gravitated to the job because of the slow pace and solitude. Quiet acted as a perfect salve for his tendency to unsubstantiated panic.

Sidney, however, seemed to have ended up there by default. From what Brian could tell through their minimal conversations, the crane operator had been driven there by child support payments and a sketchy personal history.

"I didn't sleep well last night," Brian said.

"We ain't having no bonding experience here." Sidney stuffed the rag back in his pocket. "I'm here for the cold air, not to be your shrink or nothing."

A train whistle sounded outside the yard. Sidney checked the clock on the wall. He zipped up his coverall.

"Saved by the whistle," he said. "The one-oh-five is right on time, several hours late."

Sidney left the door half-open as he departed the guard shack. Brian rolled over in his chair and pulled it closed. His phone buzzed and he pulled it out of his pocket. The screen read 'Message from 2263'.

This number wasn't familiar. He opened the message.

Awake at last.

"Damn it!" he said to himself. The New Age whatever-it-was had his email and his cell phone number. This was going to get old fast. Brian hit the Delete button, and sent the message into the electronic netherworld.

Sidney wouldn't be back until the end of the shift, so except for a few perimeter patrols and whatever truckers rolled in, he was in for a dull evening. He flicked on the tiny desktop TV. As long as it wasn't raining, the antenna picked up the three major Tampa networks and four static-filled stations with preachers touting Jesus, one in Spanish. It wasn't Netflix, but it also didn't eat up his data plan. He tuned in the local evening news.

Headlights lit the booth as a semi rolled up the long road to the gate. Brian turned down the TV volume. His minutes of mild activity had arrived. *Hip hip hooray.*

He picked up the clipboard carrying the evening's manifests.

Headlights flashed up to high beams and lit the inside of the shack like a solar flare. Brian shielded his eyes and squinted at the oncoming truck. Its diesel engine roared, loud and deep enough to make the shack shudder. The truck leaned left as it swerved head-on for the little house. The big silver grill yawned open like the mouth of a killer shark. The truck's horn blasted, not to warn, but to trumpet triumph.

Fear swept through Brian like wildfire. He jumped up from his rolling chair and sent it sailing to the shack's rear. Suddenly, feet from the shack, the truck bulls-eyed a protective concrete bollard. The post pulverised into a cloud of grey dust.

Brian launched himself out the side exit door. His foot hooked the threshold. He slammed face-first onto the oil-slicked asphalt and closed his eyes.

The truck smashed into the guard shack. It exploded in a thundering shower of wood and glass.

Everything went silent. His expected pelting by flying debris didn't happen. No semi tyres crushed his feet. Brian rolled over and opened his eyes. The guard shack still stood, completely unmolested. The access road stretched out dark and empty.

Brian's heart pounded hard. He stood on shaky legs and reentered the shack. A high-pitched, shrieking cackle sounded behind him. He spun around. A white top hat covered in yellow stars spun on its brim in the driveway. Then it vanished.

He remembered the warning about withdrawal-induced hallucinations. That little excursion into *The Twilight Zone* wasn't what Brian had envisioned. Hallucinations were supposed to be like being trapped in the Beatles' *Yellow Submarine* movie or seeing a Cheshire cat. What he'd just experienced was his subconscious trying to scare him to death. He did not want to do that again.

At the driveway's far end, headlights flared in the darkness. Brian's heart beat faster as the truck approached. He gripped the edge of the desk, ready to run when this semi spun out of control. It pulled up alongside the shack. Brian froze. A wide, redfaced driver stared down from the window, Atlanta Braves hat askew on his boxy head.

"Well, you gonna sign me in or what?" the driver asked. "Ain't got all night."

Brian shook his head and admitted everything was normal. He grabbed his clipboard and stepped out to sign in the trucker.

The remaining hours on his shift promised to be long ones.

CHAPTER FIVE

Brian sagged, bone-weary tired, by the time he made it home that night. Between yesterday's poor sleep and the long, anxiety-ridden day, he fought to stay awake. He skipped food, skipped a shower, and just collapsed onto his unmade bed. He was out the instant his head hit the pillow.

* * *

It isn't a dream his subconscious spins for him tonight, so much as it is a memory. He's a boy, or he must be because he seems small in his bed and he's in his childhood bedroom. The setting sun bathes the wall in rich ochre stripes through the window blinds' slats. The schoolbooks on the desk and the pictures on the wall tell him he is in elementary school, fourth grade if he remembers correctly. All is silent, not because the scene lacks natural sound, but because he is cut off from it, as if his dream has decided to exclude all senses but sight.

It must be one of those childhood nights where his anxiety had taken control. Perhaps he'd made a mess eating, dropped something and broken it, or embarrassed Derek and Camilla in front of company. In the pre-medication days, or during the windows when they went out of balance, such occurrences were commonplace. This was always the result, sent to his room for the night, to bed no matter the time.

The awful mix of emotions that plagued his younger years is at full boil. Frustration at his lack of control, humiliation at his familial ostracism. But over both reigns fear, a combination of acute panic, layered over a chronic trepidation that such terror will haunt him all of his life. In this present-day playback, he can so much better dissect the multiple threads that weave the screwed-up emotional tapestry of his life.

His sentence to solitary confinement only stokes the fire of his anxiety. The oncoming sleepless night, and the upcoming morning's potential for punishment, are simply more fuel for the flame. Despite the fall swelter outside, his room is over-chilled, a Sheridan family hallmark, though the cold of the family's heart needs no physical manifestation to match it. His right leg begins to bounce beneath the sheets and he knows Mr. Jitters is about to come over and play.

A shadowy figure appears, sitting on the desk. The sunset stripes divide him into red-frosted layer cake sections from the neck down. His arms and legs are both impossibly long and impossibly thin. His right leg crosses over the left, and the dangling foot dances in perfect time with Brian's fidgeting leg.

Brian startles, and yanks the bedspread out from under the mattress's foot and all the way up around his neck. The desk lamp snaps on by itself. It delivers more illumination than it possibly could, a near spotlight on his intruder.

In the light, his clothes are nearly blinding. A blazing-white jacket and over-flared bell-bottomed pants. Wide, red stripes run up the pants and accentuate his spindly legs. The jacket's vertical stripes are bright blue, a jarring juxtaposition with the pants, but not near so much as the neon-yellow T-shirt he wears beneath it. The tight shirt reveals every ripple of his emaciated ribcage. A white top hat with a constellation of yellow stars completes the ensemble. Brian remembers the hat from his hallucination in the guard shack. No strands of hair protrude from under the hat.

The jacket sleeves also flare, and from them extend hands too delicate to be real, fingers twice as long and half as thick as normal, but somehow proportional to the gangly arms and legs. The visitor's face is gaunt, his eyes wide and incredibly white, the sockets around them coated black as night. Ashy greasepaint covers the rest of his face. Black makeup paints his head in the style of a skull, complete with a toothy rictus drawn over and around his own thin lips. Somehow, an actual skull would have been less terrifying.

He is all the more horrifying because in this flashback dream of Brian's childhood, amidst all he sees and feels as so familiar, this spectre is not. Like the stain on white linen, like the black cloud in a blue sky, like the madman outside the asylum walls, he does not belong.

"Brian!" the figure shouts, his voice a high-pitched shriek. It shatters the dream's silent-movie soundtrack like a clap of thunder. Young Brian jumps under his bed sheets.

The intruder leaps from the desk, arms extended. For a second his fingertips flash as if made of sparklers, then extinguish with ten overlapping firecracker explosions. He lands upon the edge of the bed, running in place at a cartoon-character pace, sending the mattress bouncing. "I'm back, man!"

No introduction is needed. Brian has never met this manifestation, but can feel the familiar, dreaded connection. The amorphous presence he called Mr. Jitters now has a face, a body, a voice. The beat of Brian's bouncing leg doubles. Panic swells.

Mr. Jitters lets rip a high-pitched cackling laugh that sends a chill up Brian's spine. He perches on the foot of the bed. He reaches down with his incredibly long arms, and with one hand on either side of Brian's tap-dancing foot, pounds out a perfect accompaniment with the flat of his palms. "It's the beat, it's that groovy beat, can you dig it?"

He drops down and straddles Brian across the waist in a low squat. He only clears Brian by millimetres. Both Brian's legs now thrum with anxiety, jumping back and forth in a synchronised rhythm. Mr. Jitters bends close, face inches from Brian's so that white makeup and that horrid painted-tooth smile fill his field of view.

Brian's heart slams in his chest. Sweat rolls down from his temples. The adult part of him wants to scream, wants to punch Mr. Jitters in the jaw and send him flying. But he is trapped in his younger self, bound by the deeper fears and more desperate insecurity of a seven-year-old boy. He cannot move, cannot speak, and that fury he cannot release only fuels the evil rush of Mr. Jitters' transmitted anxiety. He bites the sheets bunched up around his mouth.

"No meds, no restrictions," Mr. Jitters screeches. "We're

bonding like never before. I've always been part of you. Soon you'll be part of me!"

Mr. Jitters reaches forward with one elongated finger. He stabs at Brian's chest. The finger slices between his ribs and pierces Brian's heart like a dagger laced with cayenne pepper. Anxiety radiates through him like a nuclear blast wave.

Finally, he screams.

★ ★ ★

Brian jolted awake with a shriek. He was back in his apartment, back to being almost twenty-one. Sweat soaked his T-shirt and his chest galloped like a wild horse in flight. Daylight pierced the edges of the cardboard window coverings. The clock read just after six in the morning.

"Holy shit," he whispered. He focused on taking deep, cleansing breaths, on counting heartbeats and slowing them down. He looked at all the details of the real world around him and pressed back the horrific memories of the one he'd just dreamt.

Mr. Jitters' image hung tough, unwilling to be banished and consigned as a product of imagination. In his childhood, when he'd told himself Mr. Jitters was on the way, he'd never created such a fully formed vision of his anxiety's alter ego. He was a concept, not a character. But this adult version, fueled by drug withdrawal and a more developed imagination, was far more real than Brian wanted. It was certainly more real than his seven-year-old self could have handled. He even doubted his twenty-year-old self was fully prepared for it.

No sleep could follow that nightmare, at least not now. His eyes burned red and itchy against the unwelcome daylight. He rolled out of bed to start the day.

An hour later, recharged with coffee and a goat cheese omelette, he pulled up his email. Nothing from Daniela. But two missives from the Totally You Institute awaited him. *Be More Than You've Ever Imagined!* demanded one. *Time To Grow Into Who You Should Always Have Been* ordered the other.

These self-help gurus ought to go a few rounds with Mr. Jitters. If they could keep him quiet, Brian would sign right up. He deleted the emails.

CHAPTER SIX

That evening at work felt fuzzy. From the moment he'd released Terry from day shift, Brian felt as if he was watching the world through teased cotton. The last few days, he'd barely slept and the physical and psychological effects of dropping his meds were getting worse, not better with time. The sun had set and the yard's hazy lighting only made him feel worse. He added an extra spoonful of coffee to his standard evening brew for a caffeinated boost to get him through until the night shift arrived.

Eventually, the guard shack got to everyone, even Brian. Too cramped, too stifling, and too isolated, no matter how much audio and video entertainment he tried to pump in. His two security checks of the yard each evening weren't enough of an escape, and every now and then, he just needed air, even if it was thick, humid, and tainted with the fumes of diesel trucks. His pent-up energy had to be spent. Brian had to admit to himself that the need had grown greater since he dropped his meds. Not a good reason to go back on them, but still not deniable.

No trucks were due for hours, so he left the shack. Once out of the air-conditioning, he broke out into an immediate sweat. The setting of the sun hadn't abated the heat. The heavy air seemed to crawl down his throat, intent on his suffocation. He headed down an aisle between the containers on his way to the crane.

Halfway there, tapping sounded from the top of the containers to his right. A simple rhythm. Tap-tap. Tap-tap. He paused. The sound stopped. He looked up into the gloom, and saw nothing. He started walking again.

The tapping restarted, this time from up on his left, a bit faster. Brian kept walking. The tapping paced him. Then the high-pitched, shrieking laugh of Mr. Jitters shattered the night's quiet.

Anxiety swept through him. The combis stretched twice as

tall as usual. They canted inward, ready to topple in on him from both sides. The tapping along the combi roofs accelerated to match his soaring pulse. He didn't need this, didn't need hallucinations plaguing him awake and asleep, at home and at work. He broke into a run for the end of the combis.

Footsteps pounded the combi roofs alongside him. He imagined Mr. Jitters, gangly legs and skull-painted face, matching his moves, ready to jump down and block his way. Blood thrummed in his ears. He sprinted for the end of the row.

And slammed head on into Sidney. Sidney staggered back a step, but Brian bounced backward and went sprawling to the ground. He scrambled back to his feet and scanned the combi roofs. Nothing. The tapping and the pounding of Mr. Jitters' feet were gone. The combis were back to normal size.

"Damn it, what the hell is wrong with you?" Sidney said. "Why you even out of your damn box?"

"S-some air…stretch my legs." Brian couldn't think straight, still reeling after Mr. Jitters' stalking.

"You know you been getting even more screwed up," Sidney said. "As if that was even possible." He pushed past Brian. "Now get the hell out of my way."

★ ★ ★

Brian arrived home that night to a surprise on his doorstep. Daniela. A day early.

Brian had a ground-floor apartment in this two-storey set of six. Picking one had been trying, as he had to balance his anxieties about being trapped by a fire on the second floor with having something from an upper floor crash or seep down into a first-floor apartment. The benefit of another layer of building between his place and hurricane wind damage gave a first-floor unit the win.

His apartment entrance had a small covered porch. A light illuminated the concrete pad into an amber oasis in the darkness. Daniela sat there, back against the door, knees tucked up to her chin. The light highlighted the sprinkle of freckles that graced her cheeks. Brian loved those freckles. She looked out into the darkness of the parking lot, searching.

He really wasn't sure how to feel. He teetered on the edge between happiness that she was back, and fear that she was still pissed off that he'd been out of touch. He approached the doorway, leery. She saw him and jumped to her feet. She ran out from under the porch light with a big smile on her face. She wasn't on the warpath. Brian relaxed.

She wrapped her arms around his neck and gave him a big kiss. "So glad to be back and see you."

"I'm glad you're home," he said.

He *was* glad. He didn't feel the panicked urge to recoil at her touch, a gift only she had ever been able to give him. He'd spent his life feeling uneasy around everyone; the closer people got, the more he felt like he had insects crawling under his skin, the more he wanted to bolt and find a place to be by himself. She was the first person he'd ever known who didn't make him want to run away.

But, though she'd never done anything to earn it, he could never shake a lingering feeling of apprehension, an undercurrent of fear that she would eventually flee. Everyone always did. Even before he could push most people away, they took off on their own, repelled by that anxiety-driven side of his personality, a side he barely understood to be so off-putting. Every moment with Daniela, no matter how calm and comforting, felt like a cautious step across a frozen pond, where the ice might crack at any time and send him into the freezing water beneath.

Brian led her back to the apartment door. As he fumbled with his keys, the look on her face went from joy to concern.

"Damn, Bri, you look spent."

"Well, really busy at work, worried about you up at your mother's. I guess it all adds up."

Her eyes narrowed and she gave him a closer inspection. He opened the door and they stepped inside.

He flipped on the light and realised the place was a shambles. Dirty clothes lay around like they'd been arranged by a windstorm. A greasy pizza box gaped open on the kitchen table, leftover crescents of crust lying like little tattling smirks about his temporary full-bachelor lifestyle. A spray of opened and unopened mail spread out across the coffee table.

Ah, crap, he thought as he closed the front door behind them.

"What happened in here?" Daniela said. Her face fell. "You're off your meds, aren't you?"

The easy way out of this accusation seemed like the best option. "No," he lied. "The place just got a little out of hand knowing you weren't going to be over. You *are* home a day early."

She looked like she was mulling over whether to buy his line of bull. She sighed. "Well, I'm not spending a minute here with the place looking like a frat house. Get to work on this mess out here and I'll take care of the kitchen." She poked him in the chest to emphasise each of the next words. "This. One. Time."

"Absolutely!" He hoped he didn't sound as relieved as he felt.

Daniela went into the kitchen and he attacked the rest of the living area like a sirocco. "You really ordered a pizza?" she called from the kitchen.

"Vegetable Delight. All organic from the place down the street. Pretty good, actually."

She popped her head out from around the corner. "Look at you, living a little, trying someplace new. We're going to add that to our things-to-do list."

She was perfect for him, the little push and support to put his anxiety behind him. No need to resort to drugs. He just needed to get past the last bit of withdrawal symptoms unnoticed, and everything would be fine.

He scooped the mail off the table and arranged it in a neat stack. In a week or so, he'd tell her the truth. Once they experienced an excellent week, a normal week. She'd see he was a better person unmedicated, and then maybe they could both agree that this relationship should be something more permanent.

CHAPTER SEVEN

The red velvet caresses his hand. Though his vision is black and white, the rope has that same shade of black that red always had in old movies. He lays one, then two turns of the rope across his left palm and over his knuckles.

He grasps the rope's other end with his right hand. Two twists of the wrist bind the rope about his hand. Ten fingers close and clamp this beloved instrument, this ticket to paradise, this blessed release. Thin rubber covers shield the feeling from his fingertips, but the rest of his hands can catch the sensations. The surface is soft, like a rabbit he remembers petting in his childhood. The fibres tickle his skin.

He wraps his thumbs across his fingers, and locks them in place, as if barring them from a change of heart. He senses that such an about-face is completely unlikely.

He wishes it was. He doesn't want to be here, doesn't want to be a voyeur again in another killer's point-of-view nightmare.

The cold of the car's leather backseat penetrates his shirt and sends chill bumps across his back. The parking lot floodlights add little illumination to the vehicle's charcoal interior. He makes himself as small as possible, and tucks himself into the shadows. He stares up at the fuzzy headliner. The memory flashes by of replacing the dome light lens after removing the bulb, and it is as if he can access an earlier nightmare within this one. The possibility of admittance to infinite rooms of horror turns his blood to ice.

He pulls the rope tight. The braids bite into his palms, compress his knuckles together. The power of what he is about to do surges through his hands, up his forearms, into his shoulders. He takes a deep breath and exhales, savouring the anticipation, as a connoisseur does when sampling a glass of wine's bouquet before sipping.

The emotions repel him, as if he's touching something cold,

rank and slimy. But it is worse than that, for the contact he's making is not external, but internal. This evil touches not his fingers, but his heart, his soul.

An approaching figure blocks and unblocks the light entering the car. His pulse quickens. He slides sideways and into the passenger foot well behind the driver's seat. He crosses his forearms so the velvet rope makes a loop. The door locks pop open, the headlights cast their beams across the empty parking lot. He imagines the car chirping its happy greeting, the only one it knows.

The door opens. A purse sails in and flutters a bright feather hanging from the rearview mirror. The purse lands dead centre in the passenger seat. A woman plops into the driver's seat and closes the door. She hits the locks, and seals her fate.

His pulse hammers hard and fast, like a drumroll before the cymbals' crash.

He springs up from the back seat and loops the rope around her neck. He pulls hard and leans back, knees dug into the seatback.

The vision is silent, but the rope vibrates as the victim chokes out a gurgled scream of surprise. Her hands grasp at the velvet, but her manicured nails find no purchase against the constricting braids. Her body shudders. Her arms reach back in a panicked flail and claw at the air above his head.

His heart pounds. His manhood swells in expectancy of the night ahead. He looks up into the rearview mirror, angle pre-positioned for just this moment to see the woman's face. The feather hangs still. Terror and confusion fill the woman's wide eyes. Her mouth opens in a silent, final scream.

* * *

Brian snapped straight up in bed. He shivered, though whether from the cold sweat on his face and chest, or from the afterimages of his nightmare, he couldn't tell. His stomach seemed to turn itself inside out. He threw back the bedcovers. They landed in a heap on top of Daniela. He bounded out of bed, and straight for the bathroom.

He hit the grungy tile floor on his knees and slid the last two feet to the toilet bowl. He grasped the sticky sides with his hands.

Like a striking cobra, his spine snapped up and back, then his head plummeted forward across the bowl's rim. His heart stopped as he projectile vomited what felt like his entire set of internal organs. It arced into the toilet with a splash. A second, then third attempt delivered only painful dry heaves. He awaited a fourth. When it didn't arrive, Brian slumped to the floor beside the bowl, where the pungent stench of new vomit and old urine wasn't quite as overwhelming.

The bathroom light snapped on. He squinted against the blinding sixty-watt bulb.

"You liar!" Daniela said. "You're off your damn meds, aren't you?"

She stood in the doorway, short, auburn hair a tangled mess. A tight, grey muscle shirt strained across her small, perky breasts. Lithe, freckled legs stretched up into dark blue hip-hugger panties. Brian thought this was her sexiest look, now thoroughly negated by the fury in her eyes.

"Uh, yeah," he said. His voice sounded about ninety years old through his ravaged throat.

"You promised you wouldn't do that."

"Baby, I don't need them anymore. I'm better."

She looked down at him, curled on the bathroom floor, with disgust. "Yeah, look at you, all goddamn better."

"Look, you don't know how they make me feel. All fuzzy, disconnected."

"I don't want to hear that line of crap again. I've had enough."

She stormed out of the bathroom. The bedroom light clicked on. Brian rose to pursue her. His head spun like a Chinese acrobat's plate on a stick. He swooned, reached for the bowl for support, missed the rim, and plunged his hand in the morass of his own sick. He cursed.

A zipper closed in the bedroom. A very bad sound. He jumped up, towelled his hand clean, and exited the bathroom.

The red numbers on the clock radio read 4:12. Daniela already had on her jeans and shoes. She pulled her T-shirt over her head and gave her hair a frustrated ruffle with her fingertips.

"Baby, I can do this," Brian pleaded.

"No, Brian, you can't!" Daniela pulled open her purse and rummaged for her keys. "This is so typical of me. Pick up the stray, sign up for the project man, set out on the impossible quest. I want to kick myself for being so stupid."

She yanked her keys free of her purse, snapped it shut and marched for the front door. Brian followed a step behind.

"Don't leave," he begged.

She held up a hand at him, like a traffic cop ordering a halt. "Enough. You have too many issues. Anxiety, intimacy, attention span of a puppy. I can't fix all that, especially if you aren't going to do your half and take your meds. I warned you."

She walked straight through his apartment's living room and out the front door. She nearly crushed him in it when she slammed the door closed behind her.

What little physical and mental energy he had spiralled down into some black vortex. Another wave of dizziness washed over him. He dropped onto the couch and closed his eyes.

Damn it. She'd all but told him it was the meds or her. It was going to take a lot of time and effort to untangle this mess now. If he even could.

The nightmare this withdrawal had just given birth to still gave him a case of the shakes. Not that he hadn't had nightmares before, but the first-person point of view was a new development he hoped that his subconscious wasn't going to get used to. He vaguely remembered one from a few days before, similar to this one, but nowhere near as intense, or as visceral.

He wanted so badly to get back to sleep. Today was his day off, but he would have rather gone to work than do dinner with the family. He'd need every ounce of energy to maintain a semblance of self-control. Dinner was at five. He crawled back into bed and hoped that he could sleep through until then.

* * *

He found he couldn't. He gave up about thirty minutes later and started some coffee. He headed for the bathroom medicine cabinet and had to stop himself, again. Even without doing it for so long, the decade-old morning med cycle was a tough habit to break. He went back to the kitchen and pulled cheese and eggs from the refrigerator.

A drop of water pinged into the metal sink beside him. Without looking, he reached over and pulled the faucet handle down tighter. Another drop pinged.

He turned to the sink. A third drop hit, nowhere near the faucet. He looked up. A dark, damp stain the size of a basketball spread across the ceiling. In the centre hung a bead of water. It dropped in what appeared like slow motion and splatted into the sink. Another drop coalesced to take its place.

"Damn it."

This was the moment he loved to share with others, when real-life events unfolded to validate his anxieties. The vindication usually took the edge off the actual awful incident.

The drip was over his sink, which meant that with the duplicate floor plan of the apartment above, the leak was coming from the upstairs apartment's sink. He wondered if the guy upstairs was even awake.

He turned to go outside and bang on the door to 2B upstairs. He entered the living room. A second leak stopped him cold. Another stain on the ceiling, softball-sized and growing, over his television. Drops of water already drizzled down the front of the screen.

"Son of a—!"

He ran over, grabbed the TV and moved it out of the leak's line of fire. Before he could start back for the kitchen to grab a bowl to catch the water, a third leak sprouted near the door, then a fourth over the couch. The four stains spread like overhead oil spills.

What the hell was the guy doing up there? His neighbour had to have water backed up all across the floor.

The dripping from each stain accelerated into a drizzle. A steady stream of water began to drain from the tip of the living room's overhead light. The rank smell of sewage filled the room. Brian burst out in goose bumps and shivered in disgust.

The ceiling stains darkened to black. The gypsum board sagged at each circle as the waterlogged fibres threatened to dissolve. Whatever disgusting brew the second floor harboured was coming his way.

Brian ran for the front door. He grabbed the knob. It would

not turn. He yanked and shook it. Frozen tight. He reached for the deadbolt butterfly. Stuck. Hard. The ceiling around the living room overhead light drooped down a foot, like it was made of taffy. Brian's pulse went into overdrive.

He gave the door one more futile yank. Then the ceiling burst.

An inverted volcanic eruption of foetid, grey water blasted into the room. The impact lifted furniture from the floor. The surging water sent it hurtling toward the walls. Brian dodged a lamp and it smashed against the wall behind him. The water lapped his knees in an instant. Toilet paper and human waste swirled in the maelstrom.

He shuffled to the window against the rushing water's current and tried to throw the latch. It wouldn't budge. He pounded against the glass with his fist. His blows made soft, muted thuds. The window merely flexed, as if the glass had been replaced with something shatterproof. The water's roar made him want to scream.

The water rose past his waist. The pressure forced him up against the wall. He struck the window with both fists in rapid succession, like he was hitting a speed bag. The rising water made each blow sound softer, more distant, more useless.

Panic crept into his every neuron, overloaded every synapse. Rational thought evaporated and all he wanted to do was somehow claw his way to the other side of this glass, to the wide-open outside world he could see so clearly.

Water crested his chin. The acidic stench of human waste crawled up his nose and set his sinuses on fire. Soft objects swirled around his neck, bumped the side of his face. He clamped shut his mouth, held his breath. His lips submerged, then his nose. The water compressed his chest against the window. His searing lungs screamed for him to exhale, no matter what disgusting mix he ingested in return. He stared straight across the rising water and out the window to a world indifferent to his imminent death. He closed his eyes and the water consumed him.

The pressure vanished.

He opened his eyes. His nose pressed against the window. A quick whirl revealed the room was completely dry. He exhaled so hard the effort doubled him over. He dropped to the floor and rolled on his back. The ceiling stretched out above him, unblemished and dry. His pulse coasted down to something closer to normal.

Another goddamn hallucination. The potential ramifications sent his anxiety spiking again.

What if he'd actually shattered the glass and sliced open his hands and arms? What if he'd made it outside, ranting to strangers about sewage filling his house? He'd be in full-time psychiatric care before he knew what hit him.

That excursion into hell was way worse than the guard shack incident. What would the next one be like? Where would he be when it hit him? Getting himself killed wasn't the result he was shooting for by getting off meds. Nightmare-filled sleep and hallucination-filled days were a one-way ticket to real-life crazy.

Utter exhaustion dropped on him like a set of weights. He rose and staggered back to bed.

His phone on the nightstand flashed that he had a message. It had arrived hours ago. He called it up.

An improved you gets closer every day! Be ready for change!

He deleted the latest Totally You Institute spam. He dropped on top of the sheets, and fell fast asleep until late in the afternoon.

CHAPTER EIGHT

Brian knew he shouldn't feel like this. Dread shouldn't fill him as he stood on the front porch of his adoptive parents' home that evening. Family get-togethers were supposed to be warm, joyous events. Hallmark TV movies told him so. But not in the Sheridan household.

From the outside, the home would be the envy of any stranger passing by, if somehow that stranger got into this gated community outside Tampa to start with. An expansive two-storey home sat in the centre of an acre of verdant Bermuda grass. White flowers bloomed from the Indian hawthorn bushes that lined the faux-cobblestone driveway. Potted orchids hung from the overhangs and filled the air with a scent so cloying it seemed artificial.

Brian rang the bell. Plates clanked together inside the house. Footsteps sounded on tile. He took a deep breath and tensed, as if he was about to withstand a blast of frigid air.

Camilla Sheridan opened the door. Early forties and fit, she wore a white tennis outfit, mandatory club attire whether one played or not, and she did not play. The last year and a half, her tan had deepened, and the lines on her face lessened, coincidentally aligned with Brian moving out. She managed an unconvincing smile.

"Brian! Come on in before the humidity ruins everything in the house."

"Hey, Cam." He'd slipped to a first-name basis with his parents during high school and they'd never objected.

He walked in. They did not hug. Camilla had never been much of a hugger, even less so with Brian.

Camilla followed him through the foyer and the living room to the screened back patio. Aquamarine water cast a sparkling invitation from the full-size pool. Derek Sheridan stood beside a built-in stone-faced gas grill. He wore his weekend relaxation outfit, a short sleeve button-down shirt, khaki shorts and deck shoes without socks. He prodded thick steaks with a huge two-tined fork as the meat sizzled over the open flames. He gave Brian a nod.

"Brian. Good to see you."

"Derek." Coworkers passing the water cooler exchanged more warmth.

Three chairs with topaz padded covers surrounded a glossy, circular redwood table. The fourth chair had been consigned to storage when Brian moved out. The thoughtful family had put a folding chair out for Brian's brief visit.

Ariana sat in one of the padded chairs. Brian's stepsister was in her senior year at high school, already accepted at Dartmouth. Her tennis outfit matched her mother's, but she actually played. One finger danced back and forth across her smartphone. With her head leaned forward, her shoulder-length brown hair hung like blinders on either side of her connection to the rest of the world. Brian sat down. She didn't look up.

Camilla joined them at the table. She set down a plastic tray of fresh cut vegetables ordered from the local organic grocery. Derek piled four steaks on a platter, doused the grill's flames, and took his seat at the table.

"Get 'em while they're hot," he said as he delivered a sizzling slab to each of the four plates at the table.

Ariana looked up long enough from her phone to see that food had arrived, then responded to another text message. Brian and his parents exchanged quick glances, tense as gunslingers waiting for the other to draw in some weird three-way duel. An uncomfortable silence turned tortuous. Brian waited to hear why he'd been summoned for the meal.

"I spoke to Dr. Kaufman on Thursday," Camilla said.

Brian shook his head. *Of course*. Dr. Kaufman always thought that the restriction of doctor/patient confidentiality was familial, not individual, in nature.

Relieved of the responsibility of starting the conversation, Derek raised his knife and fork. He began to study his steak, like Caesar looking for the weak spot in the Gallic lines before battle.

"Of course, I was checking," Camilla said, "because we hadn't been invoiced for last week's session."

"Because I didn't go," Brian said. Lying about it would be a waste of time.

"And this week?" Camilla said.

"I'll guess you know I missed that one, too."

"Now, Brian," Derek said. He pointed a steak knife at his son for emphasis. "That was part of the judge's conditional release."

Brian twitched, his usual involuntary response to bringing back dark memories. He tugged the sleeves of his shirt down to cover the purple, ropy scars along his wrists. "He set that up when I was thirteen."

"To run until you were twenty-one," Camilla said.

"Well, hell!" Brian said in frustration.

Ariana finally looked up from her phone in curiosity.

"That's six months away," Brian continued, "so what difference does it make?"

"Quite a difference to the courts," Camilla said.

"And you would tell them?"

"I'd be remiss not to."

"And," Derek cut in, "there's a question of liability, in case—"

Brian slapped the table so hard the plates bounced. "In case I go nuts and start killing people?"

Camilla slid her chair a few inches away from the table. "I can see you've also stopped taking your medications as well."

Brian's blood went to a boil. To still be treated like a kid.... He shot to his feet. His chair skidded back and collapsed in a heap.

"Well, family, thanks for the invite. Great catching up. I say we do the same thing next year, how's that?"

Brian marched past Camilla, through the back door, and then straight out the front. Before he knew it, he was in his car and halfway down the street, doing forty in first gear.

The idiocy of what he was doing caught up with him. He pulled over to the side of the road and shut off the car. He inhaled and exhaled deep, measured breaths. His fury ebbed.

He was twenty years old, for Christ's sake. He lived on his own, had his own job. He wasn't a kid anymore. He was livid with them for not seeing that.

He was also furious with himself. What did he expect was going to happen? Derek Sheridan was going to pop out like some 1950s sitcom dad and take him downtown for an ice cream sundae? That Camilla was going to shower him with praise for having not tried to kill himself, or even consider it, for the past seven years? Ridiculous.

He slammed his palm against the steering wheel, feeling stupid for losing it with his parents. Two nights in a row of interrupted sleep and the chemical backflips induced by medication withdrawal had put him on edge. His face flushed at realising he hadn't controlled himself.

But he was also a bit amazed by the ferocity of his response. He'd never been so forceful when he was on his medications. He'd just kept all the anger inside, muted and wrapped under that cottony veil that meds draped over his world. He'd have to keep an eye on his reactions to everyone. They might be hair-trigger in this new, sober world. He hoped this was one of the temporary side effects. Telling his parents off did feel pretty cleansing, though.

His parents were right about the court-ordered visits with Dr. Kaufman. He could really get a maelstrom started by not going. Worst-case scenario, the doc could have him recommitted. At the least, he might recommend an extension of Brian's treatment past age twenty-one. He was too damn close to freedom to let that happen.

He picked up his phone and scrolled to Dr. Kaufman's number. He thought about the standup comedian who used to do a 'You might be a redneck if...' routine.

You might be mentally defective if you have your shrink's number saved into your phone.

He sighed and made an appointment for before work tomorrow.

CHAPTER NINE

The next day, Brian gripped the arms of Dr. Kaufman's waiting room chair, as if squeezing them would somehow wring a bit of his dread out onto the floor. Having someone with an anxiety disorder spend time in a waiting room was as thoughtless as having a lung cancer patient sit in an airport smoking lounge.

Three other people waited as well. Across from him sat a mother with a child who looked about twelve. The kid's long hair swept down over his face in sheepdog fashion. Every stitch of his clothing was black. Brian consoled himself that he had never been quite that screwed up. Brian compensated for feeling like an outsider by pursuing anonymity, not embracing the outsider status. The mother flipped through texts and email on her phone, interspersed with glances up at the clock on the wall.

Two chairs down sat a frail, older man, at least sixty, balding, with his grey hair swept back in a ridiculous attempt at a ponytail. He kept scraping his bottom teeth against his upper lip, as if trying to rake his lip back into his mouth. The frayed hems of his too-long khaki pants had grazed the ground for a long time.

Brian felt like Ebenezer Scrooge, with the Ghost of Brian Past and what he sure hoped wasn't the Ghost of Brian Future around him. He'd always wondered if the shrinks really wanted people cured, or if they wanted them as stable sources of income.

The receptionist called Brian's name. He walked the familiar path past her to Dr. Kaufman's office. It reminded him more than ever of a scene from a prison film where the death row inmate made the long walk to the electric chair. The Doc was not going to be happy with him at all.

The therapy room door was open. Therapy rooms on television always looked like someone's personal study, lined with bookshelves, walls covered in diplomas. Dr. Kaufman never went in for that. The small, simply decorated room just had a couch and two easy chairs around a coffee table. Bright pictures of snow-capped Colorado mountains hung on the peach-coloured walls. Maybe some of the other rooms were decorated differently, tuned for different mental problems. Brian didn't know. He'd spent the last eight years coming to this one.

Dr. Kaufman stood behind one chair. Years of experience had told him to skip the handshake greeting with Brian. He had sandy hair, parted on one side, and wore gold, wire-rimmed glasses. He'd always struck Brian as looking like a thin Robert Redford. As usual, his face didn't betray his emotions, and Brian couldn't guess if the missed appointments had made him mad or disappointed.

"Thanks for squeezing me in, Doctor K." He took his usual seat on the couch.

"I thought it was important since you missed two sessions."

Brian winced. Even though the doctor got paid by the hour, he never wasted time. Dr. Kaufman took his usual chair across from Brian.

"Yeah," Brian said. He rubbed the back of his neck. "I'm just short of twenty-one, thought I'd see what doing without was going to be like."

"And what have you discovered?"

"Oh, well, that part's good. All good." His pants suddenly felt like sandpaper. He rubbed his palms against his thighs. "But I kind of backed off my meds."

"That was obvious. How much did you back off?"

"All the way."

Dr. Kaufman's expression turned grim. "Both the label instructions and my personal instructions were pretty clear on the dangers of doing that. How long have you been off them?"

"Two weeks. The first week was okay."

"Because the medications don't flush out of your system for several days after you discontinue them."

"And it isn't bad now. Mostly. Except the nightmares." Admitting to Mr. Jitters and the other hallucinations would be like asking for a ticket back to the psych ward. "They wake me up."

"Abruptly stopping treatment like that will always cause

poor sleep cycles, and poor sleep cycles increase the likelihood of nightmares."

Brian thought that maybe he could get something useful out of the normally reticent shrink after all. "The nightmares. Where do they come from?"

"Why do you ask?"

"Some of them are horrible. People getting killed. Lots of violence." He didn't want to add that they were getting worse. "Am I thinking up all that gruesome stuff?"

"You mean are they your personal fantasies?"

Brian nodded.

"No," Dr. Kaufman said. "The subconscious doesn't work that way. It is kind of a holding area for all sorts of things, some are hopes and desires, some are fantasies, but most are experiences. And not necessarily personal experiences."

"Like stuff from movies, or books I've read?"

"Exactly. Dreams pull on all of that, probably as a way for people to deal with stress and anxiety. If you experience it in a dream, it's less scary if there's a second time around in real life."

Brian was really hoping to never experience killing a woman in real life. "So these nightmares could be rearranged scenes from some horror movie?"

"Something like that."

"Nothing dangerous?"

Dr. Kaufman pushed his glasses up the bridge of his nose. "What do you mean by dangerous?"

Brian wasn't the shrink, but by now he knew Dr. Kaufman's tell. A push on the glasses meant that something had piqued his interest. The last thing Brian wanted was for this conversation to get interesting.

"You know, it won't give me a heart attack in the middle of the night or anything?"

"No, nightmares don't give heart attacks. That is definitely from the movies. You really should get back on your medications. Not right back at full strength, of course, you need to work up to it again. Going back on full strength will really cause havoc. It will likely amplify your anxiety, not relieve it."

"I understand," Brian said. Even though he wanted out of the office, he couldn't bring himself to lie and say he'd start taking the drugs again. There was no way he was going back to the fuzzy life under pharmaceuticals.

"Julia will have your usual prescriptions ready. Just take the pills at a quarter strength for a week. We'll see where you are at our next scheduled session and decide how much to up the dosage."

"That sounds good," Brian said. He rose. "I'll let you get to the other patients. Thanks for your help."

"Call me if things seem more than you can handle."

"I will."

Brian left the room and headed to the front desk. His prescriptions sat on the counter. He palmed them as he walked past without stopping. He shoved them in his pocket and went for the front door.

Dr. Kaufman hadn't offered anything but the same-old same-old. Back on meds. Back on the therapy schedule. Back to him making boat payments or whatever the hell he did with all his money. The two of them would just run out the clock until Brian hit twenty-one. That course of treatment wasn't going to get Brian anywhere he hadn't already been.

Brian left the building and got a blast of straight Florida sunshine wrapped in sweltering sub-tropical humidity. He headed back to his car.

The visit wasn't a total loss, though. He definitely felt better knowing that the screwed-up crap in his dreams wasn't some personal fantasy. Whatever bits and pieces of late-night horror stories his mind strung together were just that, fiction. Maybe just knowing that would banish them.

He could hope.

His phone buzzed with a text message. The sender was a new number, 5642.

Breakthrough tonight to find your true self. Awaken!

This Totally You Institute spam was getting really old, really fast. He pressed Delete so hard he was afraid he'd crack the screen. He imagined the crap they were peddling. A glorified self-help revival meeting. Somewhere to display his scars, mental and physical. He bet that Camilla had dropped his name onto this place's mailing list, trying to get him into something else that might make him less of a burden. Then again, maybe Ariana signed him up just to piss him off. How lucky he was to have his list of suspects be all family members and all with different, negative, motives.

He considered calling Daniela, then discarded the idea. Seeing the shrink was a step she'd approve of, but it wouldn't be enough. He needed to be on meds or better without them before he tried to reconcile with her. The former wasn't going to happen. The latter definitely hadn't happened yet.

The world was getting to be a lonely place again. He was looking forward to seeing the ever-abusive Sidney at work tomorrow. That was certainly a sign of desperation.

CHAPTER TEN

The dream is so vivid, it is hyper-real, even in black and white, even without a soundtrack. That partial sensory deprivation only makes it worse. There is no distraction from what he sees.

It is night. The cowl of a sweatshirt hood reduces the view to tunnel vision. Streetlights spray their meagre illumination out from the curb and across the street, but shadows command the space from the sidewalk to the rundown homes. Dilapidated fences corral tiny, weed-choked yards. The houses' sagging porches and peeling paint scream of the locality's slow decline. It looks like an urban neighbourhood, the kind of place where long ago these little one-storey homes were quite desirable. But subdivision sprawl eroded their value, and turned a community of owners into a collection of renters.

A girl walks ahead of him down the cracked sidewalk. She wears tight shorts cut to the top of her thighs. Twiggy, cocoa-coloured legs dissolve into a butt still years from being shaped by womanhood. A tight T-shirt, black, maybe purple, covers her boyish torso. In the dim light and the greyscale mode, the colours all look the same. Cornrows stretch down to the base of her neck. They bounce up and down with each step she takes. White wires trail from her ears to a small MP3 player in her left hand. Her head bounces to an unheard beat.

She should not be here, on this dark, deserted street, this little girl. He wonders where her parents are, why they let her travel through the night alone.

A chill runs up his spine. The houses sit dark, the air still. No rumbling cars prowl the pavement, no men stare from the shadows. Yet he knows the street is unsafe.

Because he is there.

His strides lengthen, each step a bit more of a stretch. No furtive movements to attract attention, no radical sprint. Just an almost imperceptible shift of speed. The distance between him and the girl closes.

His heartbeat spikes in anticipation. He wants to slow it, to quell the rush within him. He wants to command his legs to stop, better yet to turn away from the girl he senses is his target. But he is powerless.

He digs his hands into his hoodie's pockets. His right hand touches velvet. His mind recoils, the soft comfort of the cloth now associated with heinous activity. He pulls the velvet rope from his pocket by the end. It slithers out like a copperhead snake.

The girl does not react. Though the nightmare has no soundtrack, he knows the steps he takes are silent. Despite an uneven stride, he can feel how lightly his feet touch the ground, how inaudibly he moves through the air. To his horror, he senses it is from practice.

He swings the velvet executioner up and grasps the other end with his left hand. Both hands twirl in sync. The cloth cable tightens around his palms, and the sensation foreshadows what the girl will soon feel about her neck.

Revulsion spreads through his mind. He fears, no, worse, he knows what is about to come. The so-familiar rush of anxiety demands that he flee. But still he moves forward, until he is just a step behind the girl walking in her private, isolated, audio world.

They cross a driveway that stretches back into the black abyss between two unlit homes. He twists a loop in the rope and flips it over the girl's head. He yanks it just tight enough to cut off a scream. She flails her tiny arms, then scratches for purchase against the velvet braid.

He yanks her to her toes, and drags her into the darkness. Her arms slow, then drop limp to her sides. He reaches the ragged end of the pavement at the rear of the house, spins the girl by the velvet loop, and lays her down on the ground. He flips his leg across her and straddles her waist. Blood rushes to between his legs. His pants grow tighter.

The low moon sheds pale light across the scene. Sparse grass sticks up through hard, white soil. The girl still breathes, but her eyes stare off at nothing.

For a second, he dares hope it is done. That the vision will end, or that the part of him committing this barbaric act will relent, happy with the damage already delivered.

Neither expectation comes true. He yanks the red velvet killer so tight that his biceps burn. The girl's mouth opens in a silent scream. Her eyes roll up and turn bright white against her dark skin. Life seeps from her body. Her head sags, and she is gone.

He pleads, he begs that it is done, that this vision has reached its hellish climax. But the scene does not end, the credits do not roll.

He releases the ends of the rope and pulls it from her neck, like starting an outboard motor in slow motion. Hands coil the murderous weapon with undeserved reverence. He slithers down until he straddles the girl's knees. He unfastens the button of her shorts.

His mind reels with panic and revulsion. He's seen enough, done enough, felt enough. If he adds the violation of this innocent's corpse to his list of sins, he'll surely go insane.

Instead, he pulls a clear sandwich bag from his back pocket. Inside is a playing card. The face of the three of diamonds flashes in the moonlight. He pulls the card from the bag with his covered fingertips, like pulling Excalibur from the stone. He slides it face up into the girl's shorts, and closes the button. He rests his gloved fingertips upon her zipper, as if saying farewell.

★ ★ ★

Brian woke up when his head slammed into the floor. He raised himself up like he was doing a pushup. Sweat dampened his palms. His heart still raced. He must have fallen out of bed as his nightmare concluded.

The clock read just after 1:00 a.m. He'd hardly been to sleep.

This was the worst nightmare yet. It was like being in that futuristic movie where the guy had his eyelids clamped open as he watched horrific scenes. Except Brian didn't just see things, he felt them. If nightmares like this kept up long term, the lack of sleep would drive him crazy.

He stumbled into the bathroom and popped open some over-the-counter sleeping pills. He wasn't going back to the mind-altering crap from Dr. Kaufman, but a little temporary OTC assistance to get him through one night uninterrupted wouldn't be the same thing. He palmed double the recommended dose and headed to the kitchen. He opened the refrigerator, pulled out a bottle of sparkling water and popped the cap. He threw back the pills and drank half the bottle in one draw. The icy liquid hit his gut like a snowball. He slammed home the rest of the bottle. The carbonation lit up and he belched loud and hard.

He lay back in bed. Images from the vision flashed by. The rope. The little girl. Houses along the dark street. He couldn't shed the sickening, filthy feeling of having participated in such a disgusting act. The reality that he'd just dreamed it didn't matter. The fiction had been as intense as reality.

In minutes, the sedatives began to work their toxic magic. His memories blurred, his eyelids felt heavy. He fell sound asleep.

⋆ ⋆ ⋆

The edges of the room are indistinct, but not just from the darkness. They are blurred, soupy. The result is a kind of circular view, with the clearer central section in murky black and white. A flashlight beam, he realises. But there is more to it than that. What he can see is covered in a psychedelic sheen, a shifting, swirling mix of weak rainbow colours, like oil on still water in bright sunlight.

Dirt and scuff marks mar the grey, industrial-style floor. The corners of many tiles are missing, and over time, dirt has filled the jagged little triangles. Bits of acoustic ceiling tiles litter the floor, and for an instant he gets a look at a ceiling of broken neon lights in a latticework of bare metal strips. Fresh plywood covers one wall.

The view and the sensations lack the sharpness of his other dreams. The sleeping pills can dull, but not defeat the vision's broadcast. His stomach sinks as he realises this failure, and fears what acts he must now witness.

The girl from the earlier dream appears, lying on the ground. Her throat is swollen from the velvet rope's dirty work. Her eyes stare wide open and milky. The swirling overlay makes seeing her details difficult, and for that he is glad. With covered fingertips, he reaches down and grabs her wrists like grasping a wheelbarrow. They are stone cold and send a shiver through him, well out of proportion with their actual temperature. He pulls the girl to what looks like the centre of the room.

He grows terrified thinking what horrors he may be about to witness. Necrophilia, dismemberment, evisceration. The depressants in his bloodstream are not enough to quell his dread.

He walks around the girl. The scene rolls out of focus and then back in. He straddles the corpse and then drops to his knees across her waist. She is so small that blessedly their bodies do not touch. The emotion that he registers doesn't mirror his own anger, fear or revulsion. It is satisfaction.

He grabs the girl's wrists again, pulls them down to her side, and places her hands upon her chest. He tents her fingers, as if she is praying. The act is not one of reverence, but of irony, a sarcastic commentary on who really makes decisions about life and death.

The vision fades and returns. He reaches into her shorts and pulls out the waxy playing card left there before. He tucks it between her thumbs. The three of diamonds.

The flashlight snaps off. The room returns to near total darkness. The vision disappears. He wants to awaken, to let the onset of reality scrub the memory of this fabrication from his consciousness. But the drugs overrule him.

CHAPTER ELEVEN

Three in the morning wasn't the best time to get word of a murder. Theoretically, no time was good to learn of a murder. But being a homicide detective meant Eric Weissbard was among the first to get such unwelcome news. Today, he was at the top of the rotation, and the pre-dawn call was all his.

He listened to the details from dispatch. A woman, late twenties, found in a car near Croom Wildlife Management Area. That was all dispatch had, but if it had been death from natural causes, she wouldn't have woken up Weissbard. He hung up, then slipped back the covers and tried to slide out of bed without drama. Middle-aged weight gain made that impossible.

"So what is it?" Maryanne said from the other side of the bed.

His wife hadn't moved a muscle, but her voice was clear, strong, wide awake. In thirty-five years as a cop's wife, she'd honed the same instantly alert skill he'd mastered.

"Possible homicide, woman found in a car out at Croom." He'd stopped sugarcoating work events with her after his first year in uniform. She liked being a cop's wife, revelled in learning about his job, devouring all the details, hearing about the darker side of humanity.

"I'll make you something to go."

"Don't bother, I'll grab something on the way."

"Yeah, something stupid like a cliché cop donut. Not gonna happen."

She threw back the covers, rolled out of bed and headed for the kitchen. She didn't even turn on the light. She fluffed her curly dark hair out of habit as she walked.

Weissbard shook his head and smiled. For an overweight fifty-six-year-old man, he was doing okay. After retiring from the NYPD, he and Maryanne moved to Tampa. But a month into his golden years, he missed the thrill of solving crimes. He had a feeling Maryanne did as well, because when he mentioned applying to the Tampa PD, she practically filled out his application for him.

He rubbed his head as he walked to the bathroom. He'd told Maryanne he cropped his hair real close because of the heat, but that was only half of it. He thought he looked more intimidating this way, and first impressions mattered when questioning suspects.

Goober, their black Labrador, bounded in from the living room. He stopped alongside Weissbard and licked his hand.

"How come whatever time we get up, you think that it's breakfast time for you?" he asked the dog. He waved in the direction of the kitchen. "See if you can convince her."

Goober yipped and ran off to the kitchen.

In the bathroom, Weissbard rolled on the hot water in the shower and started his well-practiced fifteen-minute-exit routine.

★ ★ ★

A mile down the dirt fire road at Croom, Weissbard's headlights lit up a pair of nose-to-nose police cruisers that blocked the way. Two uniformed officers leaned against the fenders. They straightened up when the headlights hit them, and both officers' hands moved to rest on their sidearms. One of them squinted and seemed to recognise Weissbard's black Charger. He gave a little wave.

This was one of Weissbard's many disadvantages within the Tampa PD. Other detectives who'd moved up through the ranks knew the beat cops. They had often worked in the same precincts. Weissbard didn't know anyone, and the sheer magnitude of all the new faces made it even harder to overcome that weakness. Add in that he 'wasn't naturally gregarious' as his wife often said with sarcastic understatement, and fitting in had been an issue. This cop in front of him might have looked a bit familiar. He couldn't really tell. The bright headlights and long shadows didn't help.

"What have you got?" he said as he approached the cops.

"At two a.m., I had an abandoned-car call," one officer said. "I approached and saw a single white female in the driver's seat.

She was unresponsive. I opened the door, and she was dead. I backed off and called it in."

"Did you try to resuscitate?"

The other cop stifled a laugh.

"Uh, no," the first cop said. "She was *way* dead. Didn't touch a thing."

"Good job. Do you have an ID?"

"The car is registered to a Meredith Viejo, twenty-six, out of St. Petersburg."

Weissbard nodded, then walked between the cruisers and toward the Volvo.

"I think you should have tried mouth-to-mouth," the second cop whispered to the first. "You never know...."

"Shut the hell up," the first cop answered.

Weissbard checked the area as he approached. No tyre tracks, not even behind the Volvo, but Florida's daily afternoon thunderstorms would have obliterated them. The door was closed, which meant she had to be a real stinker by now for the cop to seal her back in. 'Way dead' indeed. He pulled out his flashlight.

Weissbard opened the door and was not disappointed. The foetid stench of human decay rolled out like a cloud. The interior light didn't come on. Moonlight revealed the woman in profile, her left side in shadow. A feather hung limp from the rearview mirror. He snapped on his flashlight.

A yellowing pallor and sagging skin ruined what had likely been an attractive face a few days ago. The short, no-nonsense cut of her dark hair still had a sense of style to it, a cut that said she probably had to deal with the public, but didn't need the hassle of long hair. He trained his flashlight beam on her neck.

Heavy, dark ligature marks around her throat indicated strangulation, though he'd wait for the ME to give him the specifics, including time of death. But she'd been dead days, at least. It figured that no one would find her back on this fire road.

"Then what was someone doing out here at two a.m., calling in an abandoned car?" he whispered to himself.

His gut told him that didn't sit right. In all his years as a cop, his gut had never steered him wrong. People who weren't cops didn't understand. Judges issuing warrants definitely didn't understand. But the same way a good farmer could tell that it would rain in an hour, a good detective could tell when facts didn't mesh just right.

He played his flashlight across the body. No bleeding, no wounds. The usual post-mortem faecal discharge soaked the seat bottom, but he also noticed a broad swath of it crossed the centre console, and there was a circular stain on the other seat. She sure as hell didn't switch seats back and forth after she stopped breathing. Not without help.

So the killer strangled her in the car, probably from behind in a surprise out of the dark. Then he threw her into the other seat, and drove the car way the hell out here, then put her back in the driver's seat. The son-of-a-bitch was one dedicated psycho to take the wheel of a car carrying a dead body while sitting in a seat full of fresh diarrhoea. And he likely had an accomplice to drive him away from here after he'd set up this little scene. Killers were crazy, but not dedicated enough to walk miles after the murder.

He played the light across her lap to see if the murderer had gone to the effort of belting the corpse back in. His heart skipped a beat. Her hands were clasped together in a very unnatural way and a playing card stuck out from between them. An eight of spades. The red backing had a drawing of two women in togas in front of oak trees, one in bloom, one nothing but branches. One woman was head up, one head down. The head-up woman with the dead tree behind her held a skull in one hand.

He didn't like the look of that at all. Killers who left signatures were the worst kind. Self-assured, ruthless, narcissistic, fully disconnected from the enormity of the crimes they committed. They generated a media circus that made a decent investigation twice as hard. The last thing he needed was one of those on his watch.

Which meant he needed to find this perp right now.

Another set of headlights flared at the end of the fire road. Even in the gloom, he could make out that it was a TV news van, satellite dish across the top ready to soar skyward and gleefully tell the citizens of Tampa that they had something new to fear.

Wonderful, he thought. He hoped the uniforms had enough common sense to keep the crime scene details to themselves.

CHAPTER TWELVE

That morning, Brian awakened groggy from the sleeping pills.

Now they have an impact, he thought. *What about last night when they couldn't take me deep enough to escape the second installment of the nightmare double feature?*

He had no idea how long these withdrawal symptoms would last, and he prayed that's all they were. If being haunted was a permanent result of being unmedicated, he'd have to go back to the meds, and that was the last thing he wanted. He wanted to just power through this and end up normal.

Priority One tonight would be to hit the sack damn tired. He clicked on the lights in his room. He'd stay up as long as he could, no sleep until well after work today, late into tomorrow morning. That would make him tired as hell.

Priority Two. Up the sleeping pill dosage to comatose level. He needed to be able to snore through a hurricane.

He turned on the TV. The early morning local news came on. He rarely watched it. The weather was always the same, hot with afternoon thunderstorms. The news was always the same, various acts of human stupidity.

Two picture-perfect Barbies delivered the usual litany of grim news from the day and night before. An apartment fire in St. Petersburg. A man arrested for leaving his toddler in the car at midday while he went to a strip club. A missing woman found dead in her car outside Brooksville. Maybe horror movies didn't power his nightmares after all. The daily news provided plenty of fodder.

Half an hour later, he was showered and dressed. He started coffee, then lingered over the choice of fruit or eggs for breakfast. He opted for both. A long day would need a lot of energy.

His phone buzzed. Another message from a strange number. This time, 4175. He tapped it.

Are you ready to start enjoying life? the Totally You Institute asked.

"Goddamn it!" Brian shook his head. Hadn't he signed up for some kind of no-damn-spam list with the government? These ads were pissing him off enough that Ariana moved to the top of the list of suspects. He deleted the message.

★ ★ ★

Later that night at work, the clock had just passed 8:00 p.m. when Sidney handed him the train manifest through the window. "Signed, sealed, delivered. Last load of the night."

"You're clocking out?"

"No, I'm gonna hang out with you, get caught up on your dull-as-shit life. I gots women who need to be serviced, looking for the Sidney Slam. Open the damn gate."

After Brian passed Sidney out of the parking lot, he checked his outbound roster. No one due until the next shift. That wasn't going to make his stay-awake-forever plan any easier. He poured himself a cup of coffee.

He turned on the tiny TV at the desk. The local all-news station came to life.

The first piece was about a female teacher having sex with a high school student. Brian wondered what planet that woman was from where she thought that story wouldn't spread fast as lightning through the male student body. The next story was about the dead woman found in a car outside Brooksville. The report started with an establishing shot of a white Volvo wagon parked on a sandy trail though scrub oaks. A fence of yellow crime scene tape hung from surrounding trees. Recorded earlier in the day, the reporter described how restaurant manager Meredith Viejo was found in her car by two police officers in the Croom Wildlife Management Area.

The report cut to a picture of the woman when alive, always easier than ever to get off the internet. Meredith was attractive, mid-twenties with short, dark hair and smiling, brown eyes. The jaded side of Brian guessed that only attractive murder victims made the news. If it bleeds, it leads, as long as it's photogenic.

The story cut to a shot of the driver's side of the car. The door hung wide open, the corpse thankfully removed. Brian froze. His cup of coffee slipped through his fingers and hit the floor.

A yellow feather hung from the rearview mirror.

And it wasn't just a feather, it was *the* feather. The one from the nightmare he'd had days ago. Just lighter looking in his uncoloured nightmare, but this yellow version was a dead-on match.

He shivered. He remembered the dark leather seats, the headliner. The dome lamp. All the same. How could that be? Hell, he'd never even been in a Volvo.

He flashed back to memories of the woman in the nightmare. Velvet braids around her neck. He never saw her face, just her eyes, wide with fear in the rearview mirror. The same eyes from the picture of Meredith Viejo.

Brian's left hand started to shake. He grabbed it with the other to hold it still. This couldn't be. He thought he'd had a nightmare. Instead, was it some kind of premonition? Deny it all he wanted to, there was no question he'd witnessed this woman's murder.

Then a realisation far darker surfaced. He remembered reading about anti-anxiety meds that turned users into sleepwalkers. And not the kind in movies where the person wandered about, arms out, eyes closed, mumbling. The drugs spawned coherent, deliberate sleepwalking. People had cooked food, driven cars. He thought one sleepwalker has committed a crime somewhere.

His anxiety began to simmer. He stood inside the tiny office and wrung his hands. His breath came in short, sharp bursts. What had he done? Did he relive his experience in that nightmare? Or was that his live version? When did he dream that? When was she killed?

The story had run its twenty-second-long course and now the Rays' latest loss filled the TV screen.

He grabbed his phone and did a search on the internet for Meredith Viejo. Local stations in Tampa and one in Orlando all had stories. He flipped through one, then another. The same story, over and over. Days ago, she closed up the restaurant where she worked. Security video had her locking the front door at 1:00 a.m. But the parking lot didn't have video surveillance. Police didn't know whether she met with foul play there, was carjacked elsewhere, or drove willingly to the Croom Wildlife Management Area. Employees who'd departed before her had no recollections of anything out of the ordinary happening at the restaurant that night.

Brian ran an internal mental diagnostic. Could he have done this? His immediate thought was no. He'd been bullied and treated pretty poorly his whole life, and never once responded violently. He went out of his way to avoid confrontations.

But he'd been having those dark, sadistic dreams since he'd gotten off his medications, not to mention those damn hallucinations. Then there was the uncharacteristic fury he'd unleashed on his parents at dinner. Had some repressed side of him been set free, some Mr. Hyde manifestation of himself? People snap all the time, even without medication withdrawal to light the fuse.

But wait. The rope. He didn't have a velvet rope. He'd never seen one until it entered his dreams. How could he kill someone with something he didn't own?

Well, maybe he'd hid it. If in his altered state he could plan a murder, he'd surely plan to hide the murder weapon.

But he couldn't hide everything. There'd be evidence of the crime somewhere.

His anxiety went to a boil. Brian grabbed a flashlight from its charger, left the guard house, and went to his car.

The corpse-laden Volvo had been dumped on a dirt road. He played the beam around the outside of his car, under the fender wells. He didn't see anything that looked like he'd taken his little beater on an off-road adventure. Then he remembered the sandy soil from the video footage. That wouldn't have stuck to his car anyway, certainly not for days.

He opened the back door. Anxiety amped him up and he rummaged through the clutter in the rear seat at a hyperkinetic speed. He tossed some T-shirts and empty plastic shopping bags around. He reached underneath the front seats. Nothing. He popped open the centre console between the front seats. Auto registration. A dozen McDonald's napkins. A yellowed fold-up map of Florida he'd gotten from the Welcome to Florida centre about two governors ago. Nothing new. Nothing murderous.

He hit the trunk release and dashed around to the back. A

rusting folding beach chair lay alone in the trunk. Sand salted the black, fuzzy trunk liner. Was it from some beach excursion or from a crime scene? He yanked out the chair and tossed it aside. Up went the mat to expose the empty spare tyre well. The car hadn't had a spare when he bought it. He thrust his hands down into the recess between the rear fender wells and the trunk floor. Empty.

He sighed, tossed the chair back in the trunk, and slammed the deck lid. His pulse slowed down. He rested his sweating palms on the car's cool metal and took a deep breath. Not finding anything was better than finding something, but far from conclusive proof of his innocence.

The idea of calling the police occurred to him. He dropped it like it was on fire. What would he say? He had a dream about a feather? The statement sounded stupid even to him, and he knew it was true. And if he did witness the murder, what details could he add to help solve the case? None.

He headed back to the guard shack. Maybe there was way less to this than he thought. He'd read a lot about the strength of the power of suggestion, the ability for the mind to fill in the blanks. The nightmare he'd had was terrifying, but what he saw now as specific details were pretty generic. Black car seats. A dark night. A woman attacked by an assailant from the shadowy back seat of her car. The whole thing was a horror-movie cliché. Was it more likely that he committed a murder he couldn't explain, or that a few details of a murder matched a nightmare? Billions of women have brown eyes.

The feather? Was it a feather in his dream? Looking back, how clear was that image? Had he just made it a feather when he saw the one on the news? It could have been anything in the nightmare. Dreams are just a sea of shifting, half-formed images.

And the police didn't release the cause of death. No one said this woman was strangled. She could have been shot. Had a drug overdose. A heart attack.

Plus, this murder had occurred days ago. He wasn't even sure what night he'd had that nightmare. The last two unmedicated weeks were kind of a blur.

By the time Brian closed himself back into the guard shack, he'd come up with a decent list of reasons why he was overreacting.

Overreaction made the most sense after all. Working the meds through his system left him a little unbalanced, a little prone to make two and two add up to five, maybe a little paranoid as well. That was in the side effects list, wasn't it? He'd check when he got home.

The rumble of a diesel engine broke his train of thought. A truck turned into the driveway and lit up the shack with its high beams for a second before cutting the lights to a low setting. It pulled up to the door. Brian opened it and stepped out, carrying the manifest list. A woman in a CAT Diesel cap leaned out the window.

"I'm a bit early for my load." She handed him her manifest. "You cool with that?"

Brian thought a little normal human contact was the perfect thing right now. "Cool as can be." He raised the gate. "I'll even walk you back to it."

CHAPTER THIRTEEN

Weissbard's yesterday had started early and ended late. The first day of a homicide investigation always did. That initial day sometimes even took forty-eight hours to complete. At 3:00 a.m., he'd started with no leads in the case. By the time he shut it down last night, he hadn't moved forward an inch.

Meredith Viejo had worked at Sheehan's Grill for over five years. Employees were grief-stricken to a person. She was apparently the Mother Teresa of restaurant managers, always helpful, supportive, and infallibly flexible when personal problems arose. There were no recently terminated employees with an axe to grind. There were no pissed-off customers who wanted revenge for an overcooked steak. By the time he was done interviewing everyone at the restaurant, Weissbard couldn't decide whether he wanted to take Maryanne there for dinner or just throw it all in and get a job at the place.

The first suspect was always the husband/boyfriend/significant other, and nine out of ten times, that guess was dead on. Murder was most frequently a crime of passion. Her doting boyfriend was a restaurant favourite, with an airtight alibi at his job, and no insurance or other motives. Weissbard interviewed him and he came across as genuine. He'd follow up with a little more background on the guy, but Weissbard was definitely trusting his gut on this one, and his gut said the guy didn't do it.

Weissbard could always hit a new day fresh. Whatever setbacks the previous day had brought, he could always begin the new day with the wholly unsupported certainty that today he'd make great progress. It was a necessity as a homicide cop. He set out this morning certain he'd uncover something to blow this case open.

Detective Sergeant Roman Francisco approached Weissbard's desk. The senior homicide detective had been on the Tampa PD practically since birth. He sported a thick head of perfectly coiffed silver hair, a body that obviously still spent hours at the gym each week, and a permanent ruddy Floridian tan. His chiselled good looks often made people assume at first sight that he was a jackass. He always lived up to that expectation.

"Today's progress, Swissbard?" Francisco thought mangling Weissbard's name was hilarious. He'd accidentally done it the first day they met, and then stuck with it to keep from admitting his mistake. Even now, when it was just the two of them.

"A lot of potential suspects have been eliminated," Weissbard said, which was the most positive spin he could put on the day.

"Which means your suspect list is at zero, I take it." Francisco exhaled an exaggerated sigh. "You know, we like to solve the murders down here in Tampa? It's kind of a thing."

This was one of the many times that nothing but low tenure and a mortgage payment kept him from kicking some of the shit out of Francisco. The sergeant always acted as if Weissbard's solve rate in New York had been zero, when actually it had been above the Tampa Bay PD's. Well above. But Francisco's insinuations made the required impression, and from the beginning, the other detectives wondered if Weissbard could pull his weight. Francisco had chalked up Weissbard's two-for-two solve rate so far as beginner's luck. The prick.

"There's still the playing card to figure out," Weissbard said.

"Please, do you think this is some Hollywood serial killer? Nobody does that shit in real life. Follow the boyfriend. It's always the boyfriend. Ten-to-one he's got some side action he wants to move to the spotlight. Mark my words."

Every time Weissbard had 'marked' Francisco's words, they'd been dead wrong. He had no idea how such a blowhard had risen to high rank in such a good department.

"You heard I closed that double homicide with those Bloods gangbangers, right?" Francisco said as he walked away. He paused and turned around. "Oh, yeah. That was covered in the morning briefing. I forgot." He sauntered out through the squad room doorway. As he did, he flicked the lights on and off twice, just because he was Francisco.

Screw him, Weissbard thought. The playing card did mean

something. It being the eight of spades might mean something as well. The damn thing didn't flutter out of the sky and tuck itself between the dead woman's hands.

He typed up an internet search for 'strangled woman playing card' but paused before he hit the last key. His bruised ego rooted for vindication with a dozen hits throughout Florida, but the cop part of him hoped the search would come up empty. He touched Enter.

He got ads for decks of sadomasochistic playing cards. Nothing more relevant than that. He felt relieved, and was glad that unlike that sphincter Francisco, his cop side had his ego side in check.

But his gut said the card would matter yet. Just wait.

CHAPTER FOURTEEN

Weissbard's positive psychological start, though marred by Francisco's acting like the ass he was, hadn't made his morning any more productive. Meredith Viejo had the hallmarks of being a random victim, murdered by someone with a detailed plan. A scary proposition if true. It meant there would be no predicting the killer's next victim, no way to make the murderer's opportunity for a second kill more difficult. And he was certain if this guy wasn't caught, there'd be a second victim. The murderer was either out there for sport, or answering some voice in his head. Either way, success would never satiate him. It would just embolden him.

His gut piped up and said this wasn't the killer's first show. Too much had gone too well, his plan had been overly intricate, not a nervous first attempt. Weissbard had done a quick, specific internet search for playing cards and strangled women. Now he'd try a more general search restricted to the local databases. Plenty of crimes never got any press coverage. Even murders.

He scribbled the word 'unsolved' on top of the note pad beside his desk and prepared to make a list. He knew the Tampa Bay backlog by heart and there wasn't an unsolved female strangulation in the past three months. He checked Naples to the south, Orlando to the east, even as far as Gainesville to the north. A couple of possibilities, but in each one, something jumped out that made him discount the case, details about the scene or the victim that didn't mesh with what the old gut check said he was looking for. Then he pulled the surrounding counties' backlogs and got no better results. Then, while he was there, he decided to change up the search, and look at solved cases.

One jumped up right away. Weeks ago in rural Brewster. Karen Strong, white female, sixty-two. Found strangled in her trailer on a country lot, well away from town. Weissbard looked down the evidence list. His heart stopped when he saw that Item 22 was a playing card, the seven of clubs. He wondered if the backing matched the card found in Meredith's hands. He scribbled all this down on his note pad as he clicked over to the record of the accused, who had been arrested six days ago.

Wendell Wrassie, a white male drifter in his late forties. Weissbard could tell by the mug shot alone that some serious mental issues must have led to his homelessness. When the picture was taken, the guy's last shower, shave and haircut were likely distant memories. His rap sheet carried two prior felonies for meth manufacture. This scumbag was going to see the horizon through razor wire fence for the rest of his life.

Two playing cards at two murders in two weeks was no coincidence. But this guy was in jail when the Viejo killing happened, which meant he was either the wrong guy, or perhaps Meredith's killer had been Wrassie's accomplice, now freelancing solo.

He was going to have to find out which. He transferred his notes from the pad by his desk to his notebook and added the address of the nearby Polk County jail. Time to pay Wendell Wrassie a visit.

★ ★ ★

Weissbard tapped his pen against his notebook in increasing irritation. He'd been cooling his heels alone in the Polk County interrogation room for almost twenty minutes waiting on Wendell Wrassie's arrival. Every minute wasted here was one more minute Meredith Viejo's murderer walked free.

Police professional courtesy had been profoundly and uncharacteristically absent from the moment he tried to set up this interview. The county sheriff had made him get his chief to back up the request, and then Weissbard had to give a lot of details about how it might be tied to an active case in Tampa.

Once he'd arrived, he had to sign off on some bullshit judge's gag order about releasing any information about the interview, as if he'd do that anyway. The desk sergeant gave Weissbard the frosty treatment reserved for defence attorneys, not cops. They only allotted him a limited amount of time to look at the collected evidence, but all Weissbard cared about was Item 22, the card.

His stomach sank when he saw the backing design. It matched the one in Meredith Viejo's hands.

Then the perp hadn't been delivered at the appointed time to interrogation, even though the cellblock was one hallway over. Weissbard had done a little search before coming over, and Wrassie's arrest had been front-page news in the local outlets. You'd think they'd be proud to show off their trophy.

The door opened and two overweight, green-clad deputies dragged a spindly, orange-jump-suited Wendell Wrassie in between them. Wrassie looked smaller than Weissbard had expected, his face more gaunt, his eyes wilder. Sores ringed his lips. Some newer bruises peeked out beneath his grey beard. He wore more chains than an ice trucker's tyres. The deputies locked him in place across from Weissbard.

"You got ten minutes," the fatter of the two deputies said.

"What? I was scheduled for eleven to eleven thirty."

"And it's eleven twenty. Ten minutes and he has to be back for headcount and lunch in isolation. We don't do room service around his visitors."

"You brought him here late," Weissbard said.

"We're busy. Got a whole jail to run. Big surprise that an out-of-county cop's interview with a murderer might not be at the top of the priority list?"

The two deputies left him alone with Wrassie. Wrassie gave Weissbard a nervous once-over.

"You ain't from the county?"

"I'm Detective Weissbard, Tampa PD."

"I didn't do nothing in Tampa. Just here."

Weissbard hadn't ever heard a confession before he delivered the opening question. Not from a guilty man, at least. He didn't have time to get a rapport going with Wrassie. The wall clock loudly ticked away his evaporating ten minutes.

"So what was it you did here?"

"Killed that lady, Karen. Strangled her with a rope." His hands shook against the table and set up a repeating jangle of his chains. Sweat dripped from his temples.

"Why did you do it?"

"Robbery. Needed money for some crystal."

It looked like he needed some crystal right now. "Why her?"

"Trailer was out by itself. Looked easy. Didn't plan on killing her. Didn't know she was there."

"What was she doing when you broke in?"

"Didn't break in, just walked in the open door. Guess she was in a back room or something. Must have come out and startled me."

"Then why did you have a length of rope with you?"

Wrassie thought a bit. "It was just there in the house, I didn't bring it."

The ligature marks on the Viejo woman were pretty wide. Weissbard tried to imagine a middle-aged woman with a few feet of stout rope just lying around her trailer. He failed.

"I threw the rope in the swamp after to hide the evidence," Wrassie added helpfully.

This guy couldn't possibly do more to solidify the case against him. Wrassie might as well have been reading aloud the prosecutor's opening statement for his upcoming trial.

"You know Florida still has the death penalty for murder, right?"

Wrassie's eyes went wide. He yanked his chains hard against the table's anchor point. "Uh, uh! Got a plea. Life, no parole. Max security. They don't fuck with murderers in there."

"But Wendell, this is tied to a Tampa murder as well. That's a separate crime, a separate trial, a separate sentence. We don't plead down murder."

"Didn't do nothing in Tampa! Ain't got no car! How the hell would I get to Tampa?"

Especially when he was in jail during the Viejo murder, Weissbard thought. But he pushed anyway. "Your buddy drove you to Tampa, the one with you when you killed Karen Strong."

"Wasn't no one with me. I did this on my own. Didn't kill no one else. Ain't taking no other rap."

His time was almost up. He'd wanted Wrassie to bring up the connecting evidence, but Weissbard would have to force it in himself.

"Then why the playing card?"

Wrassie paused. "The what?"

"The seven of clubs. What was with leaving the seven of clubs?"

"What the hell you talking about? No one said nothing about no deck of cards."

Commotion sounded outside the interrogation room door. It burst open. The two deputies rolled in and began to unlock Wrassie from the desk.

"I thought I had ten minutes," Weissbard said.

"Been ten minutes plus by my watch," the fat deputy said. "He needs to go back in the hole."

The deputies yanked Wrassie up from his seat. He looked genuinely scared. "No one said nothing about some goddamn seven of clubs! What's with that? I signed my deal!" They trundled him out the door and back down to the cellblock.

Weissbard slapped his notebook shut and left the room, fuming. He headed straight for the duty sergeant, another beach ball in forest green. The smug look on his face made Weissbard even angrier.

"Good luck with your case there in Tampa," the sergeant said.

"Good luck with yours here," Weissbard said. "You've got the wrong guy."

"Signed confession says otherwise."

"Any defence attorney worth a shit will get a meth-addled confession tossed. He's still detoxing now."

"His DNA is all over the crime scene. Had her wallet and cell phone and DVR when we picked him up."

"Well, he's too small to have subdued her, too whacked out to have planned it. He can't describe the murder, and you've got no weapon. He probably walked into the place after she was dead, and stole that shit to get high. Plus he doesn't know anything about the seven of clubs."

Worry crossed the sergeant's fat face. "The what?"

"The card shoved in the woman's dress. Did anyone find the rest of the deck lying around the house? Did they look? The next card in the deck ended up on a vic in Tampa."

The cop's face returned to blasé. "Signed confession. Signed plea goes to the judge this afternoon. Wrassie gets life with killer status. Three hots and a cot and he's happy to be off the street, back to what he thinks is home. County residents see a murder solved and feel safer. Everybody wins here."

"And the killer who's still on the streets?"

"Sounds like he's on Tampa streets, Detective. You might want to go home and catch him."

Weissbard got as far as cocking his fist before exercising enough self-restraint to keep from beating this worthless excuse for law enforcement. Instead, he headed back to his car.

After all, the worthless excuse for law enforcement was right. He still had a killer to catch.

★ ★ ★

Weissbard walked back into the detectives' warren of desks. Detective Sergeant Francisco stood at the far end of the room, already mid-pontification. The rest of the detectives on duty, a few uniforms and their boss, Sergeant Bertram, surrounded Francisco in a loose semicircle. Francisco's police-issue dark blue golf shirt looked starched for the occasion. Weissbard stopped at his desk, well within hearing distance, but not so close that he looked like he gave a damn about whatever Francisco was spouting. Because he sure didn't. His invitation to this little shindig had been lost in the mail, as usual. All he had to do was catch his killer. Whatever was going on in Francisco's world could just keep spinning. He took a seat behind his laptop, cleared the screen saver, and called up his email.

"So," Francisco said. "There's a good chance each of you will be getting some detailed assignments from me over the next twenty-four hours. The chief was very specific when he placed me in charge of this investigation. He wants this solved now, before the general public makes Tampa Bay synonymous with a serial killer."

Weissbard stopped scrolling through his email. He looked up at Francisco. He must have whitened his teeth for the day because they were damn near blinding. There was another set of patterned killings going on in Tampa? What was bringing out the crazies?

"Now so far," Francisco said, "only two unsolved murders have been linked by the playing cards."

Weissbard's jaw dropped. *How the hell could Francisco know...?*

He glanced to the note pad beside his laptop. The top page, where he jotted down the details of the Karen Strong murder, was gone. *That son of a bitch.*

"Let's keep there from being a third," Francisco continued. "Someone has come into our city to make a name for himself. That's not happening on my watch."

Francisco nodded, as if somehow that meant he'd given everyone some sort of useful instruction, and then strutted back to his office. Weissbard followed Francisco in before Weissbard even realised he was out of his chair.

"What was all that?" Weissbard said.

Francisco looked up, feigning he just realised Weissbard was there. "Swissbard? Eventually made the briefing, I see. In summary, once the chief saw the breadth of the Viejo case, he thought it should be in more experienced hands. Serial killers are serious work."

And high profile, Weissbard thought. This jackass was just angling for the chief's job, and the publicity around this would sure get him one step closer.

"You took the notes from my desk," Weissbard said.

"I don't know what you mean." Francisco grinned. "Just doing good old-fashioned shoe-leather cop work, and I turned up another unsolved case."

"You know that case is solved, right?"

Francisco's smile caved in on itself. "What?" He'd apparently taken the scant information from the note pad straight to the chief before checking into any of it himself. Typical.

"Polk County got their guy. Full confession."

"Copycat," Francisco rationalised.

"Yeah, a prequel copycat. Good luck with that."

"I'll need whatever notes you have on the case," Francisco said.

"I've filed everything with my reports."

"No, personal notes. Things are going to get heavy now that local TV has wind of this."

Weissbard's anger went from blazing to thermonuclear. There was only one way the reporters would have any idea what was going on. Francisco had to have let them know. Which of course, he would have.

"I'll be sending you leads generated by the hotline calls," Francisco finished. That was his way of saying he was completely in charge, and Weissbard was now an errand boy.

For the second time in under an hour, Weissbard walked out of a room before he punched a member of Florida law enforcement.

CHAPTER FIFTEEN

It is night, but enough light reflects off the water to make out the area, a nondescript shoreline somewhere on Tampa Bay's south side. The city's skyline rises in the distance across the water, glowing shafts of concrete and steel that stretch for the stars. Noiseless waves lap the edge of a cracked concrete ramp in this silent vision. A warm breeze tickles the hairs on his legs. He's wearing a T-shirt, swim trunks and flip flops. The situation feels off. This is the wrong time of day and the wrong kind of beach for these clothes.

His focus shifts as he grips a key in his hand. Brian sees the dreaded rubbery covers on his fingertips. He recoils in panic, knowing that unfathomable evil is about to unfold at his hands, and he will be powerless to stop it. The tingle foreshadowing an anxiety attack sets in.

He slides a key into the cylinder on a car's silver trunk lid, right under the Toyota logo. The trunk pops open. A Florida licence plate flashes by. A dim light flickers on and illuminates the trunk interior. The inside of the trunk lid has a big reflective safety decal that shimmers in the light.

Inside, an Hispanic woman lies curled in the foetal position. A leather skirt too short to be attractive reveals legs scarred with track marks all the way down to her bare feet. One small breast hangs exposed from a cheap tube top. Black zip ties bind her ankles and wrists. A broad band of shiny duct tape covers her mouth, but underneath it, purple bruises are forming where she'd earlier been knocked unconscious. Beneath her, a thick, clear plastic drop cloth covers the trunk interior.

He reaches in and shakes her. Her head lolls, her eyelids flutter. He shakes her again, harder. Brian can feel that he is yelling, sense the vibration in his throat, though he cannot hear a thing in this black-and-white world. He pulls her tube top up to cover her breast.

She stirs to a level of coherence. Her eyes clear, focus on him, then widen in realisation of her dire situation. Tendons in her neck go tight as steel cables as she screams into the duct tape gag.

He reaches into his back pocket and pulls out the velvet rope. Brian doesn't need to see it. He knows it now so well by touch alone, an enticing softness now turned repulsive. Brian tries to override his hands' actions. In his mind he screams against the malevolence they are about to commit. The hands wind around the rope anyway. He is just a prisoner in this body, his orders as useless as grabbing jail cell bars and howling at uncaring guards.

The woman tries to rise, tries to somehow affect an impossible escape with all four limbs bound. In his mind, Brian roots for her. But the emotion he senses tied to the hands he watches is one of excitement, of anticipation.

He whips the velvet executioner around her neck. She jerks and squirms against the heavy plastic tarp. Last time, he killed quickly, crushed the airway shut like slamming a door. This time, the constriction is more measured, the pressure strong, but not overpowering. The terror in the woman's eyes shifts to pleading.

He leans into the trunk a bit for leverage. He rests against the edge of the car. His manhood swells tight inside his bathing suit, hard, throbbing.

Both detached and immersed in this horrendous act, his disgust morphs to anxiety-ridden terror. He realises the kill itself is no longer enough to satisfy. The malicious hands gripping the velvet must slow their work, so the killer can savour the woman's panic as long as possible. It now makes sense why he risked awakening the woman first, instead of killing her as soon as he opened the trunk.

But all good things.... The rope cinches one last time. The woman's begging eyes fill again with horror, a look that says she knows, though unimaginable an hour ago, that Death reaches for her. Her skin pales. Her lips darken. Her eyes go still.

Brian's mind reels, repulsed by the murder, sickened by the torture, and disgusted by the sexual thrill it's given his body. He prays that whatever power fuels this satanic vision lets him awaken, and break this awful connection.

He picks up the woman from the trunk and slings her over

a shoulder. He carries her to the shore. When he steps off the concrete pad, soft sand yields with each of his footsteps toward the retreating tide. He wades into the warm water.

Waist-deep, he slides the corpse off his shoulder and lowers it into the bay. There is no reverence in the act, just the practical avoidance of a splash. He reaches into his back pocket and pulls out a playing card in a plastic baggie. The four of hearts. He slips the baggie inside the corpse's tube top.

A mental shiver runs through Brian. The killer protects the card, wants it safe from the corrosive bay waters. Wants to take credit.

With one hand around the hem of the corpse's skirt, and one at the base of its feet, he launches the body out into the bay. Its head breaks tiny waves like a ship's bow. The body rolls face down. The tide catches it and pulls it away.

He returns to the car's open trunk and slams it shut.

When he does, the rear window comes into full view. In it Brian sees a reflection, ghostlike and translucent, but almost indecipherable. A young man. Caucasian. Short, ultra-blond hair done in a porcupine of spikes. The face is a blur.

The man sees his reflection and breaks into what looks like a smile. It seems at first a narcissistic action, a little moment of personal pride. It dawns on Brian that it is much more, much worse than that. Though he can't clearly see it in his face, he can feel it in the man's reaction. He is not proud of his appearance, he is instead proud to share it, to make a final reveal.

He knows that Brian can see him.

* * *

Brian yelled and jerked awake in his bed. He threw off the covers and jumped to his feet, as if he needed to affect a physical, as well as a mental, escape from the nightmare.

The vision was so real, so tactile. Even worse than the ones before. He swept his hands down his legs, certain that the waters of the bay would still drip from them. His legs were dry.

The revelation didn't calm him. The vision had been too vivid for his imagination to spawn it alone. It must have had help from reality. Or insanity. Was one option worse than the other? Had he just seen another murder, or had his imagination stitched one from the cloth of his last nightmare?

He'd only been asleep a few hours, but his brain didn't care. He was too wired, too scared to even think about getting back to bed. He flicked on the TV. Normally the late-night programming grated on him, but now he needed it. He wanted something, anything, to take away the sense of being alone, of being stalked by some killer inside his own head.

* * *

The clock hit 7:00 a.m. and Brian ran out of excuses. Daniela would be awake, dressed, ready to leave for work. Any longer and she'd be at work, and he'd have a fresh excuse why he shouldn't call. For the tenth time that morning, his finger hovered over the button on his phone to call her. He took a deep breath, and pressed it.

Five rings in, he imagined the scene on the other end, Daniela staring down at her phone as it rang, deciding whether to pick up or not, deciding if Brian was worth the headache.

"Hello?"

The sound of her voice startled him. Scared him in fact. He didn't speak.

"Brian?"

"Yeah. It's me."

"You sound...spent."

"Rough night." He paused, dreading the question he knew she'd ask.

"Are you back on your medications?" she said.

"Daniela, hear me out. I'm not. But it's more than that. There's something else wrong—"

"Brian, no meds. That's what's wrong. When you were on them, you could sleep. No nightmares. You were good. We were good, or at least getting there."

"If you could let me explain, let me talk to you."

"I want to help you, Brian, I do. But I won't help you if you aren't going to help yourself. You step back up to where you were,

I'll step back to where I was, and we'll figure all this out."

It sounded so simple, seemed to make so much sense. Dr. Kaufman's prescriptions were in his apartment somewhere. Once filled, the white capsules could take him back to that hazy, half-living state.

"Baby," he said, "the pills are not an answer. They're part of the problem."

"You can't get right with that attitude. If you can't see how much better you were with the meds, you're just in denial. And I can't help someone in that level of denial. Meet me half way, I'll meet you half way. I have to go to work. Think about what I said. I'll help you. I won't enable you."

She hung up.

He was officially and completely on his own.

CHAPTER SIXTEEN

Detective Eric Weissbard hated the First Amendment.

Not the whole thing. Just the phrase 'freedom of the press'. If he had a time machine, he'd go back to 1787, and hold Congress at gunpoint until they deleted it. That would probably make the Founding Fathers rethink the Second Amendment, but he'd take the good with the bad.

Nothing screwed up police operations like the local press, especially television. Every reporter saw the Tampa market as their launching pad to someplace bigger, and everyone wanted a scoop to use as the rocket.

You give them information off the record. You beg them to hold back some details. You explain how delicate some investigations are. You go out of your way to be polite, to use all that empathy everyone was always pushing down police officers' throats. You do all that, and what do you get? Some idiot coins the term Playing Card Killer and you end up centre ring in a goddamn circus.

But Francisco had made sure that this circus opened. Hell, he raised the tent as soon as he leaked the playing card connections, something that would have made much more sense to keep quiet. But he couldn't ride a wave of publicity if he didn't create the swell. The backlash from Polk County around the scab of their 'closed' Karen Strong case being ripped off whipped through at the highest levels yesterday. Francisco had been kind enough to redirect the fury to Weissbard, the detective who had visited Wrassie without authorisation.

And this morning, the Viejo murder was on every station. The nationals hadn't picked it up yet, thank Jesus, but that was just a matter of time. Weissbard sat on the armrest of the sofa in his living room and watched the ultra-bright HD TV in the otherwise dark space. The station already had a special banner for the killer, complete with a little suicide king playing card icon. Corrine Donovan stood in front of the police station, face framed by her preternaturally-glistening dark hair and plastered with a layer of makeup excessive for this early in the morning. Her breathless delivery sang with all the hot-button words like 'terror' and 'lurking' and a dozen more designed to make the public feel unsafe. Weissbard wanted to make *her* feel unsafe.

"Why are you sitting in the dark?" Maryanne asked from the doorway.

"Honing my night vision."

She flicked on the light. "Knock it off, Batman. How did all that detail get to the press?"

"Detective Sergeant Ramon Francisco, Tampa PD. Rectum Extraordinaire."

"That's good. You needed another reason to hate the guy. Looks like he was put in charge."

"Looks like it."

"It's going to piss him off when you solve the case out from under him, isn't it?"

"It most certainly will."

★ ★ ★

Weissbard was only at work twenty minutes when Francisco rushed into the squad room. "New body, washed up on the bay near St. Pete. Female and it looks like she's got a card." Weissbard rose and rolled open his desk drawer for his service weapon.

Francisco ticked off the names of the two most junior detectives. "You two are with me on this. The rest of you keep following your leads. Swissbard, you stay put here to follow up on anything hot off the tip line."

Weissbard slammed his desk drawer closed. It hit so loudly nearly all eyes in the room turned to him. Francisco smiled and the two 'lucky' newbies raced out after him. Weissbard settled back down in his chair. Another round just went to Francisco.

CHAPTER SEVENTEEN

Around 9:00 a.m., the television droned on as background noise while Brian lay on the couch and tried to escape from himself in a paperback sci-fi novel. It had been lying around unread for who knows how long. His other option was a horror novel about a couple moving into a haunted house in Tennessee, but he figured his imagination didn't need any paranormal boost.

He was on page fifty-five, with an alien race about to rain hellfire down on planet Earth, when a sentence from the morning newscast caught his ear.

"Police today pulled the body of a woman from Tampa Bay, the latest work of an apparent serial killer."

Brian's breath caught in his throat. He dropped his book, sat up and glued his eyes to the television screen. A police boat sat at dock. Near it, a paramedic rolled a gurney bearing a covered corpse to a waiting ambulance.

"A fisherman noticed the body as he headed out to his traps this morning and alerted the police. Authorities identified the victim as Carmen Alessandro."

The screen cut to what was clearly a mug shot of a young girl, the kind who life had turned adult too quickly. Brian mentally superimposed the duct-tape gag, and caught his breath. She was the woman in the trunk.

"Police confirmed a part of the story broken by our own Corrine Donovan, that the victim was found with a playing card on her person, and that this wasn't the first local murder victim associated with the person now dubbed the Playing Card Killer."

The scene shifted to a harried-looking female police officer behind a microphone. "The last thing we need is to sensationalise this perpetrator, to feed a media frenzy by giving this twisted psycho some hyped-up nickname."

"Earlier victims include Ms. Meredith Viejo," the TV anchor said, "whose body was found days ago in her car outside Brooksville, and Mrs. Karen Strong, an elderly widow found dead in her trailer home in Brewster last week."

"Holy crap," Brian exhaled. The woman in the Volvo, with the yellow feather. And he'd had another dream before that. It wasn't as sharp, but an older woman was strangled in it as well. It was probably that woman in Brewster. He'd seen every one of these crimes in his dreams.

"Ms. Alessandro had a history of minor drug and prostitution offences," the reporter continued, "and was currently on parole. Police are asking anyone with any information about her whereabouts last night, or any information about the other victims of the Playing Card Killer, to call or text them through Tampa Bay Crimestoppers."

He cursed himself and wondered what the hell he had been thinking when he rationalised the yellow feather 'coincidence'. It wasn't a coincidence. It couldn't be. A smack in the head with a baseball bat would have been less obvious.

Then a worse thought occurred. The little girl from his other nightmare. She wasn't on the victims list. But he'd seen her murder as clearly as two of the others. Who was she? Where was she?

He pulled out his phone and started a search. He found a database for missing children and pared the results down to the Tampa area in the past two weeks.

A list popped up. His heart sank. Five kids. Five kids missing in fourteen days? There were over four million people in the Tampa area. Out of that, maybe five wasn't many, but that math didn't make the number seem any less enormous.

He scrolled through the list. A teen girl, a teen boy, two children presumed abducted by an estranged spouse. The last one was a little girl. Her school picture was next to her name, a lovely little girl in cornrows with one front tooth growing in to fill her big smile. Keisha Valentiner. Age six. Last seen over a week ago in north Tampa. The girl from his nightmare.

Brian knew what happened to her. But the police didn't. They hadn't found her in that abandoned building with the filthy floors, lying with the three of diamonds tucked between her thumbs.

He couldn't rationalise this anymore, couldn't escape the responsibility that lay on his shoulders. He had to tell the police. He knew what the killer looked like. Sort of. He knew he drove a silver car with a pretty big trunk. Whatever little he knew, it was more than the police had in their files.

First, they'd guess he was crazy, then be completely convinced of it if they found out about his past. He looked down at the scars on his wrists, those reminders of his weakest moment. If he was going in to talk to the cops, it was going to be a long-sleeved-shirt day. He wouldn't talk about himself at all. He'd just tell them what he knew.

But he'd have to tell them *how* he knew. Well, he'd just explain very rationally that he'd seen it in a dream. Hell, that alone would make them think he was crazy.

He'd have to somehow convince them he wasn't. Make them listen. Before the Playing Card Killer struck again.

CHAPTER EIGHTEEN

Weissbard bent over his desk and ran his fingers across the stubble on his scalp. Even without the glare of media attention, homicides were tough to solve. Most of the victims were poor. Most of those victims had records. Hardly anyone ever admitted to seeing anything. The ones who did often lied about everything. Every clue, every piece of evidence had to be constantly rearranged and reevaluated. Add in how quickly a promising lead's trail could go cold, and every case was a race against the clock.

And Weissbard sat manning a desk in the precinct, as far from any real police work as possible.

Sergeant Bertram walked up to the detective's desk. A shit-eating grin nearly split his face in two. Another born-and-raised Floridian, tight with Francisco and the Tampa Bay Boys Club. "Got a hot tip coming in, Detective."

Weissbard looked up at him in dejection. "Aren't they all? Every lunatic for three counties has the hottest lead, the keenest insight, the final piece to the puzzle. What's this one got?"

"He's solved all three murders for you. Seen the killer himself."

"C'mon, Bert. It's already been a long day."

"Francisco says follow every lead," Bertram said.

That explained it all. That jackoff Francisco had made sure Bertram steered a few crazies his way, and good-ol'-boy Bertram was happy to oblige.

Bertram turned and motioned someone to come forward. A slight twenty-something in faded jeans and shaggy hair under an Orange Star Trucking baseball hat stepped up beside him. Bertram shuffled back. "This is Brian Sheridan, your new lead."

The kid looked nervous. He kept tugging at the sleeves of his shirt. Who wears a long-sleeved T-shirt in Florida in the summer? Well, hell, he saw guys this age wearing ski caps, so who can figure out what people wear. Across the office, someone dropped a box with a bang. The kid flinched like it was a gunshot. Bertram stifled a laugh, winked, and walked away.

Weissbard knew he was going to have to go through the motions here. He'd take some notes, then send the loon on his way. He just didn't want to do it with an audience. He grabbed a pad of paper from his drawer and a pen. He rolled back from his desk and levered himself out of his chair. He winced at the weight he'd gained since he left the NYPD. He gave the kid a weary wave forward. "Follow me."

He led Brian into an interrogation room and closed the door. Brian took a seat at the table in the middle of the room. Weissbard dropped the tablet on the table and it hit with a slap. Brian shuddered. Weissbard collapsed into the other chair.

"So, Brian. Tell what you can about these series of murders."

"This is going to be hard to believe...."

Weissbard tried not to roll his eyes. If he had a dollar for every nut job who started his statement with that phrase....

"But I've seen them happen," Brian continued. "All three murders. At least I think it was three, but definitely two."

"So you're some kind of psychic?"

"No, nothing like that. I've never had visions like this before, not while I was on my medications."

This time Weissbard did roll his eyes.

"I can tell what you're thinking," Brian said. "Crazy guy off his crazy meds."

"No, I wasn't thinking that at all. Just tell me what you saw."

Brian started to tell him about the Viejo murder, reciting details already covered by every news outlet. Weissbard jotted down a few notes, mostly about errands to run on the way home.

"And where did the killer leave the playing card?" Weissbard asked.

"I don't know. I woke up before I saw that part."

Weissbard nodded. A convenient excuse. That detail from the investigation hadn't leaked out yet. "And you had this dream when?"

"About six days ago."

"Why didn't you come forward with this information then?"

"I thought it was just a nightmare, until I saw it in the news. I still waited, though. I figured you'd think I was crazy."

Not like I do now, Weissbard thought.

"But then I saw the other death, and I had to take the chance. I saw the killer murder a woman in the trunk of a car by the water."

"What kind of a car was it?"

"I don't know. It was dark. Wait, it seemed to be silver. Pretty big. Oh, a Toyota something."

"Didn't happen to catch the plate?"

"No, but it was from Florida."

That narrowed it down to several million Florida Toyotas. Weissbard's stomach growled that lunch was overdue.

"I saw the card on that woman. Tucked into her top before he put her in the water. A red card."

Fifty-fifty odds. Lucky guess. "And where was that?"

"On the south side of the bay. It looked like a boat ramp that hadn't been used in a long time."

That piqued his interest a bit. Given the currents, they suspected the body had floated up from the south.

"You saw all this, but you didn't see the killer? Is he wearing a mask?"

"No." Brian paused. "I see these things through his eyes, his point of view. I can see his hands. That's how I know he's white. And I saw a fuzzy reflection in the car window this last time."

"What did you see?"

"Seemed a little taller than me, blond hair, short, spiky. Dark eyes."

Weissbard took a few notes, then cursed himself for letting this guy send him on a goose chase. He was a patient off his meds, after all. He clicked his ballpoint pen and retracted the point. He rose from his chair.

Panic spread across Brian's face. "Look, it's wild, but you've got to believe me. You've got to help me. He's going to kill someone else! I don't want to see it. I don't want to feel that velvet rope again."

Weissbard froze in place. "What rope?"

"The braided rope he uses to strangle them. I can feel it in his hands as he tightens it around their necks. I don't want anyone else to die, but I really don't want to *feel* anyone else die ever again."

The cause of death for any of the women hadn't been released, and Weissbard hadn't seen it leaked on the news. But absolutely no one knew about the velvet rope. He'd only found out about an hour ago when the ME, Chamberlain, briefed the morning meeting and said they'd pulled red fibres from the necks of both victims.

"What colour is the rope?" Weissbard asked.

"Red, I think. It's hard to tell."

Weissbard lowered himself back into the chair. He clicked the ballpoint pen back into action. "Okay, let's start from the beginning."

CHAPTER NINETEEN

Detective Weissbard had left Brian alone in the interrogation room for almost forty-five minutes. It seemed a lot longer to Brian. If someone wasn't crazy, the Tampa police's interrogation room could drive them to it. Silent. Empty. Grey. The place was little different from the holding cells down the hall.

His image in the one-way glass along the wall looked like hell. His appearance hadn't helped him sell his story, a story he barely believed himself. But by the end, he was sure the detective believed him.

A tall man in a charcoal suit entered the room. He wasn't the detective Brian had spoken with earlier. He carried a file folder and an aura of authority. He was mid-fifties with one of those trim haircuts straight out of a TV commercial. He delivered an artificial smile Brian knew all too well.

"I'm Kent Williams," he said, without offering his hand. "Detective Weissbard asked me to speak with you."

"You're a shrink," Brian said with a sigh and put his head in his hands.

"I am a psychologist," Williams said.

"There isn't time for this," Brian said. He looked up into Williams' eyes. "The Playing Card Killer is going to murder again. We need to stop him."

"And you can help us?" Williams said.

"That's why I'm here."

"You've lived here all your life," Williams said. He flipped open the file. "You've never had any contact with the police. You called off work to be here. Your information must be important."

Weissbard must have spent the time out of the room doing a little Brian Sheridan research while someone rustled up this shrink. Brian hoped that his medical records weren't part of the package.

"I can give the police details about the killer," Brian said. Williams looked at him with feigned interest. "The news said that they didn't have a description, but I do. He's a white male, young, a little taller than me, with blond hair."

"And you saw the killer...?"

Brian really didn't want to do this part of the conversation again.

"In my dreams," Brian said.

"He came to you in a dream."

"No!" Brian yelled. "I already explained this to the detective."

He got hold of himself so his frustration would not come across as lunacy. "Days ago, I started having these dreams."

"You dreamed you kill people?"

"No, I watched the murders through the killer's eyes."

"And what have you seen in your dreams?"

"More than I want to, but not as much as you'd like."

"But your description of the killer is vague."

"I only caught a glimpse of him in a reflection. But I see his hands, so I'm sure he's white."

Williams nodded, more in acknowledgement than in acceptance of the story.

"Are these dreams premonitions?" Williams said. "Or do they happen after the killing has taken place?"

"As near as I can figure," Brian said, "they happen in real time, or just afterwards. It's hard to tell."

"Have you spoken to your therapist about your dreams?" Williams said.

This was just what Brian had dreaded. Some idiot would take his whole life out of context....

"I don't have a therapist."

"Dr. Kaufman seems to think he still has a patient, though," Williams said. "Your mother says you've missed some sessions."

Of course! he thought. *Camilla would certainly be thrilled to give the cops every damning detail she could.*

"I'm months away from being twenty-one and then my obligation will be done," Brian said. "I was fine."

Williams just stared at him.

"I'm not crazy," Brian said.

"I didn't say you were," Williams said. "How long have you been off your medications?"

"A week or two," Brian snapped. He paused and ran his fingers through his messy hair. "That's immaterial. I'm not imagining these things. They're really happening."

"When did you last sleep?"

Brian clenched and unclenched his hands into fists three times, rapid fire. He could feel Mr. Jitters warming up in the bull pen, ready to get into the game.

"I get a few hours each night. Can you blame me? Would you want to go back to sleep and watch another victim get strangled?"

"Anything else odd happening to you?" Williams asked. "Headaches, heart palpitations, blackouts, hallucinations? All of those would be common if you've been without decent sleep so long."

He imagined the shrink's reaction if he shared his hallucinations with him, gave him a little intro to Mr. Jitters. "No. Look, I came here to help. I tried. If you don't believe me, I'll leave."

"Wait here a minute," Williams said. He left the room.

Brian was so damn tired. Physically tired from lack of sleep. Emotionally tired from watching hell unfold at his hands when he finally did sleep. And especially tired of people thinking he was insane.

★ ★ ★

In the interview room's observation area, Weissbard watched Brian rest his head in his hands. Williams walked in.

"Well, Doc? Nut job?"

Williams sighed and shook his head at the pejorative term.

"It's hard to be definitive," Williams said, "with him so sleep deprived. But I have a theory. He's got a list of psychological issues stemming from an awful prenatal environment. His adoptive family says that he was always troubled. He was under the care of a therapist for years, but quit recently and got off his meds because he considered himself 'cured'."

"A little premature on that one," Weissbard said.

"A deep-seated need to be important and accepted could easily manifest itself in this minor break from reality," Williams continued. "He sees all the news about the Playing Card Killer, and then convinces himself that he's seen it all before. Given the depth of local coverage on it, he'd know the details."

"But we *have* found red velvet fibres on two of the victims' necks," the detective said. "We never released that information."

"Coincidence," Williams said. "Red as the colour for murder? A subconscious cliché. Plus…."

Williams pulled out his phone and tapped in a search. He showed Weissbard the result, a movie poster with a picture of two leather-gloved hands pulling a red rope around a woman's neck.

"*Tied in Knots* did eighty million at the box office this year. Who knows how many times he saw it? Even if all he saw were the ads for it, it would sure prime his subconscious pump to create a red rope killer."

Weissbard sighed and leaned back against the wall. "I thought maybe…."

"Then, add in the vague description of the killer, the man he only saw in a reflection. The description matches his own, except the killer had blond hair and Brian's is dark. He's taller, a subconscious cue for better. A reverse image thing, but one good, one evil. That's also his subconscious, manifesting the guilt of fabricating this whole thing.

"Plus, he has a job as a security guard. Most security guards are wanna-be cops. He also gets to live out that fantasy by helping the police."

The records showed that Sheridan had once applied for the high school Police Explorers program. Weissbard rubbed his temples. Had a hundred worthless leads made him grasp at this one blindly?

"Eric, seriously," Williams said. "Do you think he can see visions through the eyes of a killer? Do you think a judge will issue warrants based on that?"

Weissbard had to admit defeat. He wanted to kick himself for even entertaining the thought. "Safe to cut him loose?"

"He's no threat to himself or others," Williams said. "A solid night's sleep and he'll feel a hell of a lot better."

The detective looked at Brian with regret. "Great. Another dead end."

* * *

Brian stepped out of the police station completely dejected. Most people would be elated to hear a detective tell them 'You're free to go.' But that wasn't what Brian had gone inside to hear. He'd admit to some relief when the shrink's little interrogation didn't get him committed, but that wasn't enough to outweigh the feeling of failure. He'd tried and failed to forge the horror forced upon him each night into a weapon to end it. He would have to live with it on his own.

He walked to his car in a daze. He didn't want another nightmare, another vision, another whatever it was that ripped his sleep to shreds. Last night's self-medication still hadn't been enough. He'd bump up the dose, maybe double it. He'd make himself catatonic if he had to, but he never wanted to see, to feel, that velvet rope again.

His phone buzzed with a message. Another unknown four-digit number. He knew it was spam, but summoned the message anyway.

Your new beginning is right around the corner read the message from the Totally You Institute.

He was too depressed to get angry. A part of him wished the fortune cookie-like spam was true. He could use a new beginning right about now.

CHAPTER TWENTY

Weissbard slipped out of bed the next morning without rousing his wife. He was so proud of the accomplishment he almost woke her up to brag about it. He shivered and put on his robe. Maryanne grew up in Buffalo, couldn't stand the Florida humidity, and, as far as he was concerned, kept the house two degrees above freezing. Of course, she'd never wanted to move here at all, so he sucked up having cold feet, wore a robe in the summer and paid the high electric bill.

He entered the kitchen and flicked on the light. Goober shook himself awake, rose and sauntered over for some morning affection. Weissbard reached down and thumped his side. The dog grinned and wagged his tail.

Maryanne stepped into the doorway and leaned against the frame. Apparently his stealth skills weren't as good as he thought. She fluffed her long, curly dark hair with her fingertips and squinted at the overhead light. Even over fifty, even in flannel pyjamas, he thought she still looked hot.

"I tried not to wake you," he said.

"Why are you up so early?"

"I don't know. The case, I guess." He refused to use the phrase Playing Card Killer.

"What are you thinking?"

"That guy who came in midday yesterday? The crazy one? What if he wasn't crazy?"

Maryanne stepped into the kitchen and started filling the coffeepot with water. "You mean he really saw the murders happen through the murderer's eyes?"

"Yeah, but not the way he thinks. What if he was the murderer?"

"You think?"

"Not at first. He was such a wreck. Didn't think he could pull a few murders off. But now..."

She started the coffee maker and pulled a pan from under the sink.

"You making breakfast?" he said.

"As long as I'm up, you're eating eggs. I let you leave the house hungry, you head straight for Dunkin' Donuts. And that goes straight where?" She pointed to his waistline.

No one had more love in their nagging than Maryanne. Even after thirty years of it, her good intentions kept it from getting on his nerves.

"That kid," he continued. "He knew some stuff. Specific stuff."

"I thought it was coincidental."

"Maybe. Maybe not. Good cops—"

"—never buy coincidences," they said together.

"So why would he come down to the station?" she said. She dropped two eggs in the pan and they started to sizzle. The coffee machine spit and gurgled.

"Maybe he's playing us. Wants to feed us enough clues to give chase. Thinks he can outwit us."

"Maybe he really is crazy," Maryanne said, "and doesn't even know he's turning himself in. Some kind of split personality."

Weissbard smiled. He had been the envy of the other NYPD detectives. While their wives resented and often even hated the job, Maryanne embraced it, talked shop better than some partners he'd had, and at times had some pretty keen insight.

"Could be. His background sure as hell isn't stable. Either way, I ought to check into it some more. Just to be sure."

Maryanne poured a cup of coffee and set it in front of him. He slid the sugar bowl over and popped the top. The grains looked all wrong. Artificial sweetener instead of sugar. She was a doll. He raised a spoonful at her.

"You trying to keep me alive or something?"

"At least until you start drawing a second pension from Tampa." She kissed the top of his head. "After that, I stop worrying so much."

* * *

Two eggs and two cups of coffee later, Weissbard piloted his black Dodge Charger down country roads south of Gibsontown. According to the details he'd gotten from Brian Sheridan, Sheridan could see the Tampa skyline from where the killer dumped Carla Alessandro. If that was true, it would be along this shoreline. Somewhere.

The morning hadn't turned blazing hot yet, and he had the windows rolled down. A light breeze swept the tang of salty water through the car, along with a whiff of algae. After the cold of his house, it felt pretty good.

He kept an eye on the GPS, and one after another, explored whatever road nudged closest to the water. Marshes blocked the view at most spots he found, marshes that would have trapped Carla's body before it ever got to the bay. Each discovery added to his sense of failure, compounded by knowing, even before he left on this quest, that the county had no records of any boat ramps in the area, past or present.

The road turned south. An old orange grove stretched out on the left, filled with knurled trees long past their fruiting prime. Sandy scrub sloped down and away from the road to the right. A distant tree line blocked the view of the bay beyond.

The blacktop curved back to the left, but to the right ran the twin sandy ruts of an old farm road. The ageing grove had probably once covered this side of the road as well, until creeping salinity had poisoned the roots of the trees. On a whim, Weissbard spun the wheel and turned right.

The GPS barked a warning message to turn around. Weissbard silenced it. The car's stiff pursuit suspension bounced and bucked along the rough road. As he approached the tree line, a chain-link fence became visible beyond it. The section across the road had been cut and peeled to the right like a page in a book. He slowed as he passed through the opening. Rusty edges on the fence indicated that the breach was years old.

The strengthening sun beat down on the car's roof and the interior began to get stuffy. He continued a slow drive west.

According to the map at the precinct, this spit of land was owned by an oil company, but it functioned as little more than a broad barrier for the docks and facilities to the south. He doubted any employees checked on it much. They certainly hadn't noticed the broken fence.

His car rolled out of the trees and into an open, grassy area. He followed the tyre ruts in a sweeping right-hand turn. A thousand yards up, he stopped at the edge of Tampa Bay. His pulse quickened. In the distance rose the city's towers. They looked far away in the daylight, but at night, all lit up, they would look much closer.

He got out of the car and walked toward the water. A gust ruffled the long grass at his feet. Tiny, gentle waves caressed the thin, sandy shore. Seagulls squawked over some prize at the water's edge. He caught his breath as he spied a prize of his own off to the right.

The slab foundation of an old beach house stuck out of the weeds. Years ago, it laid flat, probably set well back from the bay. But tides and currents had scoured away the shoreline, and now it canted down toward the water, water only a few feet away.

Weissbard walked over and stood on its dry, upper edge. Damp black algae blanketed the lower half, nurtured by wind-driven spray. He imagined the scene at night, in low light, at a higher tide. This would look like a boat ramp. Out ahead, the water swept out between two small spoil islands. He shaded his eyes with his hand. Even at this distance he could see the retreating tide creating a current that rushed between the islands and out to the bay. A corpse, a light corpse like Carla Alessandro's, would be gone in no time.

He pumped a fist in victory. His joy was short lived. His discovery wouldn't prove anything to anyone else. Nightly thunderstorms had washed away any possible evidence. This location would be one of many the forensics guys could confirm as possible sites where Carla's body could have been dumped. All pretty circumstantial, all useless by itself.

This little revelation certainly strengthened the possibility that Sheridan was telling the truth about what he saw. But it didn't put Weissbard any closer to knowing how Sheridan saw it. Was it because he did have some special supernatural vision, or was he just another psycho killer? The cop part of him dismissed the first option out of hand.

It was time to start investigating the second.

CHAPTER TWENTY-ONE

A few hours later, Weissbard beat his fist against Sidney Johnson's apartment door. Sometimes it paid to start with intimidating, and work his way down to friendly from there. Sometimes he didn't need to work his way down.

"Sidney Johnson!" he shouted. "Detective Weissbard, Tampa PD. Open the door!"

"Shit! Don't bust down the door! Coming."

The door opened a crack, stopped by a flimsy chain. Sidney Johnson's sleepy face peered out, squinting. Weissbard shoved his badge in front of the man.

"Oh, hey," Sidney said. "You got the wrong guy. I didn't do nothing."

Weissbard's experience was that people who said they didn't do anything were the ones who certainly did something. "I'm not here about something you did, Sidney. I need to talk to you about Brian Sheridan."

"Shit, that figures." The door closed an inch and the chain dropped away. Sidney opened the door wide. "C'mon in."

The apartment looked like the usual bachelor disaster zone Weissbard had seen a thousand times. Homes might look neat and clean in the movies, but Weissbard knew that in real life, people were pigs. Sidney sat down on the edge of a beat-up couch. Weissbard stood, again to keep the intimidation factor up, but the apartment's generally low level of sanitation was a good reason all on its own. He pulled out his pocket notebook.

"You work with Brian Sheridan?"

"Yeah. He's a security guard at Orange Trucking. I run the crane."

"You seemed the furthest thing from surprised when I said I wanted to talk to you about him."

"The dude's kind of weird, you know. All jittery and shit. I'm out there because it's a job. He's there because it fits him. He actually likes being alone in his little box."

"Have you seen any recent changes in his behaviour?"

"Well, he's been getting weirder these last weeks. More jittery than usual, and he's jittery as hell to start with. Kind of distracted."

That was a little too coincidental with the start of the Playing Card Killer murders for Weissbard. He noted that. "What time do you two get off work?"

"We don't do nothing together." Sidney sounded indigent at the assumption. "Shift ends at ten p.m. Me, sometimes earlier if there ain't no trains due."

"Where do you guys hang after work?"

Sidney looked repulsed. "Hang? Ain't you listening? We don't *hang*. Like I said, the guy's weird as shit."

Weissbard paused to let some silence ratchet up the tension.

"So you've been off parole, what, five years now?"

Fear crossed Sidney's face and Weissbard knew he hit the jackpot.

"That's all in the past," Sidney said. "All of it. I'm straight, I'm clean. Don't go pinning me with whatever shit Brian's got going down."

Sidney seemed credible, his answers consistent, his fear genuine. Weissbard finished up with a few innocuous questions and handed Sidney his card.

"What'd the guy do?" Sidney asked.

"Probably nothing," Weissbard said. "Just checking some background information. Routine. Still, you should keep our conversation between the two of us."

"You got it."

Weissbard left Sidney and went back to his car. Sidney didn't look like he bought Weissbard's lame explanation for his visit. Perfect. That meant Sidney would tell Brian all about it. That might lead somewhere interesting.

Weissbard picked up his phone and started to dial. He needed a warrant.

CHAPTER TWENTY-TWO

Brian's stomach felt like he'd dropped a pound of lead into it.

He'd skipped breakfast and opted for a mega coffee from a convenience store instead. Now all that liquid bathed his stomach in an acidic bath of caffeine and sugar. He reclined the driver's seat of his car and tried to give his stomach a little room to digest.

The over-the-counter sleeping pills hadn't been worth a damn. Since he'd called in to work yesterday to talk to the cops, he'd taken a double dose last night and hoped for eight hours of blacked-out sleep. Instead, he tossed and turned all night and got zero. Drugs had held his hyperactivity at bay for years. Maybe dropping them now released all of that pent-up energy.

He knew that wasn't true. A mix of adrenaline and frustration had kept him wired and ready all night. He bounced between books and television and surfing the net and none of it made him any more tired. From the moment he left the police station, his anxiety had hit a new high, and for him that was saying something. He'd put everything out there for Detective Weissbard, and been rewarded with a visit from a criminal shrink. His quick escort out of the building afterwards told him everything he needed to know. Weissbard had handed him his card and said to keep him updated. But Brian knew they'd pigeonholed him into the harmless-whack-job box.

He'd kept one thing to himself, his visions of Keisha, the little girl strangled and left in the decaying building. The police hadn't found her yet. If he'd brought that up, it might have sounded weird, or worse, incriminating, giving Weissbard something that sounded more like a prediction than a confirmation. Weissbard seemed to believe him for a while near the interview's end, and Brian had considered telling him about Keisha. But then the shrink arrived, and Brian knew exactly where he stood.

There was the possibility Keisha had been found and hadn't made the news cycle's cut. That would lift a weight off his shoulders. Brian accessed the Tampa Police Missing Persons website from his phone. Keisha was still listed.

No matter how they treated him, that didn't mean the police shouldn't know where that poor girl was, didn't mean her family shouldn't get some closure. The Playing Card Killer seemed meticulous, but he still might have left a clue at that crime scene. Everyone makes mistakes.

Brian needed to relay more concrete information the next time he talked to the police, more than an embarrassingly vague vision like 'the trunk of the car was silver'. He knew that little clue was useless the minute he shared it.

He pulled the old Florida map out of his glove compartment. He preferred the way he could look at a bigger picture than his cell phone could give him. He needed to see if this murderer left a pattern, one he could hand to the police. On his phone, he called up the article he'd read earlier on the murders. He found the locations where Meredith Viejo and her Volvo were last seen, and where Karen Strong lived in Brewster, east of the city. He circled both. Karen's body was found in her home, but Meredith's was left in the Croom Wildlife Management Area. He found the park and circled that. It wasn't far from where she'd gone missing. That made sense. The killer would have had to walk back to his own car after leaving her car and body in the woods. Perhaps he'd gained some confidence after killing Karen.

Then Brian found Keisha's home address. According to her parents, the girl couldn't have been far from there when she disappeared. Brian had driven through that neighbourhood off Hillsborough Drive a few times. It matched the feel of the houses he'd seen in the vision. He circled her house.

The killer had murdered Keisha, and then taken her to the abandoned business, probably in his own car. He could have taken her anywhere. But on the other hand, how comfortable would he have been crisscrossing Tampa with a cooling corpse in his trunk? Brian guessed the killer would have stopped at the first place he saw that would meet his deranged standards. Or, if the man was a master planner, he'd found the place to dump the body first, then hunted a convenient, close target of opportunity. Either way, Brian's guess was that the two locations would be near each other.

He moved his seat back upright and burped something with an unappetising flavour. He shuddered, started the car, and set out for north Tampa.

* * *

Hillsborough Avenue cut across north Tampa like a six-lane C-section scar, and like the blemishes from each stitch, small, borderline businesses populated the edges. Ageing, lower middle-class ranch homes on unkempt sandy lots filled the uninspired street grid along both sides. If there was an antithesis of the Florida lifestyle sold on late-night TV commercials, north Tampa was it.

The late-morning traffic was light enough that Brian could take his time cruising the right lane without starting a road-rage incident. He tried to recall the background of his vision, not an easy task when the terror in the foreground was so all-consuming. He could remember the floor, dirty, grey industrial-style tile. White specks from decaying or broken drop ceiling tiles were everywhere, like a snow flurry on frozen blacktop. The rest of the room that he could see was empty, the walls bare, one of them covered in plywood.

That was no help. The building could have been anywhere.

Well, not anywhere. It was definitely unoccupied, and the poor condition of the room made it unlikely that it was one abandoned unit in the middle of a bunch of occupied ones. The room was in a vacant building. And one that wouldn't attract attention, because the poor girl's body hadn't been found yet.

Brian made it all the way to I-75. He hung a U-turn and headed back west. The oppressive midday sun kept the sidewalks deserted. Fear that some of his assumptions were incorrect began to creep in. He strummed his fingers against the steering wheel. He couldn't spend all day driving around here. He *had* to go to work today. He couldn't miss two days in a row and expect to stay employed.

The light ahead turned red. Brian slowed the car to a stop. A motorcycle rumbled up beside him. Unmuffled exhaust cracked and sputtered outside his door. Even with his window rolled up, the jagged noise set his teeth on edge. He stuck one finger against his left ear and looked away, wincing.

Just a half-block down the cross street stood a closed convenience store. The corporate logos had been long ago stripped away, only the frame of the upright sign by the curb remained. The roof over the ravaged refuel island sagged as if exhausted. A chain-link fence circled the property.

That place might fit the bill. Brian turned right on the red light and stopped across from the store.

Plywood covered the windows from the inside. Perhaps that's what Brian had seen in his vision, not a plywood wall, but plywood over the windows. Yellow warning signs hung on the fence, declaring that trespassing was forbidden due to toxic chemicals.

Brian remembered a lot of stories in the news about old underground gas tanks that had leaked and contaminated the soil around them, and even poisoned the ground water in some soggier places of the state. Even crackheads might have enough functioning brain cells left to steer clear of this place, and leave the killer a little more time for any clues to degrade before someone found his victim.

Brian pulled down a side street and up along the rear of the security fence. Near the far end, a few twisted metal ties held the chain link in place against a stainless-steel pole. The ties were much flimsier than those in the rest of the fencing. Someone had gone to the effort to remove the stronger ties, break in, and make it pretty easy for someone else to break in afterwards.

Brian's phone buzzed and startled him out of his concentration. The thought of it being another Totally You Institute message irked him. He picked his phone up from the car's console. The incoming number was from Orange Star Trucking. He answered.

"Hello?"

"Hey, it's Terry." The day-shift security guard sounded worried. "Are you coming in today?"

"Yeah, of course. Why?"

"Dude, you missed yesterday and I had to stay over at the last minute to cover you. I don't need the OT, and I've got my son tonight. I need to know way earlier if you're going to screw me over again."

"No, I'll be there. I'm feeling much better than yesterday."

"Okay. Don't go getting no 'relapse' between now and then."

Terry hung up. Brian shoved his phone in his pocket and shifted his concentration back to the fence. He could just call in a tip to the cops and have them check the place out. But what if this wasn't the spot and he stopped looking? Keisha might not be found for who knows how long. He considered coming back when it was dark, then guessed this neighbourhood at night wasn't anywhere he wanted to be. He had no choice but to check it out now. Just a quick look around, and then he'd be back in his car.

His left leg began the anxiety bounce. His heart fluttered. The dread of an impending anxiety attack bubbled up inside him like poisoned water.

From the back seat came a rhythmic thud in sync with his bouncing leg. Then his seat rocked in the same cadence. Brian panicked that he was not alone.

"Well, dig this groovy locale!" Mr. Jitters screamed into Brian's ear.

Brian jolted forward and slammed his chest against the steering wheel. The horn blared, startled him again, and he slammed back into the headrest.

Mr. Jitter's long, spindly arms shot forward over Brian's shoulders. Bony hands clamped against his chest. They compressed Brian into the seat so hard he could barely breathe.

Mr. Jitters screeched out a laugh and stuck his head across into the front seat. His top hat touched the glass. His painted face stopped almost cheek to cheek with Brian. A stink like rotting roadkill rolled off Mr. Jitters in waves.

Brian flinched away. Mr. Jitters yanked him back.

"You know what's in that sweet little building?" Mr. Jitters said. "Rats. Mould. Broken toilets filled with meth addict shit. Rotted floors ready to collapse. All waiting on you."

Mr. Jitters' nails jabbed into Brian's chest and sent ten pricks of fire radiating across his skin.

"Best thing though? That girl. She's going to be there. Staring right at you with the same eyes you saw when she died. But buddy, the rats will have had a feast. Climbing all over her, climbing inside her. Hope you liked your last meal, because this place is going to bring it back up for a second taste."

Brian closed his eyes. The images Mr. Jitters described filled his imagination and he was certain every one awaited him.

"You aren't real," Brian whispered in desperation. "You aren't real."

The fingernails dug deeper into Brian's chest. Hot blood oozed from the wounds.

"Does that feel real, man? Does your pounding heart, ready to burst, feel real?"

Brian reached for the door handle. Mr. Jitters slapped back his hand.

Brian's blood pressure spiked and his head felt ready to explode. Sweat seeped from every pore but his skin felt wildfire hot.

"Better yet," Jitters said into Brian's ear. Even his breath felt oily, malevolent. "The killer might still be there. Knowing you'll come. Waiting to make you the next corpse holding a playing card in your stiff, cold hands."

In panic, Brian lunged for the door. He threw it open and tumbled out into the weedy parking lot. He landed on all fours. His head swam.

He turned and looked back into the car.

Empty. No terrorising back seat passenger.

A pat of his chest revealed no blood where he'd felt Mr. Jitters' nails pierce him. He focused on his breathing, on calming his racing heart.

Everything Mr. Jitters said could be true. All his nightmares could soon play out in that closed convenience store.

He rose to his knees.

But he couldn't let fear stop him. No matter what was in there, he had to look. Someone had to find little Keisha Valentiner. He staggered over to the fence. The area was deserted. He untwisted the top and middle ties. With one shove the fence peeled back enough to let him in. He stepped over the bottom tie and into the convenience store lot.

Two restroom doors interrupted the flat, concrete-block surface of the store's windowless back wall. Large, rusting padlocks secured both of them. Brian approached the store with a short sprint, and then worked his way around to the side. He tried to move in something less than an attention-grabbing dash, and not so close to the wall that he looked sneaky. He guessed he failed at both.

He approached the corner. Two voices came from the front of the building. He backed up against the wall and froze. He realised that while everyone did that in the movies, it didn't make him any less observable in the real world. He felt like an idiot.

The voices came from two boys. Between the street slang and the Haitian accents, he couldn't make out the words. But the tone was conversational, joking. Brian peered around the corner. The two boys appeared on the sidewalk, one in basketball shorts, the other in sagging jeans that exposed bright boxers. Neither wore a shirt to cover their bony torsos. They walked away from him, down the street, with light, bouncing steps.

He sighed in relief. The boys moved out of sight, and Brian turned the corner. The street was empty. He headed for the front of the store.

Weeds sprouted through cracks in the sidewalk along the building's edge. Black mould stained the formerly white walls. In the parking spot in front of the door, just the faintest outline of a blue handicapped symbol remained. Brian stepped to the twin entrance doors. Two keyed deadbolts secured them, but jagged silver scratches gouged the surfaces of both faces. Faded decals on the glass offered the advice to push or pull, and another set displayed a half-dozen credit cards the store used to take. Like the big windows further down, plywood covered the doors from behind.

But the plywood stopped just short of the door's bottom. Brian knelt and peered through the two-inch gap. He couldn't see into the store in the darkness, but he could see the floor near the doorway. That was enough to get his heart pumping harder.

The tiles matched the ones in his vision.

A sound caught his attention. Low, muted, droning. He placed one ear against the slit between the two doors. Buzzing. Lots of buzzing.

He shuddered and pulled away. His mind filled in the picture. Flies. Hundreds of them. They wouldn't be there without a food source, and nothing fresh had been in this place in years. Except the corpse left inside by the Playing Card Killer. He conjured an image of Keisha's decomposing body, then quickly wiped it away.

Anxiety spiked to new heights. His skin crawled at the thought of being so close to a dead body. His breathing accelerated. He didn't want Mr. Jitters adding his play-by-play to this scene. He scrambled away from the door, and went straight back to the gap in the fence. He snagged a shoelace on the open fencing and nearly landed on his face. He finally made it to his car and locked himself inside.

He didn't need to see the corpse. Circumstantial evidence would be plenty good enough for him here. He started his car, and went straight for Hillsborough Avenue, ready for some distance between him and the dead little girl. He stopped at the red light, barely cleared himself for the turn, and headed east.

He reached for his phone to call Detective Weissbard, then realised how stupid that would be. He didn't need to be in this serial killer mess any deeper than he already was. He could instead call the anonymous tip line the news report mentioned, but he didn't trust it. It would have to have caller ID. He could do it online from his phone. He wasn't sure, but he doubted that was any more anonymous than a phone call.

Two blocks down, an internet café operated in a shopworn strip mall. Around here, the cafés had replaced the banks of pay phones immigrants used to use to keep in touch with family back home. That place seemed like a safe option. Even if someone traced the internet connection back to one of those computers, the trail would end there, not with him.

Brian pulled into the parking lot. A quick search didn't uncover any security cameras. A good sign. He got out of his car.

Inside the café, rows of low-end laptops sat on folding tables. Wires and cables snaked away to power strips and wall sockets. An unwholesome collection of men occupied some of the cheap, white plastic seats in front of the computers. This was the other end of the spectrum from hipsters hanging out online in an upscale coffee shop. But there weren't any security cameras here either. Apparently, users wanted their privacy, though he was certain for far darker reasons than his own.

This place would do just fine. He started to compose the message in his head, the details, the location, and a specific mention that it was for Detective Weissbard.

CHAPTER TWENTY-THREE

The day-shift guard, Terry, sighed with relief when Brian arrived at Orange Star Trucking, apparently still wary that another afternoon of forced overtime might be in his future, no matter what Brian had promised. Twenty minutes after they changed shifts, a whistle screamed to announce a train's arrival at the yard. Brian checked the manifests. Two were due tonight, and a bunch of trucks. That was good. A busy night would keep his mind off all the events he'd set in motion in north Tampa. His online tip was too specific for anyone to get it wrong.

Sidney burst into the guard shack.

"Shouldn't you be unloading that train?" Brian said.

"Screw that shit! I need to know what the hell you done. Why you have the cops calling at my apartment?"

Brian's stomach dropped. "What cops?"

"Some fat detective. Asked me about you, about working with you. Man, you doing some illegal shit? Stealing stuff from the combis? Shipping out drugs? I don't need none of that. I been off parole five years, don't need no police shit going on."

Panic began to build in Brian. What was Weissbard doing looking into him? Brian thought the cop had dismissed him as a screwball. What had elevated him to the status of suspect? And what stupid answers had Sidney given that probably drove the cop's suspicions even higher?

Brian hadn't known before this that Sidney had been on parole. He thought fast.

"What did *I* do?" Brian said. "I should ask you the same question. That same cop was at my place, asking about you."

Sidney's expression shifted from confrontational to paranoid. "What the hell? I ain't done nothing!"

"The cop didn't seem so sure. What did he ask you about?"

"Work schedules, whether you're a freak, that kind of shit."

That wasn't good news. "Same thing he asked me about you. I bet something's going on here, like you said. And the first guy they look at is the guy with the record."

"Don't you know it!" Sidney said. "Been that way ever since, and my stuff was misdemeanour shit. Bet it's one of those night-shift guys. Don't trust any of those vampire types far as I can throw 'em."

"Yeah, we need to watch our backs," Brian said. "That cop comes back with more questions, I'm not saying a word, and I'll tell you about it right away."

"Yeah, same here."

The train whistle blew again, this time with more insistence.

Sidney kicked open the door. "Yeah. Keep your shit together. I'm coming." He stomped off in the crane's direction.

"Damn it," Brian whispered to himself. His whole body burned with an anxiety rush. How could Weissbard think he was a killer? He started his breathing exercises and tried like hell to calm down.

* * *

About 9:30, Brian did his end-of-shift yard check, and he needed the release. Sitting in the guard shack, worrying about Weissbard cooking up some whacked theory of Brian's guilt, was eating him alive.

High overhead lights underlit the yard. It always reminded Brian of London in Jack the Ripper movies, just enough light to get by, just enough shadow to put him on edge. He walked the lot between rows of containers, shining his flashlight on the metal strip door seals then down underneath each mounted container to look for leaks or flat tyres. Sidney had been busy and the lot was full. He couldn't hear the crane now, so the rail cars must have finally sat empty.

Near the end of the row, a metallic clank sounded from the edge of the yard. Brian's senses went on alert. A few months ago, some teens had snuck in while the back gate was open for the rail cars' delivery. They had bags of spray paint and Brian had cut short their planned tagging festival on the combis. Something like that was the last thing he needed tonight.

He played his flashlight beam far down to the end of the row and saw nothing. He quickened his pace. Metal on metal clanked again somewhere up ahead and off to the right. He jogged to the end of the row and stopped.

He played the light to the right and lit up a collection of inverted, empty steel drums and the big blue dumpster beyond them. Nothing moved.

"This is the yard security," he yelled. His voice had a little too much nervous squeak to be as commanding as he hoped. "The police are dispatched and on their way. Come out before they get here and things get hairy."

No response.

Brian moved in closer. Sweat beaded on his upper lip. Situations like this were why he'd asked management to let him at least carry mace on the job. The lawyers said no. He shined the light up the narrow space between the rows of drums. Empty.

From behind the dumpster came the rustle of motion. He cocked one ear that way. Footsteps on leaves? A body brushing palm fronds? Muffled by the steel walls of the drums and dumpster, he couldn't tell. The hairs on his arms pricked to attention.

He sidestepped across the dumpster's front. The heavy metal lid lay closed. At the corner, he looked down the side and lit up the row of scrubby palms along the yard's edge. He took a step forward.

Fronds rustled and something burst from between them. Brian jumped back, startled. The flashlight's beam danced in his shaking hand. Two beady eyes flashed at him.

A raccoon. Bolt upright on its hind legs like a miniature grizzly bear. It bared its teeth, dropped to all fours, and sauntered off through the leaf litter.

Brian exhaled like a deflating tyre. The killer's visions had him strung tight as a harp string, and had sent his imagination somewhere dark. Two weeks ago, he'd have assumed it was a raccoon from the start, not some lurking psychopath.

He wiped the sweat from his brow and continued his inspection. He passed the silent crane. The rail cars were empty, but the light in the crane cab still burned. Sidney was nowhere to be seen. Brian figured he must have stoked Sidney's paranoia pretty good if he'd taken off so fast after he finished that he left the crane lights on.

Brian returned to the guard shack. Sidney's car was gone from the lot, departed while Brian was chasing wildlife around the empty drum maze. Brian guessed Sidney wouldn't be sleeping well tonight either.

Things could turn around, though, he hoped. Cops following his tip should be swarming that closed convenience store about now. Maybe they would find some evidence, evidence that would point Weissbard well away from him.

CHAPTER TWENTY-FOUR

Red and blue lights sliced through the night along Hillsborough Avenue. Not an uncommon sight, but the multiple cruisers and the roadblocks were enough to draw a crowd. Weissbard waited inside the barricade for the inevitable arrival of Detective Sergeant Francisco. Weissbard getting here first was not going to make the guy happy. At all.

A black, two-door, late-model Cadillac with flashing blue lights embedded in the grill came tearing down Hillsborough Avenue from the west. Weissbard took a deep breath. Francisco had somehow gotten himself assigned that car out of impound last year. The Caddy pulled up outside the barricades with a screech. Francisco stepped out and a uniformed cop practically fell over himself passing the detective through the barricade. Weissbard shook his head and walked over.

"How is it you ended up here before me?" Francisco said.

"I was screening items off the tip line, at your direction. One tip said there'd be a body in this abandoned convenience store. Turned out to be right."

"Why didn't you notify me when you went to investigate?"

"Most of these things turn out to be nothing. I didn't want to waste your valuable time."

Weissbard kept in just a whiff of sarcasm, enough to keep Francisco guessing.

They walked through the now-opened gate to the convenience store and passed the coroner's van. They stopped at the front of the store. Both doors were propped open. The stench rolled out like a fog. Portable lights lit the interior.

"When did you get here?" Francisco asked.

"About an hour ago," Weissbard said. "Went in through a slit in the fencing around back. As soon as I saw her, I called in backup and the coroner."

Inside, Cal Cambridge, the coroner, knelt over the body of a girl. African American, in short shorts and a tight T-shirt. Flies buzzed around Weissbard's head like fighter jets. He tried to wave them away. A gurney stood ready at the corpse's side.

"Hey, Cambridge," Weissbard said.

"Weissbard." Cambridge stood. He was about six feet tall, shaved bald with high cheekbones. In the right light the coroner had the unfortunate tendency to look cadaverous. This was the right light. He noticed Francisco at Weissbard's side. "And Sergeant Francisco's here, despite a lack of media attendance."

One of the things Weissbard really liked about Cambridge was his completely undisguised disgust for Francisco. Being in a separate chain of command was liberating that way.

"Screw you, Cambridge," Francisco said. "What do we have?"

"Young girl, about six years old. Probably going to match that missing-person report from this area a few days ago. Looks to have been dead about that long."

Being a homicide detective inured Weissbard to a lot, but dead children always hit him hard. "Cause of death?"

"No sexual assault, thank God for her. No obvious wounds, except ligature marks around the neck. And you won't be happy to see what I pulled from her hands."

Cambridge passed Weissbard a clear evidence bag. The four of spades sat inside it.

"Damn it." Weissbard sighed.

He handed the bag back. Francisco snatched it away. Two CSI technicians walked up behind them.

"I want every millimetre of this place screened," Francisco said, and waved them in. "The killer left us something."

But one look at the place set Weissbard's expectations low. A filthy, empty room, with the body in it for days. And the Playing Card Killer had watched enough episodes of crime TV shows to never leave much in the way of clues. Out of hand, Weissbard wrote off finding a fingerprint on the playing card.

He stepped out into the fresher air and leaned back against the wall of the store. Inside, Francisco gave unnecessary direction to everyone. Weissbard knew he could walk away and Francisco would never ask where he went.

This was becoming a homicide detective's nightmare. Four killings with the same signature and method, but with everything else different. Save gender, there was no commonality in the victims, the abduction locations appeared random, as were the locations where the bodies were found. No evidence but playing cards and a velvet rope to tie these things together. But three of the victims had something in common.

Brian Sheridan knew all about them. That screwball guy who Sergeant Bertram had dumped on him was going to turn out to be the lynchpin to solve this case. And Weissbard would do it well under Francisco's radar until the very last minute.

Some unknown tipster called in about this body. Weissbard's gut had a hunch who that concerned citizen might be. Time to track down that anonymous internet tip.

CHAPTER TWENTY-FIVE

As the sun rose hot and overbearing over Tampa the next morning, the detective squad room thrummed tight with tension. Chalking up a serial killer's victims wasn't the department's mandate. They were supposed to be preventing them. And whether each detective idolised Francisco or thought he was a jackass, they all wanted this killer caught. Leads went all over the place and detectives were fanned out across the county trying to uncover the identity of the serial killer.

Weissbard had kept Brian Sheridan to himself. First out of embarrassment for buying the story of someone Dr. Williams thought was one step from certifiable. But since last night, he'd kept it to himself because he was more and more convinced that betting the mortgage payment on Sheridan would pay out. One piece after another said that kid was tied to the killings. When it all proved true, he wanted the credit. He'd have fun shoving that back in Francisco's face. Then he'd get the last laugh on Sergeant Bertram for sending Sheridan to him in the first place.

His precinct desk phone rang. The ID was from Washburn in what Weissbard called the Forensics Geek Squad. Computers, phones, internet, tech. What SWAT did with brawn, those guys did with brains. Weissbard picked up the phone.

"Weissbard."

"It's Washburn. I've got the IP and an address for that computer used to connect to the tip line."

Weissbard flipped his notebook open to Sheridan's apartment address. "Give it to me."

Washburn read an address on Hillsborough Avenue. Weissbard cursed. He scribbled down the location. "How about those phone records I asked for?"

"Not here yet. I'll call you when they are."

Weissbard hung up. He searched the address on his desktop. Lourdes' internet Café. Damn it. The bit of information he thought would seal the case against Sheridan instead practically disproved it. It made perfect sense that someone, anyone, could have found the body, then walked a few blocks down Hillsborough and sent in the tip.

"Oh, hell," he said to himself. "I followed it this far. Might as well confirm it was a waste of time." He pulled himself out of his chair, and headed for the parking garage.

★ ★ ★

Weissbard's view through the front window of the internet café revealed rows of laptops lined up on folding tables. They stretched the length of the shotgun strip mall storefront. Half were in use, mostly by people Weissbard could stop for probable cause on appearance alone. Criminal intent has a look all its own. A Pakistani clerk sat at a desk beside the front door.

Weissbard stepped inside the internet café, detective's badge displayed prominently on his belt beside the buckle, pistol sitting high on one hip. Faces turned in his direction. Eyes went wide with fear. A cacophony of keystrokes filled the air as browsers closed and users deleted histories. Weissbard smiled. Just the effect he was looking for. He turned to the clerk by the door.

"I'm Detective Weissbard, Tampa PD. Are you the manager?"

"Yes. I'm Rashid." The clerk had a shrill, fast clip to his accent.

"Rashid, we had someone involved in a criminal investigation possibly use one of your computers. Do you have any records of who was logged on yesterday afternoon?"

"I'm sorry, all our client information is treated with the strictest confidentiality," Rashid said twice as loud as necessary.

Tension eased from many of the faces at the laptops. Weissbard's blood pressure ticked up. He leaned in closer to Rashid.

"You aren't running a doctor's office, or a confessional. You're running a sleazy little shop where people download the porn they don't want their wife to see, or wire money for whatever marginally legal business they conduct."

"And all it takes is a warrant to see as much of that as you want," Rashid said.

Rashid had obviously been well-coached by whatever consigliere the owner kept on retainer. Weissbard loved a challenge.

"Sure, I can get that. And it would have to be for a pretty broad period, maybe a week to be safe. Confiscating all the hardware would probably be the easiest way to check everything. Narcotics, Sex Crimes, INS and Homeland Security would probably want to look at it all, I mean, as long as it's lying around. It's the end of the month and we all need to make our arrest quotas, you know?"

Weissbard paused to let his vision of the future sink in. "Or you can voluntarily show me who was logged in on one IP address at twelve-oh-three p.m. yesterday. I'll quietly finger my murder suspect, and your scumbag clientele over there won't be any the wiser."

They stared at each other. Then Rashid blinked and swallowed. Apparently coming back with a warrant wasn't what he wanted Weissbard to do after all. He cleared his throat and retrieved a ledger from the side of the desk. He quietly opened it up to yesterday's page without looking down.

"With discretion, please," he whispered with a furtive glance back to his customers. "What is the IP address?"

Weissbard read it to him. He looked down a list.

"Station 21."

Weissbard ran his finger down the ledger to Station 21. Mickey Mouse was signed in. Most of the names around it were bogus as well.

"I guess you don't ask for ID," Weissbard said. "This is useless."

"But I can get you something else," Rashid said. He turned back to his computer and began to tap keys. "Every laptop has a camera. Every camera takes a user picture for each session. Covering our ass in a worst-case scenario."

"And that's just the scenario you're in, Rashid."

Rashid tapped a few more keys. A printer behind his desk powered up and started to print. It spit out a picture. Rashid inspected it, spun it around, and slid it over to Weissbard.

"That was the gentleman on that terminal at twelve-oh-three," Rashid said.

Weissbard looked down at the scared-looking face of Brian Sheridan.

CHAPTER TWENTY-SIX

From the moment Brian got home from work last night, he hadn't slept. The anxiety alone made it impossible. He worried about all the things going on around the city, completely out of his control, and ready to come crashing into his life. What were Weissbard and the Tampa PD uncovering about the Playing Card Killer that pointed to Brian? What new murder was the killer planning? Was there a victim being stalked right now?

If anxiety hadn't been enough to keep Brian awake, that final fear of a new innocent victim would have been enough by itself. Was someone else about to become the killer's prey? He didn't want to know about it, didn't want to fall asleep and see it.

And he'd actually have to do worse than see it. He'd experience it. And while seeing through the victim's eyes would be terrifying, seeing it through the killer's eyes was horrifying, nauseating, and repulsive, all rolled into one. Brian had no doubt that the killer wasn't about to stop. If he didn't sleep, Brian couldn't dream it.

After noon, he started to load on coffee laden with sugar. Every one of his doctors had told him to do the exact opposite to fight his anxiety and ADHD. But now he had to work against a short-term problem, staying awake through work. He'd get back to long-term problems eventually.

An hour into his shift at Orange Trucking, Brian started to nurture a new worry. He hadn't seen Sidney. According to the time clock, the crane operator had arrived early, which was the polar opposite of a standard Sidney work day, where he clocked in to the second, even if that meant standing around for five minutes at the time clock waiting. Brian checked the schedule and two trains were due that evening, so Sidney would be busy, but by now he'd always worked in an excuse to pop in and tell Brian he was worthless.

Every reason he could come up with for Sidney's distance seemed spawned from Brian's own paranoia. Maybe the police had questioned him again. Maybe Weissbard had told him about Brian's dreams, and now Sidney was scared to be in the same room with him. Maybe he really was doing something illegal at work, and the police investigation spooked him into keeping others at arm's length. That would actually have been poetic justice after the guy had been such a long-time dick at work.

Brian picked up the phone to call back to the crane. A black Charger pulled up to the main gate. A Tampa PD squad car pulled in behind it. Weissbard exited the Charger and headed to the guard shack at a brisk pace for such a fat guy. He had a look of immense satisfaction on his face. Two uniformed cops got out of the cruiser and followed right behind him. Brian dropped the phone. It missed the cradle.

"Oh, hell." His fight-or-flight reaction came on full force. The guard shack suddenly felt skin-tight, airless. He grabbed the doorknob and yanked the door open. Weissbard blocked his exit. Both cops behind him had their hands on their guns.

"Brian Sheridan, you are under arrest for the murders of Carla Alessandro, Keisha Valentiner and Meredith Viejo."

Brian dropped into a level of shock. Weissbard spun him around, and pulled Brian's hands behind his back. Handcuffs ratcheted behind him and twin rings of cold steel clamped around his wrists.

* * *

The Tampa PD interrogation room scared the hell out of him this time around. Same table, same chair. But this time, shackles held Brian's arms to the table and his legs to the floor. The door out of the tiny room seemed miles away. Weissbard towered over Brian from the other side of the table. The detective wasn't the disinterested, then disappointed, listener he'd been during their last conversation. He'd transformed into an aggressive badass, out for Brian's blood.

"Did you really think we were that stupid? That you could come in here, tell us all about the murders you'd committed, and we wouldn't know it was you?"

"It wasn't me. I couldn't be."

"It could be, and it was. How else would you know all the details of the crimes?"

"I told you. From my dreams."

Weissbard laughed. "Yeah, right. And a Ouija board and a crystal ball. Juries love to hear all that. They believe every word of it."

Brian imagined twelve incredulous faces staring at him from a jury box as he explained his visions. He didn't like how it looked.

Weissbard slid the picture of Brian from the internet café in front of him. "Are you going to deny that you contacted the tip line and told us where Keisha's body was?"

Crap, he thought. *How could I think anonymous could really be anonymous in the Information Age?*

"Yeah, that was me," Brian admitted.

Weissbard pulled a piece of paper from a file folder and laid it on top of the picture. It was a call log of Brian's cell phone. A call at 11:50 p.m. was circled in red.

"And just before that, you received a call. We triangulated from the towers and it places you, coincidentally, at the site we found the murder victim. So if you see all this in visions, how come you had to be there in person?"

"The visions aren't completely clear, just the view through the killer's eyes. I only see what he sees."

"Whoa!" Weissbard sprouted an I-hit-the-jackpot grin. "That's even more convenient, and damning. So if you couldn't see the convenience store, how did you find it?"

"I knew where she was kidnapped, and started looking for the place the killer left the body."

"Hey, now!" Weissbard reached over and stroked the security-guard patch on the shoulder of Brian's uniform. "You've promoted yourself from rent-a-cop, zoomed past police officer, and straight to detective. How did the Tampa PD ever miss the chance to recruit you? Oh, wait...."

He flipped open the file folder and thumbed through a few pages. Brian recognised his application, years ago, for the Tampa

PD Explorers Program. Weissbard ran his finger under the Reason for Denial box.

"Psychological instability. That was probably it."

Brian sagged in his chair. Weissbard pulled another page from the folder and put it in front of Brian. It contained timestamps and a list of websites and search parameters.

"Another little tidbit. The day before, you did a few internet searches from your phone. Coincidentally, and that word comes up a lot with you, searches all about Keisha Valentiner. You aren't going to deny *that,* are you?"

There wasn't any point. Brian shook his head.

"So you start your killing spree, dropping bodies around the bay area. You leave your stupid playing card breadcrumb trail to get whatever sick credit you want for your handiwork. As soon as some idiot in the department leaks that part out, you drop by with your so-called 'visions' to make sure that we don't miss a detail. But we hadn't found Keisha yet, and it just stuck in your craw that you weren't going to get that bit of sickness added to your resume."

Weissbard pulled an eight-by-ten-inch colour glossy from the file folder and slapped it down in front of Brian. It was one of the CSI shots of Keisha's corpse on the convenience store floor. Maggots crawled from her eyes, ears and nose. Her bloated, ashen face barely looked human. Dark bruises wrapped around her neck. Brian gagged and looked away.

"Yeah, that's what you turned that little girl into, you sick bastard. Take a long look at that."

Brian was glad he hadn't taken the effort to see inside the convenience store. A picture was bad, seeing it in real life would have been unbearable.

"So," Weissbard continued, "you search the internet to confirm that we know she's missing, then you check that no one has moved the body. Once you're satisfied with that, you drop us a line so that we can tie all four killings together."

"No, she just deserved to be found, her family deserved closure."

"You're worried about her family?" Weissbard pounded on the photo. "What about her?"

"I didn't kill her," Brian sobbed.

Weissbard leaned back, dialled down his anger. "Prove it to me. Where were you the night she was killed?"

"After work, I went home."

"Anyone see you?"

"No."

"How about the nights Karen, Meredith, and Carla were murdered? I guess you went home those nights also?"

"I don't know, I guess so. I can't remember. I don't even know what nights you're talking about."

"I can fill that in for you. On each of those nights, you left work. And on each of those nights, there's no record of any phone calls, internet usage, nothing that places you in your house until late the next morning."

Brian didn't doubt that was true. Since Daniela walked out, every night after work had been straight home alone. No calls. No internet.

"We're searching your house and car now. That's only going to give us more evidence. But I don't need it. I've gotten guys convicted with far less. If Polk County wasn't so obstinate, you'd be charged with Karen Strong's murder as well."

Brian hung his head. A thought occurred to him.

"Motive," he whispered.

"Say again?"

Brian raised his head. "Motive. If I did this, what's my motive?"

Weissbard smiled ear to ear and flipped the file folder shut. "Motive? You're goddamn crazy, how's that for a motive?"

Brian imagined those same twelve jurors again, and thought that particular motive would sound pretty good to them. His chest constricted with anxiety. It doubled when the idea that a visit from Mr. Jitters might happen at any moment. There was no way he wanted to deal with that in front of Weissbard.

"I think I need a lawyer," Brian said.

CHAPTER TWENTY-SEVEN

No sooner had Weissbard stepped out of interrogation than Detective Sergeant Francisco descended on him like the cartoon version of the Tasmanian devil, but there was nothing funny about him.

"You mind telling me what the hell is going on here?" Francisco's beet-red face radiated heat.

Weissbard seriously considered that the detective might lose control and start throwing punches. He consciously toned down his usual sarcasm. "There's a break in the case."

Francisco stormed over to the video feed of the interrogation room. Sheridan now sat alone, disconsolate, staring at the floor. "And who the hell is he?"

"Brian Sheridan. One of those walk-in tipsters I had to deal with." Weissbard figured he'd better work in somehow that this whole investigation wasn't completely behind Francisco's back, before the guy really blew a gasket. "Has way too many intimate details of the crimes."

Weissbard gave him a condensed version of Sheridan's convenient knowledge of the Playing Card Killer's activities. Francisco walked himself back a few steps from apoplexy.

"I've got forensics, motive, opportunity," Weissbard said.

"How about a confession?"

"Not yet."

Francisco smiled. Weissbard imagined the little wheels turning in his head. Francisco's extraction of a confession would become the lead story, no matter who made the arrest.

"I'll take care of that," Francisco said.

Francisco turned for the interrogation room door. Weissbard put a hand on his chest. "Sheridan saw what was at stake and lawyered up."

"Son of a bitch. And why is it I didn't know about this arrest?"

"It all unfolded pretty fast. I was going to bring him in from his place of work. I wasn't even sure he'd be there. It all happened quicker than I'd planned."

Francisco wasn't buying that line of crap. Weissbard didn't either, and he was the seller.

Francisco's eyes narrowed. "If Sheridan doesn't pan out, it's all on you."

And if he does, it will be all about Francisco, Weissbard thought. "He's the perp. No question."

"Get him to agree with you. On the record."

CHAPTER TWENTY-EIGHT

The next few hours passed in slow motion. Brian felt like he was viewing a tornado via television. Everything seemed to be flying all around, while he stood still and watched in utter dejection and disbelief. He got his one phone call, called his parents, and went to voicemail. The story of his life. Next stop was a holding cell with two dozing drunks.

Anxiety bit him like a tiger and refused to let go. The confined space, the proximity of strangers, the seen and unseen filth of the cell, they all conspired to spawn a host of interconnected fears, all amplified by his complete sense of powerlessness. His body screamed to pace the cell and burn some of the energy that seemed to flare from every nerve ending. But he dared not wake the sleeping drunks, and instead rocked in one corner, wringing his hands until the skin felt raw.

In the morning, a frazzled-looking public defender in a rumpled suit showed up. He arrived at his cell door to take Brian for arraignment and bail. He volunteered that he'd never tried a capital case before. Brian's leg started to twitch.

In court, Brian followed his pseudo-lawyer to the defence table. The gallery was full to standing room. The Tampa PD had caught the Playing Card Killer, and everyone wanted a peek. Brian wished he were dead. He and his lawyer took seats. The lawyer pulled a manila file folder from his bag. It had two pieces of paper in it. Brian didn't think that would be enough to mount much of a defence.

A silver-haired man with an aura of power stepped forward from the gallery. His pinstripe suit was so sharply cut it could probably slice paper. He stopped beside the table, towered over the public defender, and bored into him with two piercing blue eyes. The public defender's jaw dropped in recognition. So did Brian's.

There probably weren't many people in Tampa who didn't know who Chance Monroe was. The offices of Monroe and Monroe advertised on nearly every taxicab in the city, as well as billboards in dozens of prime locations. His self-narrated TV ads always ended with 'Monroe and Monroe. Take a Chance without taking one.'

"I've got it from here," he said to the public defender. He turned to Brian. "Your parents hired me."

The public defender scooted his chair straight back from between the two of them. "He's all yours." He dashed out of the courtroom like it harboured anthrax.

Monroe took the chair and moved inches from Brian. "Okay. Say 'not guilty, Your Honour' when asked, and then shut the hell up."

Judge Enger entered and all rose. He was stout, with a receding hairline and a black robe that looked a shade too long. Just like a TV drama, the prosecutor read the charges, three counts of murder, three counts of kidnapping, and a host of lesser charges. The judge asked Brian for his plea.

"Not guilty," he answered. Given the list of charges and the evidence, it even sounded ridiculous to him, and he knew it was true.

The prosecutor asked for remand, citing the heinous nature of the crimes.

"I agree, Your Honour," Monroe said.

Brian looked at him in shock.

"And when they find the person who committed these crimes," Monroe continued, "that would be a great decision. But the Tampa PD has arrested my client with virtually no evidence. Nothing physical links him to crime scenes or the victims. In a rush to show progress on a high-profile serial-killer case, Mr. Sheridan was a quick, convenient scapegoat. He has no criminal record, no history of violence, but he does have a history of mental confusion."

Brian was about to dispute that, but remembered his instructions to shut the hell up.

"The worst crime my client could be reasonably accused of would be spinning a fantasy to the police to gain attention under the influence of drug withdrawal. A police psychologist already diagnosed him as delusional days ago. I have multiple, credible grounds to dismiss much of their so-called evidence, as well as the charges themselves. I move for release to the custody of his parents, as well as a detailed psychological evaluation before returning to court."

An unkind murmur swept through the gallery. The judge banged a gavel for silence and paged through some notes. Brian figured he was screwed. The public would crucify a judge who let the accused Playing Card Killer loose on the streets.

"Good points on both sides," Judge Enger said. "This case is weak. One million dollars bond, released into his parents' custody with electronic monitoring, and I'll take you up on the psychological evaluations, Counsellor. Both one from your psychologist, and one from the state's."

He banged the gavel. The crowd emptied the gallery to spread the news. Brian still felt like he was watching a tornado, but now from the inside.

★ ★ ★

The police fitted him with an ankle monitor, which was only slightly less comfortable than having a brick duct taped to his leg. He was processed out of custody and Chance Monroe led him to the courthouse doors.

"Keep that shut-the-hell-up thing going a little while longer," he whispered.

Monroe's trademark white limousine waited at the base of a long set of marble steps. Between Brian and the car buzzed a swarm of reporters, television cameras, and the macabre-curious. Brian spent a lifetime trying to blend into a crowd. Having one waiting for him sent his adrenaline spiking.

Monroe broke into a smile and stopped a few steps down at a conveniently placed six-microphone set up. TV cameras surrounded the microphones, looking like giant black eyes, like a pack of hungry Cyclops. Monroe addressed the crowd like a king, and pontificated about injustice, sloppy police work, and Brian's obvious innocence. Then he hustled Brian down the rest of the steps and into the back of the limousine. Derek Sheridan was waiting for them in the spacious rear seat. Monroe pulled the door shut and the limo leapt from the curb.

"Derek?" Brian said. "Thank you for getting me out of there."

"Camilla took some convincing," Derek said.

Brian thought it more likely she still wasn't convinced.

"You two can catch up later," Monroe said. He loosened his tie. His look shifted from beaming lawyer to something way more thuggish. "My retainer is deposited?"

"As of nine a.m.," Derek said.

"No one talks to the goddamn press, and I mean no one. No social media posts, nothing. My office handles all of that." He focused on Brian. "Don't screw with that jewellery on your ankle, and don't leave the house. I don't care if it's burning the hell down. You die in it."

Monroe pulled a flask from a pouch in the door and took a swig. He swallowed and pointed the container at Derek. "How are you fixed for security?"

"The community has a private service of off-duty police. The neighbourhood is secure."

"Not secure from people outside the house." He waved the flask at Brian. "From someone inside the house. You need to keep your guard up. This kid's probably guilty."

CHAPTER TWENTY-NINE

Since the birth of his sister, Brian had dreamed of getting out of his parents' house. From about the age of sixteen, he longed for it, counting the days. Now, after only two years on his own, he was back. And the experience this time was far worse. Before, his restrictions were mental, internally limited by his anxieties, but with the distant hope for a future escape. Now, the restriction was physical, enforced by the state, and the only event that loomed in his future was confinement someplace even worse.

The clock read past 11:00 p.m. as he sat in his father's den. He wasn't the only one still awake. Though the den was at the far corner of the house, it still wasn't far enough away to miss overhearing Derek and Camilla's intense conversation about his state-ordered internment.

"We owe it to him," Derek said. "He's our responsibility."

"Owe it to him? What haven't we already done for him? What haven't we already sacrificed?"

Brian rolled his eyes at Camilla's definition of sacrifice. He'd never made himself an imposition over the past twenty years. He'd been closer to invisible.

"He made his own decisions," Camilla said. "He stopped going to therapy. He stopped taking his medications. He created whatever he's become. It's just like I told the police."

That revelation sent Brian seething. Of course Camilla would paint him in the worst possible light to the cops. When a jury sent him to the electric chair, she'd probably volunteer to throw the switch.

"Be that as it may," Derek said, "Chance Monroe warned there was a question of personal liability. If, when he moved out of the house, we knew he wasn't competent, we're wide open to lawsuits from the victims' families. We're leaving ourselves at risk if we don't show we're trying to be part of a solution."

"So we're going to let him live here, under the same roof as Ariana? And me? You remember he's killing women, right?"

"Holy hell," Brian whispered. His so-called family wasn't in this to defend *him*, they were defending themselves. They were all convinced he was guilty. If people who knew him his whole life thought he was a serial killer, what chance did he have convincing a judge or jury?

He couldn't deal with any more of this. He got off the couch. The monitoring bracelet slid down and rubbed his foot, as if to say 'Hey bud, remember you aren't going far.' He left the den and went upstairs to his bedroom.

Or what had once been his bedroom. Camilla had wasted no time redecorating it as soon as Brian moved out. Really all she did was clean it out. She stripped the walls bare of anything he'd left and tossed the rest in the trash. The shelves, dresser and desk were as empty as a furniture store display. The bedclothes he'd used were gone, burned he presumed, and a new set, creases still crisp from the factory two years later, covered the mattress.

His suitcase sat on top of the dresser, as if not unpacking it meant he wasn't really staying here. Next to it were two bottles of prescription meds, thoughtfully provided by Dr. Kaufman at Camilla's request, and heartily recommended by Chance Monroe.

Fat chance. No matter how lousy things got, he wasn't backsliding and taking those. Whatever was going on with him wasn't caused by being clean, so dissolving those toxins into his system wasn't going to fix him.

He kicked off his shoes and dropped onto the bed. The new, unwashed cover scratched against his skin.

Exhaustion fell over him like a lead-lined blanket. He'd barely slept the last three days, and hadn't slept at all last night in holding. His eyes drooped. Then fear gave him a sudden jolt back awake. Nightmares waited on the other side of consciousness, visions of murder, faces frozen in terror at the moment of death. All day, his world had fallen about him and shattered into a million pieces. He didn't have the mental strength to subject himself to any more sick, twisted experiences.

But his body only had so much to give. Before he could stop it again, his eyelids rolled shut, he exhaled deeply, and sleep took him somewhere else.

CHAPTER THIRTY

He recognises the pond. Even at night, he knows this place. He must be a boy in this dream, because that was when he used to sneak back here. His parents' development borders a wildlife area, where sinkhole ponds dot the landscape. The trees are tall, long protected from a woodsman's axe and developers, first by intervening swamps, and then by local law. This place used to be his escape from the claustrophobia of his family.

After leaving the pond, he makes his way back to the house. He remembers the urgency he used to feel, knowing that he must be back in bed before sunrise so his parents would find him there when they woke him for school. The trail is soggy in places where a thunderstorm's rain slowly drains to the stagnant pond. Palm fronds threaten to block his way, like giant hands with a dozen long fingers. He pushes them aside until their stems snap.

The trail ends. He steps from the woods into the Ferguson yard. The old man living here always seemed perpetually on watch, appearing out of nowhere the second a ball or Frisbee landed on his perfect grass. Tonight that house is dark.

He skirts the yard anyway. Motion sensor lights hang beside the garage door, and even if they don't wake old man Ferguson, the lights shine near his parents' bedroom, and waking them would be far worse. He had been grounded for lesser crimes than sneaking out of the house. Who knows what punishment this transgression would earn?

He works his way back into his own backyard. The grass crushes thick and cushiony beneath his feet, silent. He realises this whole dream is silent as well. The neighbourhood is always quiet at this hour, but he should have heard the thrum of insects and the bellow of frogs down by the pond. Perhaps he had, and it hadn't registered.

At the back door, he wipes his feet on the bristly mat. He taps the access code into the security keypad and the red light turns green. He opens the door and waits. The house is dark. He enters.

In the kitchen, he pauses beside a wooden block full of carving knives. He selects a mid-size knife, one with a sharp, serrated blade. He tucks it into his belt, but isn't at all sure why he'll need this when he goes to bed. He leaves the kitchen.

He walks down the hall, then up the stairs, and stops outside his bedroom. Once inside, he will calm his racing pulse, ditch the wet shoes that are rapidly dampening his socks, and slide back into bed. An hour or two of sleep will take off some of the edge before going to school.

He pushes open the bedroom door and waits. For what he doesn't know. He reaches in his pockets, extracts a bottle and a white cotton rag, like a tiny diaper. He pours the contents of the bottle on the rag.

This part of the dream confuses him. He doesn't know what these items are, why he has them. He walks forward to the bed. In the murky darkness, he can make out a lump under the covers. Someone, something is already in his bed. It moves under the covers.

He starts to scream.

★ ★ ★

Brian woke up with a shudder. Goddamn nightmare! He'd pulled his covers up over his head in his sleep. He whipped them down to his waist.

His heart leapt into his throat. A face loomed over him, pale against the darkness. His terror reached even deeper inside him, his fear for his own sanity reached an epic height. The face, inches away, was his own.

"Hello, brother," the intruder said.

The intruder jammed a soft, white cloth over Brian's face. Brian struggled, but the cloth reeked of some sharp chemical, and the scent invaded and weakened him. The face above him, *his* face above him, smiled, and Brian went unconscious.

CHAPTER THIRTY-ONE

Detective Weissbard cursed every mile of the way to the Sheridan house. He thought it was stupid to let any murder suspect out on bail to begin with, and even stupider to let Sheridan out. As soon as that media-whore sleazeball Chance Monroe took the case, Weissbard knew it was going to turn into a total zoo. The call that woke him thirty minutes ago confirmed it.

Francisco himself had ordered Weissbard to report on Sheridan's escape. Weissbard had crawled out alone on the limb to pluck Sheridan as the suspect. The second that fruit turned sour, Francisco was ready to chop off that limb, with Weissbard still on it.

He pulled down the Sheridan driveway and stopped behind the black-and-white that had responded first. Every outside light was on, but this was the kind of neighbourhood where everyone did that all the time anyway. Oh, the irony of people in a secure little enclave like this keeping security lights on all night, while crime-ridden neighbourhoods on the other side of Tampa were all shadows and darkness. Weissbard stuffed his tiny flashlight into his pocket and went to the front door.

A uniformed cop opened it before he could knock. Weissbard recognised him from the precinct.

"Diaz," he said. "What's the story?"

"Hey, Detective. Call came in just after three a.m. that Sheridan's ankle monitor broke contact. The monitor and the parents are upstairs."

Weissbard slogged upstairs, every riser reminding him he carried too much weight and managed on too little sleep. He stopped in the first open doorway. The bedroom wasn't much more than that, a room with a twin bed and an empty desk. A wad of sheets and a blanket lay snarled at the foot of the bed. The ankle monitor lay in the bed's centre, its strap sawed through. A mid-size carving knife lay beside it. Derek and Camilla stood at opposite sides of the bed looking down at the monitor. They displayed the same disgusted look they'd have if someone left a steaming pile of shit there. They both turned to Weissbard.

"I don't understand," Derek said. "How did the officer know Brian was gone? The monitor is still here."

"It sends a signal if it senses it's been taken off," Weissbard said. "Not just its location."

"Oh, I see," Derek said, as if the revelation was something profound.

"When was the last time someone saw Brian?" Weissbard said.

"At dinner," Derek said. "Then he came up here. We went to bed at eleven p.m."

"And you're sure he didn't leave the house?"

"The alarm was set even before dinner," Camilla said. "We're quite concerned about the press and whatnot. All this unwelcome attention."

Not to mention victims' families wanting to string up your son, Weissbard thought.

"Opening any door or window would have set it off," Derek added. "It was on when we went to sleep, but off when the police officer woke us up."

Weissbard checked the bedroom window. The upper right-hand corner had a wireless alarm sensor. The window was locked from the inside. He looked out and down from the window. A straight drop onto undamaged holly bushes. Sheridan hadn't escaped that way.

He looked at the monitor on the bed. The kitchen knife beside it didn't make sense. If Sheridan was going to bolt in the middle of the night, why not just go to the kitchen, cut himself free, and leave? Maybe he needed the privacy to saw through it. It wasn't easy work.

A look around the room confirmed that Sheridan hadn't made any effort to move in. Some clothes and basic toiletries sat in an open suitcase on a dresser. An open, lightweight backpack lay on the floor underneath the chair. The rest of the room seemed sterile, like no one had gotten around to decorating it.

The pile of personal articles didn't sit well either with Weissbard. Who goes on the run and brings nothing with him? Especially with a convenient backpack available and plenty of prep time to pack it?

"I'm going to look around," Weissbard said. "Don't touch that monitor or the knife."

He checked the interior perimeter of the house. Other than the front door, only the back door was unlocked. He stepped out onto the patio. The next-door neighbour's yard backed up to some woods. If Sheridan was going to make a break for it, that would be the way to go, not wandering out through the development's front gate.

Weissbard snapped on his flashlight and checked the grass between the patio and the fence. It looked like there were footsteps crushed into the thick turf. Nothing he could get an impression of, just bent blades that were already bouncing back into the upright perfection this place's home owner's association probably mandated.

Derek walked up behind him. "Did you find anything?"

Why, yes, Weissbard thought. *And my first inclination is to share it with the idiots who freed their son to jump bail.*

"What's that woods back there?" he said instead.

"A swampy wildlife preserve. Highway 58 runs on the other side of it."

And that was that. Sheridan would be through there without being seen and out on the highway. Thumbing a ride, picked up by a friend. Wherever he was, he wouldn't be anywhere near here by now. But Weissbard needed to check anyway. He went back inside and found Diaz. He told him to get some backup and search the area between the house and Highway 58.

Weissbard went to his car for two evidence bags for the knife and the monitor. He contemplated showing them to a certain bail-granting judge before booking them as evidence.

CHAPTER THIRTY-TWO

Brian's head slammed against hard metal. He came to, blinked, and tried to focus. His brain felt like it was covered in shredded paper and rolling inside his skull. His fuzziness dissipated, but the motion didn't stop. He was moving in the darkness.

Thick, humid air enveloped him. It reeked with the chemical smell of new vinyl. A blindfold covered his eyes. He tried to reach for it, and found that his hands were bound behind him. His ankles were as well. He lay upon a thick, plastic drop cloth. It felt sticky against his face and hands. Duct tape covered his mouth.The road noise of cars and the rumble of tyres surrounded him. He bounced up and down. He had a bad feeling he was in the trunk of a car.

He rubbed the side of his head against the plastic over and over, until millimetre by millimetre he inched the blindfold up over his eyes. Enough light leaked into his enclosure to tell him more than he wanted to know.

He wasn't just in a car trunk. He was in *the* car trunk. The inside of the trunk lid had a big reflective safety decal on it. The same one from his vision, the one where he saw Carla Alessandro before the Playing Card Killer set her corpse adrift in Tampa Bay. That sure as hell didn't make him feel good about his potential next stop.

He was still wearing the sweat pants, socks and T-shirt he'd fallen asleep in. He remembered being drugged and taken from his bedroom. He remembered a flash of the kidnapper's face. Of his own face?

He had to get out of this trunk. Now. Trunks had an interior release. One pull and he'd be out. He struggled against his bindings. They didn't flex. He realised he shouldn't have wasted his strength. The Playing Card Killer had way too much practice to be sloppy there.

He remembered scenes in mystery novels where the kidnapped person told the cops about what he heard or felt during his kidnapping, and the cops used it to track down the killer. Nice idea, but nothing around him sounded unique, and anyway he'd have to live through this experience before he could ever talk to the cops. His bound legs shuddered as an anxiety attack began to gather steam.

Something bumped against Brian's knees.

"Road trip!" screamed Mr. Jitters.

His cry echoed inside the trunk like a cannon shot. Brian slithered backwards like a sidewinding snake until he hit the sides of the trunk.

Mr. Jitters' disembodied head sat in the corner of the trunk. Without the hat, he looked even more like a living skull, completely hairless, skin painted white everywhere with only the black skull pattern marking his face. The creepy painted smile now stretched up and back below his ears. The two eye sockets looked like black abysses.

Panic clamped Brian into paralysis and constricted his chest so tightly that he could barely breathe.

Mr. Jitters' eyes popped open. Two unbelievably wide, unbelievably white eyeballs stared into Brian's soul.

"Face the facts, buddy." The red in his mouth was the colour of fresh blood. "Your clock is ticking down fast. This guy kills everyone he kidnaps. He has to. Can't leave a witness. And you're officially a witness."

Mr. Jitters' detached hand appeared beside Brian's neck. It grabbed his throat and squeezed. Brian choked behind the duct tape gag.

"Can't you feel it already? That velvet rope you felt in your hand now tightening around your neck? Choking you off from the land of the living?"

Brian wanted to flail around the trunk, to shake free the hand and drive the head into the side of the trunk with his knees. But between the bindings and his panic, he was helpless.

The hand released him.

Then the head began to spin. In an instant, it became a blur of flashing black and white. Like a child's top, it zipped across the trunk. It jerked to a stop inches from Brian's face. Mr. Jitters' eyes locked onto Brian's. He exhaled a stink like percolating summer garbage.

"Of course you may not live that long," Mr. Jitters laughed. "The trunk here isn't exactly first class seating. So cramped, no air. You could suffocate before he even opens this rolling coffin."

The air had turned stale, hot, thick. Brian's breathing had humidified the tiny space and now his heart laboured in his chest under a sweat-soaked shirt. The rising heat of the day would only make this worse.

"Now let's get cosy," Mr. Jitters said.

Mr. Jitters' head began to swell. Like an expanding balloon it filled the space between Brian's face and knees. It kept growing and pressed him hard, squeezing him into the sides of the trunk. The deck lid hinge gouged the back of his head. Mr. Jitters' cheek pressed against Brian's nose and cut off his air. The rest of the swelling head blotted out any remaining light and enveloped Brian's body. The pressure squeezed the last bit of air from his lungs.

The car hit a pothole and lurched hard down, then up. Mr. Jitters popped like a soap bubble. The pressure disappeared. With relief, Brian sucked air in through his nose so hard it made his head hurt.

The vehicle slowed. Brian bounced a few more times in the trunk and then the car stopped. Somewhere in front of the car, a garage door screeched open. The car drove forward a bit, stopped, and the door screeched downward again. The engine cut off.

The car door opened and slammed closed. A car remote chirped and the trunk lid popped open. Brian blinked against the brighter light. A man's shadow blocked it. Brian's mouth went dry and he quaked, waiting to feel a velvet rope around his neck.

"Awake!" the killer said. "Wonderful!"

He pulled the blindfold from Brian's forehead. He moved to the side and Brian could make out his face. He couldn't believe it. He hadn't imagined the last fleeting image he'd had in his parents' house. Except for the shorter, spiky blond hair, this guy was Brian's dead ringer. He looked over Brian's wet shirt and damp hair with derision.

"Dude, you looked way better when I put you in here."

He pulled the tape from across Brian's mouth. It felt like a lot of skin went with it.

"Ouch!" Brian spit some residue from his lips. "Who are you?"

"I'm your id. Your alter ego. Finally surfaced."

Brian's face screwed up in horror. He really was going insane.

The killer smiled and slapped him on the shoulder. "Just fucking with you! Long story. But we have time. C'mon."

The killer pulled a large pocketknife from his jeans. A lifetime of hard use had left nicks and gouges in its thick, cherrywood handle. The killer snapped it open to reveal a thick blade nearly five inches long. Unlike the battered handle, the blade's edge sparkled where it had been honed to perfection.

The killer bent over and cut Brian's ankles free, but not his hands. He helped Brian out of the trunk. Brian's knees creaked as they stretched back to a more human position. They stood in a two-car garage. A battered red Honda compact with Virginia plates sat in the other parking spot. A few older lawn tools hung on one wall, with a rusting push mower beneath them. A dusty home gym took up the front of the garage, the type with a stack of weights at one end, a bench at the other, and a pull-down bar suspended over the bench. Nothing in the garage looked like it had been moved in a very long time.

The killer led him into the main house. Brian shuffled in as feeling returned to his legs, but the killer's gait was odd as well, with a little drag from his right foot. They stepped up into the house and into a tiled, spacious kitchen.

Four high-backed chairs with woven wicker bottoms surrounded a glass-topped kitchen table. The closest chair had the middle of the wicker seat chopped out. A set of locking rollers crudely attached to the legs raised the seat an inch or two higher than the rest. The killer yanked Brian's arms behind him so they hung over the chair's back. He sat Brian down on the modified chair. Then he grabbed several zip ties from the kitchen counter and added a second round of constraints to fix Brian's bound wrists to the back of the chair. That jerked him into a painfully upright position.

The killer grabbed more zip ties from the counter, and bound Brian's ankles to the chair. The frosty air-conditioning cut through Brian's thin socks and chilled his feet.

The killer pulled another chair opposite of Brian. He spun it around, straddled it, crossed his arms over the top, and rested his chin on them.

"Now, you have a million questions," he said. "Let me answer half of them before you ask. First off, I'm Tyler." He extended his hand for a handshake, feigned a look of embarrassment, and gave Brian a chummy slap on the shoulder instead. "My friends call me Ty."

Tyler laughed, a really off-kilter snorting laugh, like this was some big inside joke. Then he straightened up and took a deep breath.

"I'm guessing you noticed our stunning family resemblance."

Tyler turned profile, then lifted his chin in an aristocratic pose. He didn't just resemble Brian, he damn near duplicated him. His face was just a bit fuller, his body was certainly more robust. But there was no way he could be Brian's....

"Yes, indeed," Tyler said. "We're twin brothers. Separated at birth by the callous hand of man, reunited by my tireless efforts."

"That can't be...."

"Central State Hospital, Petersburg, Virginia. April 17, 1999." Tyler pointed at himself. "Two-oh-three a.m." Tyler pointed at Brian. "Two-oh-nine a.m."

Brian couldn't deny that Tyler was his doppelganger. But the details of the location and exact time of his birth were something new. "I didn't know any of that."

"Of course not," Tyler said. "Those double assholes Derek and Camilla demanded a closed adoption. The agency said they never even asked about any siblings, just wanted you cut off from your birth family, forever. You have a redacted birth certificate, dude, like you're some secret government project."

"How did you know about me?"

"Well, while you got adopted, I just got borrowed. Fucking foster homes, every one another step deeper into hell. My records weren't sealed and I could see that I had this baby brother out there somewhere. One bitch social worker tried to tell me that you died at birth, but I knew that was a load of shit. I could *feel* that it wasn't true."

"I don't get it."

"Haven't you had the sensation of being, like, partial your whole life? Like there was something missing, some reason you didn't really fit in?"

Brian considered the word *partial*. For the first time, a foggy feeling he'd had forever became perfectly defined.

"Let me answer that for you," Tyler said. "Yes, you did. Because I did. We spent nine months together in a womb, dude. We shared blood. There's no bonding like that anywhere else."

Tyler stood and started to pace the kitchen. The drag of his right foot didn't slow him. His face became animated. Jerky gestures punctuated his words.

"Then, when I was like eleven or twelve, I was put with the Dunhams, a family who didn't give a shit if I went to school at all. A sweet setup, for sure. I stayed up all night, slept until noon. I started seeing shit in my dreams, like another life or something. I thought they were just dreams, but they were so seriously boring, I didn't think my imagination was that totally lame.

"Everything I saw fit the real world too much for these visions to just be dreams. I did internet searches of signs and stuff that I saw each night, like your middle school, your address on mail, stuff like that. Gradually, I pieced it together. In my dreams, that more pathetic version of myself I saw wasn't me at all. It was you, my long-lost bro."

"That dream connection didn't happen to me," Brian said. "Not until recently."

"That's because your adopted overlords kept you drugged, bro. A system full of chemicals suppressed your abilities. Once you dropped off them, I could sense you tagging along with me, the way I had for years with you. I might have had a string of foster parents who treated me like an ATM for state aid, but in their neglect, they did me one favour. No one shot me full of mind-killing meds."

That fit the timeline. Brian had started having the visions when he quit taking all the medications.

"See what they did to you, dude?" Tyler stepped next to him, tapped Brian's head, then Brian's chest. "Those drugs, they stunted your brain, stunted your growth. You're supposed to be like me."

Brian watched Tyler flex a pretty healthy bicep. Brian had spent a lot of embarrassing gym-class periods wishing he had half the muscle mass his brother displayed.

The phrase *his brother* kind of bounced around in his head a few times as he got used to the idea.

"Because, really, you're me," Tyler said. "I'm you. Identical twins. Same blood type. Same DNA. Now even with that, I *am* the big brother, so it falls on me to help you out, to help you up."

"How about untying me, for starters?"

"When you're ready, bro, when you're ready. First you need to see what you're missing, have me clue you in on why I'm strong and you're weak."

Reality reasserted itself, and Brian remembered he wasn't talking to a long-lost brother. He was talking to a serial killer.

"I've seen what you've been doing," Brian said. "I don't want anything to do with it."

"That's because you've only seen it. You haven't experienced it. I'm going to give you the full behind-the-scenes tour, let you savour every step from start to glorious finish. Then you'll understand, see your full potential, see *our* full potential."

Tyler pulled Brian's cell phone from his own pocket, tapped in the passcode and called up Brian's email. "See, I've been prepping you for this for weeks." He swiped through the email list and frowned. "Oh, dude, you deleted them. The messages from Totally You, about your upcoming new beginning."

"The spam? That was you?"

"Absolutely! Totally You. T-Y. Ty. Get it?" Tyler let out another snort-laugh.

Brian realised how easy it would have been for Tyler to get into his phone, his email. He'd seen every password through Brian's eyes. That had to be how he knew the passcode for the Sheridans' home security system.

Tyler pulled the velvet rope from his pocket. Brian's jaw dropped. That was it, the instrument of death that had starred in all his nightmares. Totally real.

Tyler swung it around over his head with one hand, like a cowboy with a lasso. "You and me gonna round 'em up, pardner! Yeehaw!"

"Ty, look, I—"

Tyler's face went crimson. He stepped forward and cracked the rope like a whip against Brian's neck. The end carried around, wrapped over Brian's Adam's apple, and continued over to where Tyler caught it with his other hand. He gave the two ends a little yank. Brian's windpipe collapsed. Tyler bent to Brian's ear.

"Only my friends call me Ty," he whispered, "and I don't have any friends."

When Tyler's face reappeared, he'd reapplied that artificial salesman's smile. Brian shivered. The velvet rope went slack and Tyler pulled it from Brian's neck. The friction left the slightest of burns.

"Now," Tyler said, "I've got some errands to run, some shopping to do. I'll have to leave you, but want to make sure you're comfortable."

Tyler went behind Brian. For the briefest moment, Brian held out hope that he was about to be untied. Instead, Tyler grabbed the back of the chair and held it steady as he released the locks on the wheels at the base of the legs. He pulled Brian backwards and down the hall.

"You know," he said, "I was this close to getting a wheelchair for this phase, but then I realised it so totally wouldn't work for this."

Tyler opened a door to a half bathroom and snapped on

the light. The room was just big enough for the toilet and a small sink on the left. The toilet's lid and seat were missing. He spun Brian around and backed him in over the john. The chair cleared it by an inch.

"See," Tyler said, "this is the part they always skip in the movies. The prisoner's got to take a piss and a shit every now and then. Just human nature. And any one smart enough to engineer a kidnapping isn't stupid enough to spend time cleaning all that up."

Tyler pulled his knife from his pocket again and snapped it open. A shocked look crossed his face and he paused.

"Whoa, kidnapping. That was an unfortunate choice of terms I used there. You aren't a prisoner. This isn't a kidnapping. This is a reunion. A reintegration. You'll see."

Tyler bent and with the knife, sliced through the hem of Brian's sweats. He slit them up one leg, then the next, all the way to the waist. With a rough yank, he pulled the flayed sweats free. Two more slices and Brian's underwear was gone as well.

The conditioned air raised chill bumps across Brian's ass, exposed through the missing seat. He felt his exposed manhood shrivel and his testes beat a quick retreat somewhere deep inside his pelvis. His face flushed in humiliation.

"Oh, dude," Tyler said. He raised an eyebrow as he looked at Brian's crotch. "Might be something we aren't identical in after all." He snorted back a laugh. "Seriously, can't have you sitting around with your wee-wee out, can we?"

Tyler pulled a towel from the rack. He flapped it open and across Brian's lap like a blanket at a country picnic.

"Ta da! I'll be back soon and we'll really get to know each other. Sit tight." He let slip another snort-laugh as he amused himself. "Sorry! Oh, I just kill me sometimes."

Tyler backed out of the bathroom and closed the door.

The shredded wicker seat dug into Brian's bare butt cheeks. His shoulders ached. Despite the chill in the room, beads of nervous sweat rolled down his sides. It was all too much to process. Serial killings. Kidnapped. A twin brother. The hope that this was another one of his withdrawal hallucinations briefly surfaced, and then sank back into the morass of despair that spawned it.

He remembered as a kid how trapped he'd felt living under Derek and Camilla's roof. He didn't know what trapped really felt like until now.

CHAPTER THIRTY-THREE

The water kept the time.

Not in a meaningful way. The drip from the sink could not tell Brian whether it was a quarter past seven or half past three, but it did confirm that time was passing, a plink of a reminder every four seconds. From his vantage point he could watch each tiny sphere swell from nothing but damp to a pregnant drop overcome by gravity. Each drop fell from his line of sight and trickled down the drain, along with another four-second slice of his life. He had no idea how many of those had passed since Tyler shut the bathroom door.

To the right, a mirror filled the wall over the sink. The rest of the walls were yellow, the shade of it more suited to a banana than to home décor. A white hand towel hung on the chrome rack by the sink. The rack to his left was now empty since its towel covered his lap. The bathroom had no decorations. A few off-coloured rectangles on the walls testified that some had been there at one time. Tyler must have removed them. Was he afraid they might give Brian comfort, or that they might somehow become a means of escape? There was no telling.

After Tyler had left him, anxiety had taken him on a wild ride. He'd struggled against his bindings in a mindless bout of thrashing until muscle strain forced a halt. Exhausted, he'd given up his thoughts of escape. The attempt hadn't delivered a millimetre of slack in his bindings. His shoulders screamed at him from the exertion, amplified by hanging backwards over the chair.

The windowless room uncomfortably mimicked a tomb. It certainly sounded like one. Silence ruled the vacant house. No sounds from outside penetrated the walls, no lawn mowers, no barking dogs, no leaf blowers. He imagined he was in some cookie-cutter subdivision, maybe even mostly timeshares. Places like that had a little going-to-work traffic, a little coming-home-from-work traffic, and that was it. Florida's heat and omnipresent humidity kept everyone inside as much as possible.

The idea of shouting himself hoarse crying for help was laughable. Even if the mailman was at the front door, Brian doubted the guy would hear his screams. He reasoned that if it had been even a remote possibility, Tyler would have kept Brian gagged.

Movement caught his eye along the base of the door. One spindly spider leg peeked out from between the door and the floor tile, then another.

In slow motion, the spider crawled out. Three inches long, with so much brown hair that it looked furry. Even at this distance, its big, black eyes shined, glossy, malevolent. It crawled towards Brian.

He shuddered against his bindings. He hated spiders, all insects actually, but spiders had their own special circle of Hell. Too many legs, unblinking eyes, fangs.

He'd been bitten when he was little. He reached into his drawer for socks and felt the sting. He yanked his hand back. A spider scampered out behind it, dropped to the floor, and beat a fast retreat under the bed. It left a small, red dot on the back of Brian's hand.

Four hours later, he really felt the impact. The bite felt like someone had driven a spike through his hand. Everything from the wrist down swelled up like some scarlet balloon creation. His fever spiked to the stratosphere. Nausea rolled through him, and he vomited until he thought he'd left the lining of his stomach in the toilet. He passed out and woke up in the hospital.

His parents were there. Camilla did not look too relieved at his recovery. A brown recluse spider took the rap. The doctor said Brian had an allergy, another item to add to Brian's list of problems and anxiety triggers.

The full nightmare of a potential bite came into focus. Trapped in this chair, alone. Tyler might not be back for hours, maybe days, and might not even help Brian if he was here. Brian conjured a vision of himself alone, bound in this chair, burning up with fever, layered in his own stinking vomit.

The spider crept closer.

"Go away!" Brian shook in the chair as he shouted. "Get the hell out of here!"

The spider continued, undeterred by, or Brian thought, maybe attracted by his screaming. It crept up on the toe of Brian's sock. He imagined he could feel the spike of its feet through the cotton weave. He wiggled his toes. He jerked his foot back and forth against the bindings at his ankle. The spider advanced, surefooted as a sailor on a gale-swept deck.

The spider crawled up his sock and paused at his bare leg. Brian froze.

"No, no," he whispered, pleading. "Go away. Please."

One furry leg touched his skin. Memories of the sting of his previous bite rushed back with a vengeance. He went stock-still, worried about pissing it off and having it sink its fangs into his flesh.

The spider crawled up his calf. Its legs plucked at hairs like harp strings as it moved systematically towards Brian's knee. Every touch sent tingles across his skin and shivers up his spine. Beads of sweat formed on Brian's forehead.

The spider free-climbed his skin, slow and steady, and reached his knee. It disappeared under the towel that covered Brian's lap.

That only made it worse. With the spider unseen, but still felt, Brian's mind amplified every pinprick touch of the spider's legs, anticipated the piercing bite he feared was about to follow. The creature moved step by step up his inner thigh, and touched one of his testes.

Brian stifled a scream. If the thing bit his balls…the pain…the swelling…damn it.

Fear squeezed his bladder. His eyes went wide. Oh, no, not now. If he pissed on the spider, it would sure as hell bite, probably more than once, sinking its fangs into everything it could find underneath the towel. He clenched his teeth, and everything else he could below the waist. The pressure built to bursting.

Legs touched his penis.

He screamed and bounced in his bindings. All control was gone. Hot urine sprayed his legs, sprayed the towel. The chair banged back and forth against the toilet as he writhed in panic. He waited for the stabbing pain of the spider's bite.

Instead, it skittered down his piss-soaked leg and across his sock. It dropped to the floor, and crawled under the door.

Brian laughed. A mad, deliriously relieved laugh.

Soaked in cooling piss. Bound to a kitchen chair. His shoulder muscles burned from the panicked contortions he'd just put them through. On a day this awful, this moment qualified as a victory.

What the hell.

CHAPTER THIRTY-FOUR

Brian jerked awake at the sound of banging pans in the kitchen. He couldn't believe that he'd dozed off in such an uncomfortable position. It sounded like Tyler was back, and Brian's guess was that his brother wasn't following along with a cooking show on cable TV. Then, from another part of the house, came the sound of furniture dragging across carpet. Tyler was executing some plan, and that couldn't be good.

The embers of Brian's anxiety glowed a bit brighter. His pulse accelerated.

Mr. Jitters appeared, sitting in the sink beside him. His black-painted-tooth smile swept upwards and curled in on itself in an even more malicious grin than before. His long arms and legs poked out of the sink at add angles. His top hat hung low, shading his eyes.

"C'mon, Brian!" He laughed that maniacal cackle of a laugh. "Time to have a little fun, a little dance with the J-Man, hey?"

He leaned in close. His hot breath rushed across Brian's cheek. It reeked of things long dead.

Brian's breaths came short and rapid. His legs began to vibrate in their bindings and jiggle against the chair. He didn't need this, didn't need the incapacitation of a full-blown foxtrot with Mr. Jitters, not with Tyler on the verge of starting who-knew-what elsewhere in the house. He closed his eyes.

"Go the hell away," he said through clenched teeth.

"You forget, boy," Mr. Jitters said. "Without the prescription pharma, I've always been the one giving orders here."

Mr. Jitters was right. A sure as Tyler had him physically bound to this chair, anxiety had always had him mentally bound, always restrained from stepping out into the wide-open world the way any normal person would. And nothing but the meds he'd flushed down the toilet had ever been able to keep it at bay. Mr. Jitters had always come and gone on his own schedule. Brian's sense of powerlessness only amplified his anxiety.

Wait, this is a damn hallucination, he thought. *A damn withdrawal-induced waking nightmare.*

Understanding that didn't stop his pounding heart or chill his burning nerves. It only made him even more furious at his internal and external captivity. He opened his eyes and turned to face Mr. Jitters. Jitters was so close Brian could make out the swirls in the white greasepaint on his cheekbones.

"You're nothing!" he shouted. "Leave me alone!"

The door swung open. Brian turned his head to see Tyler standing there, with a pair of grey shorts in his hand and a perplexed look on his face. Brian glanced back to the sink and Mr. Jitters was gone. His anxiety wasn't. His shuddering made the chair rattle against the toilet.

"Bro! What are you doing?" Tyler said. "Talking to yourself? Worse, shouting at yourself? Conduct unbecoming, dude. You want people thinking you're crazy?"

In his anger, Brian almost shouted that of the two of them, his new-found brother was the damn expert on crazy. But he cut himself off. Tyler had his happy persona on. No point in pushing the buttons that turned that off. Not with Brian bound to a chair and Mr. Jitters ready to cue the arrival of a full-blown anxiety meltdown. He took and held a deep breath, then slowly exhaled to calm himself.

Tyler stepped in and looked down at the piss-soaked towel. "I left you in better shape than this. What the hell?"

Brian wasn't about to admit to the spider incident and give Tyler another weakness to exploit. He just looked away. Tyler pulled away the towel and tossed in on the floor. He pulled the big cherrywood knife from his pocket and flipped it open. He tossed the shorts on Brian's lap, a cheap cotton exercise pair. Tyler knelt and cut the zip ties from Brian's feet. The blade was so sharp that the ties snapped and flew away at first contact. Brian immediately tried to kick Tyler in the face. His leg wouldn't move, frozen in place after being immobilised for so long.

Tyler pulled the shorts off Brian's lap and slipped them up his tingling legs, under his ass and around his waist. Then before Brian knew what was happening, Tyler whipped zip ties out of his pocket and re-bound Brian's ankles.

"Damn," Brian said. "At least give me a chance to stretch."

"Opportunities abound, bro. Just moments away."

Tyler pulled the chair forward, then pushed it from behind and out the bathroom door. Relief washed over Brian like spring rain as he saw something, anything other than the four walls of the bathroom. He revelled in the open space, the daylight streaming through the window's gauzy curtains. A day, or maybe more, in the tight, silent confines of the bathroom had been more than enough.

They took a right and rolled into the living room. A tacky pink floral-patterned couch and two matching armchairs faced a central coffee table. The light blue pile carpet clashed perfectly. Family photos hung on the walls, some new, some old, lots with kids. Brian would have normally tried to connect the genealogical dots between all of them, but he hadn't the time. There'd be no clues to Tyler's past in those pictures. This obviously wasn't his house.

A laptop sat open on an end table beside the couch. A psychedelic screen saver danced around the display. Brian wished he could get his hands on that for about five minutes. He'd have the cops beating down the door in no time.

Tyler parked him opposite the couch with the coffee table between. He took a seat on the couch, and stared at Brian with barely controlled anticipation. Tyler's psyche seemed balanced on whatever razor's edge he walked between crazed killer and childlike best friend. Brian didn't want to push him in the wrong direction. He didn't say a word.

"So," Tyler said. "We've got a lot of catching up to do. Brother stuff. Some of it might seem out there, but I really think it will be fun, get to know each other better, you know? Do some real bonding."

Tyler whipped out his knife and snapped it open. He reached over and severed the zip ties on Brian's right arm. Brian tried to lift it with no effect. Tyler grabbed his wrist and lifted his arm. He rocked it back and forth, in and out. Every muscle burned with the motion. Brian whimpered as his muscles stretched after being frozen in place by inactivity.

"Oh, yeah," Tyler said. Snort-laugh again. "So been there. One foster family...." He pulled up the sleeve of his shirt to expose a series of cigarette-burn scars on his bicep. "This family here. They had this box for me, like a dog carrier. I got the box when I broke one of their asshole rules. All cramped up in there for hours and then after they finally let me out I wasn't able to move for another hour. Just shake 'em and stretch 'em, bro."

He let Brian's hand go. Brian was able to stop it before it fell all the way to his lap. He stretched his fingers as he rolled his arm in his shoulder socket in slow motion.

His mind went straight to escape. He cycled through several scenarios, but one free hand and three other restrained limbs didn't offer any good options. As he figured Tyler already knew, otherwise he'd still have all four limbs bound to the chair. His damn brother was one step ahead of him.

Tyler reached under the couch and pulled out the board game Life. Brian hadn't seen one in forever. It looked brand new. Tyler popped the top, pulled out the board and unfolded it. It had a big spinner to determine how many spaces to move. A trail of spaces ran across the board, by white plastic buildings, and over plastic green hills. Each space had a life event on it.

"If we'd grown up together, we would have *so* played games like this. On rainy days, when we were stuck inside, we'd have played for hours. This'll be excellent."

The idea of playing Life with a serial killer didn't seem at all excellent to Brian. Tyler apparently didn't get the situation's irony.

Tyler pulled out a handful of tiny plastic convertibles with holes on top of each. They were all different colours. He shoved them in front of Brian.

"Pick your colour!"

Brian couldn't have cared less what colour he had. He picked green.

"Excellent." Tyler picked red. He placed both on Start and put a little blue stick person in each driver's seat. "You go first, Little Bro. Spin it!"

Brian spun the wheel. It stopped on the number ten. The higher the numbers, the faster the game went. All tens would be great. He reached over and started counting spaces with his car. He got to the branch where he had to choose whether to go to college. He took the college track.

"Whoa, whoa!" Tyler grabbed his hand. "What the hell? We're not going to college."

"No?"

"What kind of shit are they going to teach us there? We haven't been yet and we're doing great. Well, I'm doing great and I'll be making you great in no time."

He grabbed the car from Brian's hand and tapped it forward a few more spaces. He stopped on a space that said Get Married-Get Gifts.

"All right, you dog!" Tyler said. "Hooked a hottie! Getting some action! Congratulations."

Tyler picked up a blue stick person and held it just over the passenger seat in the green car. He looked at Brian, then snort-laughed.

"Just messing with you! I know you're no fag. I've seen Daniela."

A shiver ran down Brian's spine. Tyler had stalked Daniela. Or worse, seen Daniela through Brian's eyes, maybe at some pretty intimate moments. Damn, he might have seen her naked! She didn't need to be involved with this at all, and now he was afraid Tyler already had her in deep.

Tyler put a pink peg into Brian's car. Then he took a five hundred dollar bill from the stack of cash in the box and laid it on Brian's lap. "Live large, dude!"

His brother hadn't set them up with any money to play the game. Brian wondered if he'd ever played before, knew any of the rules.

Tyler spun the wheel. It stopped on eight. His car ended up beside Brian in the Get Married spot anyway. "Look at that. Twins with a double wedding. Maybe we even married twins. Way cool. We can switch on them in bed, kind of change it up, and they'll never know."

The game crossed the line of 'borderline creepy'. Brian spun the wheel. Tyler grabbed Brian's car before the wheel even stopped and moved it forward. It landed on a space that read to collect one thousand dollars for winning a talent contest.

"Oh, yeah. That's believable!" Tyler said with a snort-laugh.

He reached across the table and grabbed the front legs of Brian's chair. He lifted them up, and then rocked the chair side to side. Brian gripped the edge with his free hand, afraid of falling partway out of the chair and having a zip tie slice into his flesh.

"Here we go," Tyler said. "A little tap dancing for the talent show!" He snort-laughed again and dropped Brian down so hard it jarred his spine. He threw a hundred-thousand-dollar bill in Brian's lap. "See, who needs college?"

Tyler spun the wheel. He advanced until he got to a space that read You Have A Daughter Get Gifts. His face went dark. He picked up a pink stick figure and stared at it.

"Well, little bitch. Welcome to the world. Daddy was using a condom, but here you are anyhow. Sit in the back and shut the fuck up." His face flushed. He jammed the stick figure into the far corner of his car. He picked up a thousand-dollar bill from the till and slammed it down beside him on the table. "Thanks for the gift, bro."

"No big deal. Nothing's too good for my brother." The last sentence nearly stuck in his throat. But he needed to try to reel Tyler back in. Tyler didn't look up, focused on the pink stick in the back seat of his little red car.

Brian twirled the spinner and it landed on seven. He gingerly tapped his car forward, like it might break through the board. He landed on a space and read the result aloud. "Buy A Sailboat-$30,000." He didn't have any money. He wasn't about to bring that to Tyler's attention.

Tyler brightened and raised his eyes from his little red car. "Excellent! Sailing the high seas like pirates!" He rooted through the box. "There's no sailboat in here."

"Everything like that isn't in the game. You don't really get a house when you have to buy a house."

"Well, that's retarded. Who spends thirty thousand dollars on a make-believe sailboat? Screw that, we're not buying."

Tyler spun the wheel and it yielded an eight. He drove his car forward, making a vroom noise. He screeched to a stop on space number eight and read the result. "Send kids to college. Pay $50,000." His face screwed up in disgust. "See? Fucking leech. Little bitch should have spent a few years with Old Man Dunham. Learned a little about having to work for a living."

Instead of footing his college bill, Tyler moved his car forward until it shared Brian's space.

"Families are just slowing us down," Tyler said. "Wives especially. Nagging us day and night. Crushing our souls, bro. This isn't how our life should be at all."

Tyler reached down and plucked the three pink sticks from the vehicles. He laid them down in front of the cars. He made an engine-revving noise, then drove his car over the three little sticks. He backed up and did it again.

"There! Free at last!" Tyler plucked Brian's blue stick out of his green car and put it in the red car's passenger seat. "Here's a plan. Brothers on a road trip. Free and easy, where we want to go, when we want to go."

He pulled out his knife, and flipped it open. Sunlight flashed along the blade's sharpened edge like a warning strobe. He thrust it into the game board, chopping the three pink sticks in half. Then he jammed the sticks into the holes on the green car, and pushed it into one of the little white buildings on the game board. He uttered a little explosion sound.

"There you go, that's all covered up," he said. "Cops won't find a thing. They were just heading to the store and had an accident." He extracted his knife from the game board, snapped it closed, and put it back in his pocket.

Brian struggled to keep an impassive look on his face, to not betray his growing repulsion at Tyler's interpretation of a perfect life. Tyler picked up the red car and moved it straight to the end where the space read Millionaire Estates. He broke into a big smile.

"And the road trip ends happily ever after!" A timer dinged in the kitchen. Tyler's face lit up. "And right on time!"

He flipped the board closed. The cars and recently deceased stick figures crunched between the boards. He threw it all in the open box and dashed off to the kitchen.

Brian exhaled, and realised he'd barely breathed while Tyler had been in the room. He felt like he'd was walking on ice during the whole bizarre scenario, afraid to say anything to disrupt Tyler's deranged stream-of-consciousness game play.

Now he had a free hand, and his mobility was back. He grabbed for the zip tie on his left hand and pulled. It didn't break. It didn't even budge. These things were tough for being so thin. He wished Tyler had left his oversized pocketknife on the table. It would make quick work of these ties, he'd be free, and out the door one second after. He had no illusions about being able to overpower his beefier twin. Escape would be good enough.

But the knife was still in Tyler's pocket. In fact, nothing useful was within reach. Even the game was on the floor on the other side of the coffee table. Tyler, as usual, seemed to have thought everything through.

An oven door banged open in the kitchen. The smell of baking cheese wafted into the living room. Brian's stomach growled and he realised how little he'd eaten. Plates and silverware clinked from the kitchen. A beaming Tyler walked back into the living room with two dinner plates in his hands, raised too high for Brian to see what was on them, but steam rose from both. Brian's mouth watered.

"And dinner!" Tyler said.

He placed the plate on Brian's lap. The warmth of its bottom transferred through his thin shorts to his thighs. On the plate sat a gooey, bright yellow pile of macaroni and cheese. Thick, bulging discs of unnaturally red hot dog poked out of the mound. Beside the little knoll of cholesterol sat a white plastic spoon, handle hanging over the plate's edge.

"Mac and cheese...." Brian couldn't remember the last time he'd eaten something so totally artificial, in colour and flavour.

"Totally, bro. From the box to you. Kid's comfort food. Two brothers sitting down to Sunday supper with the fam. Well, hell, we're the fam, aren't we?"

Tyler dug into dinner with gusto. Brian took a tentative bite. It tasted like chemicals. The pseudo-cheese was a rough approximation of the real thing, but with the hot dog he recognised nothing but nitrates and food colouring. The overcooked pasta and greasy hot dog felt all wrong in his mouth. He swallowed and the oily mass hit his stomach like a slurry of sludge. He took another small spoonful.

"Bro, what's the matter?" Tyler said.

Shit, Brian thought. He hadn't masked his look of displeasure very well. He dreaded the violent reaction he'd get from Tyler if he turned his nose up at this meal.

"You want some of the crunchy part from the top?" Tyler speared a big scab of hard, blackened cheese from his plate and offered it up.

"No, thanks. I'm just not used to eating something so…heavy. I've always eaten lots of natural foods. Camilla read that all the chemicals made me more anxious."

"Really? Honestly, I tuned out most of your meals when I was linked to you. So boring. You didn't do mac and cheese, no Twinkies, no Lucky Charms?"

"Never."

"Well, shit, bro. No wonder you're no fun. Eating like a cave man when you should be eating all the present day has to offer. Look at me. Bigger. Stronger. Taller. Did I do that on wheat germ and bean sprouts? Shit, no. White bread, mayonnaise, fried chicken, fast food. Cheap and chock full of everything you need. Eat up. You'll see. I'll bulk you up in no time flat."

Brian forced in another mouthful and chewed. He faked a smile as he swallowed and it slithered down his throat. He *was* hungry as hell, and this stuff beat starving to death.

"See, told you." Tyler shovelled in the rest of what was on his plate at a rate Brian couldn't match, even if he had liked what he was eating. Brian mentally committed to forcing down as much as he could stand since he couldn't count on Tyler giving him a regular feeding schedule.

Brian had a minor epiphany. Tyler's hair was artificially white, the food artificially yellow, the whole mood artificially congenial. Even the house they were squatting in wasn't really theirs. Everything was fake in a situation that was all too real.

Tyler looked up with a big grin when he finished. A dab of cheese hung at the corner of his mouth. "Now, the best part."

He grabbed the almost-full plate off Brian's lap. Brian reached for it too late, and it then was gone. Tyler rushed out of the room.

Plates clanked into the sink and he returned with two floating red balloons tied to a metal spatula. His other hand was behind his back. He set the balloons on the coffee table.

"We've missed so much together," Tyler said. "But there's one thing, one most important thing we've missed, something only we can share." From behind his back, he revealed a sparkling blue, conical, cardboard party hat. "Birthdays! We're twenty shared birthdays behind, twenty years of parties with kids and games and fun."

He reached down and jammed the hat on Brian's head. He stretched the elastic band under Brian's chin and let it snap back in place. The rough little cord bit under his jaw. It reminded him of the strangled murder victims and made him shudder. Tyler rushed out of the room, right foot dragging a bit even when he tried to hurry.

Something clicked on and off several times in the kitchen, then Tyler returned. He had a red version of the party hat on, and carried a white-frosted, circular layer cake. He placed it on Brian's lap. Twenty canted, burning candles were shoved in the top in an irregular pattern, breaking up the phrase 'Happy Birthday Ty and Bri' in loopy red letters. Brian pulled his face back from the flames' rising heat.

"So here it is, bro. Twenty birthdays rolled all into one. Time to make a wish."

I wish I was free and you were dead, Brian thought.

"Wait, bro," Tyler said. "Here's our wish. That these two brothers never be separated again."

Before Brian could do anything, Tyler took a deep breath and blew at the candles. All but three at one corner extinguished. An irritated look twisted Tyler's face. He grabbed at the candles and crushed the flames in his bare fist. He registered no pain. He yanked the offending candles from the cake. They pulled a clump of frosting with them and left a patch of exposed golden cake, as if Tyler had scalped the thing. He threw the handful against the couch, where it made a gooey splat. His face relaxed, all now right with the world again.

"Cake time!" He whipped out his big pocketknife and snapped

it open. With three violent thrusts, he chopped free two oversized wedges. He sat down on the edge of the coffee table, facing Brian. He pulled two forks from his back pocket, one plastic, one metal. He handed the plastic one to Brian. "Dive in, dude. The slice is just, like, a guideline. No limit!"

He drove his fork into the closest wedge and pulled free a hunk. Brian took a far smaller section of his wedge. It ended up being mostly frosting. Once inside his mouth it tasted like pure gritty sugar, flavoured with coconut. He forced it down and took a forkful of mostly cake for the next mouthful to even out the experience.

"Good shit, huh?" Tyler said as he downed a third or fourth forkful. Brian had lost count.

"Sure is!" It actually was good cake. Wherever Tyler got it, they knew what they were doing. And any food now was better than hoping for food later.

Tyler pulled the cake from Brian's lap and set it on the coffee table. He yanked the fork out of Brian's hand. Before he knew what happened, Tyler had his wrist zip-tied back to the chair.

"Oh." Brian sighed. "You don't need to do that."

"Better safe than sorry, dude. Idle hands, devil's workshop, something like that." Tyler pointed to the cake. "We'll save the rest for later. Like breakfast or something? That would be excellent!"

He wheeled Brian back into the bathroom and positioned him over the toilet. He yanked his shorts down to his ankles and tossed a fresh towel across his lap.

"See," Tyler said. "Look at all the bonding there. We're a natural fit. You'll see. I'll get you off your rabbit-food diet and onto eating real food, get you schooled in how to live to the max, and you'll be as awesome as me in no time flat. Gotta chore to do now, be right back after."

Tyler closed the door and left Brian alone to process the whirlwind he'd just survived. Tyler had concocted some TV-ad-driven outline of what brothers should share and wedged it all into twenty minutes, checking a mental box as they started each event, not caring if the event accomplished anything in the end.

Then again, maybe he didn't know that his miniature three-act play didn't create any fraternal connections. This emotionally stunted version of himself seemed to lack all empathy with, or understanding of, other people. Maybe Tyler really thought they had accomplished something.

Brian's own empathy kicked in and for a fleeting second he felt sorry for Tyler. Anger quickly snuffed that emotion. Anger at being kidnapped, anger at being manipulated, anger over the string of corpses across Florida, corpses Tyler had everyone thinking were Brian's victims.

The delayed stress of the evening made itself known. He wasn't sure how long he'd been awake, or even what day it was, but exhaustion rolled over him like a thick fog. The heavy food in his gut added its own additional call to slumber. His eyelids slid closed, his head lolled to one side, and he was asleep.

CHAPTER THIRTY-FIVE

He walks through silent, greyscale scrub brush. Distant parking-lot floodlights turn the night into murky dusk. Bits of trash litter the ground. Some, like the beer cans, no doubt left there at the end of some clandestine party; others, like the faded, shredded wrappers from roofing shingles, blown in from somewhere else. A spent hypodermic needle crushes under his boot.

Dread wells up within him. Brian knows this killer's-eye view, knows he has no control over his brother's actions, and worse, knows he will experience every second of it.

He approaches a chain-link fence. In one section, the links are cut halfway up from the bottom and the split in the metal mesh forms an inverted V. Beyond the fence rises a shadowy wall of steel. Tyler's anticipation thrums through him like a hard-rock bass line. Brian's stomach turns at sharing Tyler's twisted emotion, knowing what will transpire at the end of this hunt.

* * *

In the real world, his head jerked back up as his neck twisted to a strange, uncomfortable angle. There was a flicker of brighter light, a flash of his bathroom prison, barely long enough to register, and then he dove back into sleep.

* * *

He stands in his apartment. Daniela comes through the front door. The concerned look on her face melts away as she sees him. She rushes into his arms. He pulls her close.

"You're safe, you're free," she says.

Her little body radiates a warmth that can only be kindled by love. He holds her tight.

"I'm so glad you're here," he says.

"I always knew you didn't do it," she answers. "Now hurry, I have everything we need in my car. In a few hours we'll be two states away from here."

The idea of leaving all this mess behind and starting a life with Daniela fills him with joy. He smiles so wide that it hurts. "Let's go."

Daniela turns soft in his embrace, then insubstantial. She vanishes, and with her any wisp of happiness floating within him. His arms collapse in, and he hugs his own bony elbows.

★ ★ ★

Another bob of his head summoned him back to reality. Uninterrupted sleep in the hard, upright chair was impossible. His banana-yellow jail cell passed by in a flash bright enough to make him wince and he submerged back into unconsciousness.

★ ★ ★

A playing card fills his field of view. A six of diamonds. The sight sends a chill through him.

Confusion sweeps him. Does he see this in preparation for the kill, or afterwards? Is he really seeing visions through Tyler's eyes, or is this vision all the fruit of his subconscious, like his disappearing Daniela?

The view pulls back from the card. The fingers holding it are thin as pencils, and nearly as long. The view expands and Mr. Jitters grips the card. He waves it before Brian, his whole body swaying with rubbery flexibility. His eyes glow bright from their darkened sockets. He smiles and exposes ruby-red gums and pearl-white teeth behind the painted smile on his white skin.

"He's going to deal again," Mr. Jitters says. "One card will follow another." His screeching, maniacal laugh pierces the air. "And they'll all say it was you. The cops won't even try to take you alive."

Jitters stops swaying. He slams the playing card against Brian's forehead. It feels slimy and sticks there. Mr. Jitters grabs Brian's face in both hands. "You and I are going to dance the night away!"

The terror builds in Brian. A full-blown anxiety meltdown is seconds away.

★ ★ ★

A ring of fire around his right wrist called him to a fuzzy consciousness. He slouched in the chair as the zip tie threatened to amputate his hand. Brian shifted right to relieve the pressure, then closed his eyes again.

★ ★ ★

He stands over an open, metal, fifty-five-gallon drum. Something sits in the shadow below the rim, dark and motionless. Brian senses fulfilment at the sight through the eyes he's borrowed, and hopes that the view does not shift and afford him any details of what lays inside. A pair of hands with covered fingertips places the metal lid back on the drum. An inch-wide screw top covers an off-centre drain hole. The hand unscrews it and tosses it away. It is as if what is inside needs to breathe, but Brian is certain that isn't true.

★ ★ ★

The vision vanished behind another flare of the bathroom light and another painful twist of his sleeping body. He clamped shut his eyes and descended back to sleep.

★ ★ ★

He is at his parents' house, in the middle of the front yard. He stands naked except for the police ankle monitors, one on each leg this time. A circle of people surround him: his parents, Detective Weissbard, Sidney, Daniela, his sister Ariana, and Mr. Wickett, a hated high school phys ed teacher. They all laugh at him, trading barbs about his nudity, his guilt, his impending punishment. The abuse comes hot and heavy, louder, sharper. The individual taunts overlap until they all meld into one audio maelstrom. He screams and covers his ears.

The sound cuts off. He now wears a dark robe, with a thick cowl pulled back behind his head. His ankle monitors lay on the ground before him, smashed, their electronic guts sparking and sizzling.

His detractors still circle him, but now all sit tied in duplicates of the dining room chair in his bathroom prison, facing away from him.

Tyler appears at his side. In his right hand is a red velvet rope, the only colour in this black-and-white vision. He whips the end around and into his left palm. It slides through and he keeps repeating the process.

"They all need to die," Tyler says. "We'll kill them all. Together. A deck has fifty-two cards, you know." He leans in nose-to-nose with Brian. "That's a whole future full of fun."

* * *

Brian jolted awake. He snapped his head back and slammed into the top of the chair with a crack. He was alone in the bathroom. Sweat ran down his forehead and across his chest. He yanked both hands against the zip ties until pain flared around his wrists and he was certain that he was back in the real world, and not in yet again another deluded dream.

Reality, dreams, seeing through Tyler's eyes, he now couldn't tell what was what, which was real, which imagined. Had he witnessed part of a murder? Lack of sleep, dehydration, drug withdrawal. He felt adrift in a perfect storm of psychological chaos.

He wondered if that storm would sink him. Or worse, if it already had.

CHAPTER THIRTY-SIX

Weissbard's day had started way too early and way too lousy. A day into Sheridan's escape, the whole department had a dragnet out, but Weissbard had taken it to a very personal level. He'd worked his ass off to bring in Sheridan, and he wasn't about to let him slip away. Francisco was running the big show of roadblocks and neighbourhood sweeps. But Weissbard knew Sheridan better than anyone. While Francisco focused on locking things down on the outside, Weissbard was going to start his personal search from the inside, Sheridan's inside.

Sheridan had limited means and damn few friends. His apartment was under surveillance, but he wasn't stupid enough to go there. He'd need to find somewhere else to lay low, and only the people who knew him might have an idea where that might be.

Sheridan's phone records were so sparse that only Sheridan's weirdo loner status kept Weissbard from assuming the guy had a second phone. But there was one person he'd called pretty regularly, up until recently. Daniela Schiavetta. She'd be his first stop.

After two hours dismissing useless tip-line leads, he reenergised himself with an enormous sugared coffee and two donuts that would have sent his wife into a rant about his health. It was just after 9:00 a.m. when he entered the veterinary clinic where Daniela worked. A very nervous receptionist ushered him into one of the small, empty exam rooms, barely large enough for the stainless-steel exam table and the Formica counter tops. A heavy dose of antiseptic didn't do much to cover the musky, acidic smell of animal waste. He leaned against the wall to wait.

Daniela entered. She wore a pair of wrinkled scrubs, all wet along one edge. She looked scared. Weissbard liked that in a witness. That kind talked a lot. He pulled out his note pad.

"Oh, my God. You're here about Brian. I knew it."

"You knew what?"

"That you'd eventually come question me."

Weissbard had hoped she was about to say that she'd known he'd been a killer all along. Well, he couldn't win them all.

"How long have you known Brian Sheridan?"

"Ten months, maybe. We dated for the last few."

"When was the last time you spoke to him?"

"Days ago, when I got back from my mother's. He'd gotten off his meds and started acting really strange."

That confirmed his hypothesis, and matched the timeline of when the Playing Card Killer murders started. "What do you mean, strange?"

"Like having hallucinations, nightmares. He couldn't sleep, got angry pretty quick. I told him he needed to get back on meds or I was out of the picture."

"And you haven't spoken to him since?"

"Just one phone call, and I told him the same thing I told him in person. No meds, no me."

Just to eliminate a few more potential holes in his case, he named the dates of the four murders. "Were you with Brian any of those nights?"

She looked at the floor, thinking. "No, I don't think so. We were broken up by then." A look of concern crossed her face. "Hey, he's out on bail, but the news said he had one of those ankle bracelet things on. I don't have to worry about him dropping by, right? You cops know where he is all the time?"

Weissbard marvelled that this supposedly most-connected generation seemed to rarely be informed about the news. "As a matter of fact, that's why I'm here to see you. He's jumped bail."

"But he had one of those ankle-tracking-things. How could…" Her face went white. "Oh my God! He wouldn't come to me, would he?"

"Would he think you'd protect him?"

"No! I stormed out last time I saw him. Gave him the ultimatum."

Her face fell. She sighed and gestured to the walls around the room. "See where I work, what I do? Broken animals come in here and I take care of them, help them get better. It's my weakness, with people, too. I thought I could help fix Brian. Someday, I'll learn that animals are much better patients."

"Is there any place you think he might hide out?"

"He only spent time at home and at work. It was a big deal if I got him to a movie. I don't have any idea where he would be."

Weissbard scribbled a few notes. He put away his notebook and handed her his card. "If he calls you, you call me."

She snapped the card from his hand. "Are you kidding? In a second. You'd better pick up, too. I don't want to end up dead with a playing card stuffed inside me."

Weissbard nodded and walked out. She was genuinely scared, and genuinely convinced of Sheridan's guilt. If Brian contacted her, she'd be in touch in seconds. All that was good news.

The bad news was he wasn't any closer to finding Sheridan. It was time to see if co-worker Sidney had any more insights to share.

CHAPTER THIRTY-SEVEN

Weissbard never made it to Sidney's. And it wouldn't have mattered if he had. A call from coroner Cal Cambridge diverted him to Orange Star Trucking. Someone had found a body in a drum.

A police cruiser and two officers guarded the main entrance. They waved Weissbard in through the open gate. The coroner's van was at the far end of the lot, so he drove down and pulled up next to it.

As soon as he got out of his car, a middle-aged man in a white short-sleeve shirt and a red tie approached at a brisk walk. He had the top-heavy physique of a guy who used to spend a lot of hours in the gym. Used to. Worry creased his broad face.

"You must be Detective Weissbard," he said. "I'm Rodney Dahlgren, the manager. The officers said you could tell me when I can get back to business."

"Mr. Dahlgren, there's been a homicide here. Solving it is my only priority."

"I've got loads that need to move, loads nowhere near this part of the yard. Some of them are perishable. Moving them won't have any impact."

Weissbard had a belly full of this guy's attitude and he'd only been with him for seconds. "This whole area's a crime scene for as long as I say it is. If you want it to be a month, keep talking."

Dahlgren stepped back, mouth shut. Weissbard walked over to where some CSI members clustered around an open fifty-five-gallon metal drum. Cambridge the coroner had his head hung over the drum in thoughtful inspection.

"Cambridge," Weissbard said. "Long time no see."

"I wish that was true," he said. "I made sure you were called before we moved anything."

"Not the esteemed Detective Sergeant Francisco?"

"I seem to misplace that asshole's number. A lot."

"I sure appreciate that."

"You might not after this," Cambridge said. He pointed a thumb at the big steel drum.

Weissbard looked inside the drum. "Son of a bitch."

Sidney sat stuffed in the drum, skin grey and sagging but with a darker band of bruising around his neck that Weissbard was way too familiar with. The edge of a six of diamonds playing card stuck out of his mouth.

Sheridan disappeared off home-monitoring radar, and within a day, another Playing Card Killer victim, one who might help finger Sheridan, showed up dead. Homicide rule #1: Coincidences were never coincidences.

"The day guard saw three rats crawling into the open spout on the drum," Cambridge said. "Kind of odd since he thought it was empty. He found the corpse when he popped the lid. The victim died sometime last night." Cambridge handed Weissbard a pair of tweezers and a clear evidence bag. "I saved you the honours."

Weissbard used the tweezers to gently extract the card from the corpse's mouth. It had the signature red pattern on the back, the mirrored Greek women by the summer and winter trees. Something on the card's face caught his eye just before he dropped it into the bag. He couldn't believe his luck. On one edge was a black, greasy fingerprint. The colour was similar to the dirt around the rim of the drum.

Looks like Sheridan got a little sloppy working on his home turf, Weissbard thought. *He's finally screwed up*. Weissbard sealed the card in the bag and walked over to the fidgety yard manager, Dahlgren.

"You have an employee in a can," Weissbard said, "and you're worried about getting business back to normal? When was Sidney's last shift?"

"Last night. He didn't clock out."

"And no one knew that?"

"My evening shift guard is in jail, you might remember. The day- and night-shift guys are covering with overtime. The night guy just thought Sidney forgot to clock out. It's a signature Sidney move."

At the main gate, a news van pulled up. Weissbard shook his

head. The vultures were already alighting. The media would be whipping the public into a panic. Playing Card Killer escapes to kill again! He wondered who already leaked the playing-card evidence.

The scenario fit perfectly in Weissbard's mind. Sheridan put two and two together, and figured that his co-worker filled in enough details to get Sheridan arrested. So, to get some vengeance and cover his tracks, the first thing Sheridan did when he chopped himself free of his monitor was to kill Sidney. Sheridan knew this hunting ground like the back of his hand. He could easily sneak in, knowing the guards' routine. He also knew where the security cameras were, and how to avoid them. Then to top it off, the son of a bitch leaves a damn playing card to rub Weissbard's face in it.

That was bad news. It meant Sheridan wouldn't stop. He had somewhere to hide, but his compulsion wouldn't let him lay low. Once he'd started, he had to keep killing.

Weissbard had to find him before he did it again.

CHAPTER THIRTY-EIGHT

The distant slam of a door snapped Brian out of the dozing stupor that had overcome him. Someone was in the house. His first hope was that the owner, or a plumber, or anyone but Tyler, was checking on the home. He'd even settle for a Jehovah's Witness. Maybe neighbours had called about a strange car going in and out of the garage, and an honest-to-God member of the Tampa PD had kicked in the door to get him the hell out of here.

"Hey! Help! I'm in the bathroom!"

"Mr. Sheridan?" a deep voice called.

Brian's heart soared. "Yes, here! In the bathroom! Hurry!"

The door knob jiggled. "Mr. Sheridan?"

"That's it! In here!"

The door opened. Tyler stuck his head in. "Hello, bro," he said in the same bass voice.

Brian's heart sank.

Tyler laughed that snorting, stupid laugh and returned to his normal voice. "Sorry, dude. Just pranking you. Couldn't resist. Today's going to be busy, so we need to get started." He unlocked the wheels of the chair and rolled it forward. "Now, bro, if you need to drop a load just hold it for a few minutes, okay?" Snort-laugh. Out came the big knife and he snapped it open. He reached behind, cut Brian's arms free, and looked him in the eyes from inches away. "There you go, give 'em a stretch."

Brian wanted so bad to grab Tyler by the throat and choke the life out of him. He couldn't move his arms, still frozen along the side of the chair.

"C'mon, little brother. Shake it out."

Brian moved his fingers. Muscles slowly, painfully rippled back to life up his arms.

"Yeah, that's it, bro. You got it. Now, shirt off, little brother."

"Tyler, this isn't necessary, please."

Tyler tucked the knife blade under the sleeve of Brian's shirt. The cold blade grazed his arm. The steely, crazy look returned to Tyler's eyes. "Shirt off or I cut it off."

Brian pulled his shirt off over his head. His spine creaked with the effort. Tyler put away his knife and took the shirt. Then he pulled a washcloth from a rack, soaked and soaped it. He tossed the washcloth at Brian's chest. Brian grabbed it just before it fell between his legs.

"Clean yourself up a bit," Tyler said. "Can't have the other half of the family stinking like a crack-house whore."

The cloth was steaming warm and smelled like roses. Brian scrubbed his face and neck, under his arms, and finished with the sticky mess between his legs.

"Sink," Tyler said, pointing.

Bryan tossed the washcloth in.

"Yeah!" Tyler cried. "Three-pointer with nothing but net."

He reached outside the door and retrieved a big bag from McDonald's. He tossed Brian one, then another, paper-wrapped cheeseburger from inside. The smell of them sent Brian's mouth to watering. At this point, having fresh and healthy food took a backseat to having any food at all.

"I splurged for the cheese. Nothing's too good for a family reunion."

Brian ripped open a wrapper and practically inhaled the sandwich. The combination of fat and protein sent his taste buds tingling. He started on the second sandwich.

Tyler scooped the washcloth out of the sink with the dirty shirt and wadded them in a ball. He took them out of the bathroom. His one foot dragged and Brian noticed the uneven wear on Tyler's shoes. He wondered if the defect was congenital, something that he missed by some happenstance of birth.

"What happened to your foot?" Brian called after Tyler.

Tyler stepped back in. He closed the door behind him. Gritted teeth had supplanted the good-natured smile. "Fucking polo injury. No wait, I think it was tennis, yeah, that was it. Do you really want to know?"

Damn. I didn't mean to set him off. "No. It's cool. Sorry I asked."

Tyler's face morphed back into the cheery boy-next-door. "Hey, got something to show you. You'll love this." Tyler pulled a smartphone from the McDonald's bag. He tapped up a website and turned it to face Brian. A local news anchor sat at a desk, looking grim.

"Brian Sheridan, the alleged Playing Card Killer, appears to have struck again. After escaping from his parents' house where he was on bail, police believe he doubled back to the trucking company where he worked and made a co-worker there victim number five."

Brian stopped chewing. "No, no way. What the hell did you do?"

The scene cut to a shot of the big empty steel barrels at the edge of the Orange Trucking Company yard. Crime-scene tape fluttered in the breeze and a black coroner's van stood nearby.

"The body of Sidney Johnson was found stuffed in an empty drum at the trucking firm's yard. Unconfirmed sources say that the victim was strangled and one of the signature playing cards was found on the body."

"Six of diamonds," Tyler said. "I wish they'd be more specific about the cards. I pick them at random but I'd love to hear the crazy theories people come up with to explain what they mean."

Brian flashed back to the combination of dreams and hallucinations from the past night. Amidst all the things that barely made sense, he remembered seeing hands attaching the lid to a steel drum. And he remembered seeing the six of diamonds.

Brian felt ready to throw up his meal. "What did you kill him for? What did you kill any of them for, but especially why him?"

"Bro, when you do something, you need to commit to doing it. Take skydiving. Once you step out of the door, you're committed to pull the chute and land. This kill makes sure that you're committed. No one could ever assign a motive to you killing those strangers, but even the Tampa PD can see you killing the guy who ratted you to the cops."

"You son of a bitch."

"And you were really sloppy. Left a big greasy fingerprint on the card this time. I borrowed your finger to get the print while you were sleeping. Took me two tries to get it nice and clear. Our DNA is a perfect match, but not our fingerprints. Weird, huh? Too bad. But that print should seal your deal with the cops. In for a penny, in for a pound, right?"

Brian had thought about escape, made some wildly unrealistic plans where he ended up leading the police straight to Tyler. What good would going to the police do? The evidence against him was more than just circumstantial now, and the story that exonerated him, the story of a long-lost twin who happened to be a serial killer, hell, even Brian barely believed it. The rest of his second cheeseburger slipped from his hand and dropped to the floor.

"Oh, bro," Tyler admonished him. "Wasting food. Foster Mother #1 said that was a sin. She'd have made me eat that right off this sticky mess you made of the floor." He kicked the burger toward the door. "Lucky for you I never bought into that."

Tyler swung the bathroom door open wide. Chill bumps prickled Brian's chest as the blast of air conditioning crossed the damp residue of the washcloth. Tyler reached outside the door, brought back a T-shirt, and tossed it to Brian. Brian pulled on the shirt. A Pittsburgh Steelers logo filled its chest. Tyler smiled.

"That's like one of my favourite shirts. See how cool this will be, sharing stuff like real brothers?" The grin drained from Tyler's face. "Hands back behind the chair."

Brian sighed and hung them back where they'd been before. What was the point of resisting? What hope was there? Tyler zip-tied them back in position. He rolled Brian back over the toilet and flushed it. The water sprinkled Brian's bare ass. Tyler laid another towel across Brian's lap.

"I'm going to start scouting our next adventure. When I get back, we're going to really start having fun."

Tyler turned out the bathroom light and closed the door. A second later, the door swung open and Tyler snapped the light back on.

"Whoa, sorry, bro! Didn't mean to leave you in the dark."

Tyler closed the door, and Brian felt his spirit go black. He was so screwed. The half of him that wasn't naked wore the clothes of a serial killer. He was bound to a chair in an unknown house. The police wanted him for a quintet of homicides. At this point, even Daniela had to believe he was the Playing Card Killer. One and a half greasy cheeseburgers roiled in his stomach, threatening to make a return visit.

He wished Tyler had skipped the kidnapping, and just killed him that night in his parents' house.

CHAPTER THIRTY-NINE

The corner closest to the bathroom door had an imperfection.

Two inches off the floor, the contractor had missed smoothing out a bit of the mud that finished the drywall edges. The painter had painted over it anyway. It looked like a cancerous lesion someone had daubed with makeup to match the wall.

There was also a scratch on the side of the sink, and the baseboards in the other corner didn't meet. Brian had time to see all of this and commit it to memory. Through it all, he had the regular backbeat of the damn drip from the faucet.

A door slammed. Brian perked up and listened, closer this time. The footsteps were uneven, one solid, one softer. His brother's signature right-foot drag. Brian lowered his head in dejection. The door swung open. Tyler stood there holding a pair of shorts and a pair of socks. He tossed them on Brian's lap.

"Bro! How goes it, dude? Big event! Today we start the hunt."

"I'm not doing that."

"Sure you are. See, the problem here is you've only experienced the last few minutes, the climax. That's like only seeing the final scene of a movie. You wouldn't really get it, wouldn't be emotionally connected with the characters. So instead, you'll get to see it all. Start to finish. Behind the scenes with Ty and Bri, the Twin Playing Card Killers."

"There's only one killer."

Tyler smiled. "And according to the cops, that killer's you, bro. Might as well live up to your hype."

Tyler cut free Brian's feet and hands. Brian slowly brought his stiff arms around front. Every muscle burned. Tyler was inches from him, unarmed, but there was no way Brian could move fast enough to take advantage of the situation. And Tyler knew it, the smug bastard.

"Put on some pants," Tyler said. "And you'll learn to love going commando. Happens when foster parents don't believe in underwear."

Brian rose with all the grace of the rusted Tin Man of Oz as he creaked into an upright position. He pulled on the shorts, zipped them up, and officially disliked going commando.

"Shoes?" he asked.

"Socks will do. You aren't walking anywhere."

And you don't want me running anywhere, either, Brian thought. He put on the white socks. As soon as he was done, Tyler was beside him, looping zip ties around his wrists and ankles.

"To the garage," Tyler said.

"Tied up?"

"Sure, bro. Hop to it!" Tyler snort-laughed. "Oh, I so crack myself up."

"You've got to be kidding."

Tyler's eyes turned hard. His smile evaporated. "Just be happy you have two hopping feet. Get in the damn car."

Tyler's unnerving, instantaneous shift from frolicking frat boy to cold killer sent a shiver through Brian. He took two hops to the bathroom door. Tyler's grin reappeared.

"That's the spirit, bro!"

In the garage, the back door of the Camry hung wide open. The folded-down rear seat created a big cargo space into the trunk. Little rollup sunshades covered the rear windows. Tyler spun Brian around and sat him down on the seat's edge. Tyler grabbed a rag and a white plastic bottle from the workbench behind him. He doused the rag from the bottle and shoved it over Brian's mouth and nose. Brian's brain went into a tailspin.

"Take a nap, little brother. I'll wake you when the fun starts."

* * *

Brian woke up bathed in sweat. The car's stifling, humid air felt straight out of hell. Tyler had added a gag to Brian's bondage ensemble, a precaution that meant they were somewhere way more public than the house's garage. Brian lay on his side, feet and hands still bound, facing the trunk's rear. His watery eyes came into focus. The back of the reverse light housing had been chopped away and the bulb removed, allowing a narrow view of a ubiquitous, bland Florida strip mall. A dingy shop that sold everything for a dollar filled the centre location. Brian swept his head against the rough carpet to wipe away some sweat. The trunk liner reeked of mildew.

"Hey, wide awake, little bro?" Tyler said from the front seat. "About time. I don't want you to miss anything. Every step's got a purpose, you know."

"I'm baking back here," he managed through the gag, slow enough for Tyler to understand.

"Yeah, sorry. Can't sit out here idling the car, attracting that kind of attention. It's not so bad up here with the windows cracked open."

Brian's mind spooled up escape options. He tried to move his arms and legs, but the zip ties on both had been bound together, hogtie-style. He stretched his head as far as he could, but barely got it off the trunk floor. He turned back enough to get a glimpse of the front seats. The backup camera view played in the centre-stack touchscreen. The rearview mirror hung canted at the perfect odd angle, down at Brian. Tyler's eyes filled it, watching him.

He thought again about an interior trunk release. The little glow-in-the-dark handle would be here somewhere. He could maybe hook it with his zip-tie bindings, pop the deck lid. Someone passing by would see him bound in the trunk. Even in this rundown neighbourhood that would warrant a call to the cops. He looked all around. He stopped and sighed. Only the jagged edge of a severed cable hung from the trunk lid. Tyler was always one step ahead.

"Okay, here she comes," Tyler said. "Wearing red."

An overweight, middle-aged woman wearing a shiny red rayon top and tan pants approached the store. Her greying hair was cut short and clipped back from her face with a cheap barrette. A name tag for the dollar store was pinned over her ample left breast. She looked a bit haggard, not acute haggard like she'd had a bad night's sleep, but chronic haggard, worn down by a life that had delivered her to a job stocking the shelves at a dollar store.

"Meet Candy," Tyler said. "A prime example of a stripper's

name on a non-stripper body. Works one-to-nine, five days a week."

"Why her?" Brian tried to choke out.

"Why her, you ask? Because she's random. Different place than the others, different age than the others, different job than the others. Bro, if we want to do this thing right, we have to be random. Start a pattern, and they figure it out. They forecast the repetition. Then one day, they'll be waiting for us."

The woman entered the shop. Guilt and dread filled Brian, knowing what torture awaited this undeserving woman. She had no clue what lay ahead, and Tyler's randomness would have her die not knowing why the horror happened to her. He craned his neck to look up into Tyler's eyes in the rearview mirror.

"Why any of them?" Brian said.

"You have to ask? Because they're women. They're all destined to screw up lives somewhere down the road. We take one life, and we've saved a dozen others from being totally tanked."

"That's—" Brian stopped himself before saying, 'crazy'.

"Crazy?" Tyler said. "Get real, bro. Look at what our biological so-called mother did to us. Whatever prenatal drug and alcohol cocktail she bathed herself in gave us these little quirks we have. Then she sent us off to whatever screwed-up couple would take us in."

Tyler's face in the mirror blushed redder. His eyes hardened. "How's your adoptive mother, dear Camilla? She's a real prize isn't she? All June Cleaver and nurturing to you? And your pseudo sister? An absolute peach of a girl, right?" His voice rose, the pitch sharpened. "Don't forget, I've been living your life through your eyes for a long time. I know exactly how they are. Two prime examples of why we have to do what we have to do."

Tyler punched the cigarette lighter into its receptacle in the dash. Then he scrambled into the backseat and hung over Brian like a vulture.

"And you just have one bad mother. I've had a bunch. Manipulative, resentful, abusive. I've seen it all. Sadism runs, like, deep in the gender, bro. Can't you see that?"

The cigarette lighter popped out.

"One of mine, this was, like, her favourite thing. Talk on a trip in the car, a word, even a noise, and you got the Silencer."

Tyler pulled the lighter from the dash and pointed it at Brian. The end glowed cherry red.

"Until I was twelve, I seriously thought this thing was called a Silencer, that it was an option parents bought in a car. And if I made a peep while I was in there...."

Brian's eyes went wide with fear. Tyler jabbed the lighter into Brian's bicep below his shirt sleeve. A circle of searing pain set his arm ablaze. He screamed into the gag. Tears filled his eyes.

"...you got the Silencer. Best ADHD medicine in the world, I tell you what. And by God you were quiet after that. For days. And if you weren't...."

He plunged the lighter into Brian's exposed thigh. Brian screamed again as a second wave of pain engulfed his body.

"That bitch taught me a lot about the power of persuasion. And there were more lessons where that came from. The world's filled with one screwed up, twisted woman after another. They have it coming to them. What we're doing is a goddamn public service, that's what it is."

The fury drained from him. He looked at Brian's arm with empathy, as if he hadn't seen the rising red blister until just then. "Oh, dude. Look what you made me do. Shit. Wait here." He grinned, plucked at the zip ties and snort-laughed. "Sorry, couldn't help myself."

Tyler got out of the car. Brian whimpered in pain and rolled back to face the rear of the car. Through tear-blurred eyes he watched Tyler enter the dollar store. Tyler returned with two sweating cans of soda. He reentered the car and faced the backseat.

"Little bro, hold still." He laid an ice-cold can against each of the swelling burns. Brian's searing skin cooled like an extinguished fire. "Learned that one from another great foster parent. But he used beer. Better?"

Brian just nodded.

"You know what's really choice about this? I bought these

sodas from Candy. I mean, how funny is that, you know?"

Brian just winced against the pain in his arm and leg. Tyler slid back into the front seat.

"Well, I gotta say, this didn't work out as well as I thought. You aren't getting it. And you made me use the Silencer. Shit. I mean, where'd that come from, right?"

Brian knew exactly where that came from. The same twisted place that spawned the rest of Tyler's sadistic perversions.

Tyler snapped his fingers. "Wait! Brainstorm! I know what I missed. Oh, bro, why didn't I think of this earlier? It'll set us back a few days, but it will be so worth it!"

Brian was immediately certain that whatever this new plan was, it wouldn't be worth it at all.

CHAPTER FORTY

Detective Weissbard sat at his kitchen table and absent-mindedly stirred a bowl of granola with a spoon.

"You can stir that forever," his wife Maryanne said. "You'll still have to eat it."

"If I mash it up enough, maybe I can just drink it."

"I'll put it in the blender."

"God, no." He put a spoonful in his mouth and chewed with an exaggerated smile. "Mmm! Can you believe poor people have to choke down bacon and sausage?"

Maryanne sat down beside him. "You barely slept last night."

"It doesn't make sense," Weissbard said. "Sheridan escaped, killed Johnson, then just disappeared. In the four days since he bolted from house arrest, there hasn't been a sighting, a useful tip, nothing. His family sure wouldn't help him. He didn't have any friends to speak of. Even his ex-girlfriend was scared he'd be back to kill her. There's almost no way for a guy with no money, no support, and no transportation to hide out for this long."

"There's always the chance he was hit by a car and died on the side of the road somewhere."

"Wouldn't that be great? Save the whole extravaganza of a trial."

"Speaking of which, what about the judge who let him out on bail?"

"Suspended pending an ethics investigation. Had a few close financial ties with the defence attorney."

"Someone has to put the 'criminal' in 'criminal justice', right?"

Weissbard smiled. His wife was always good for a laugh in almost any situation. He downed the last few spoonfuls of his cereal and turned the empty bowl up toward her.

"Happy?"

"Thrilled. Now go catch the bad guys."

★ ★ ★

If there was one bright side to this whole mess, it was that Francisco had become the man in the hot seat for finding Sheridan. He was so busy scrambling to find the escapee that he hadn't had any free time to devote to his vindictive anti-Weissbard campaign. And he sure as hell didn't want Weissbard anywhere near any leads that might result in Sheridan's recapture. Which left Weissbard free to follow his gut.

Every day, Francisco extended the search ring for Sheridan, convinced that the escapee was using that time to get as far away as possible from Tampa. Weissbard knew the opposite was probably closer to the truth. Sheridan was barely comfortable in his own skin, a creature of habit that kept to his crappy apartment, his crappy job, and the route between them. His girlfriend said she could barely talk him into going to movies. He wasn't about to take his anxiety-riddled life on the road. Weissbard was betting he'd gone to ground here in Tampa, right under all their noses.

Weissbard pulled into the police station. His phone rang. The caller's number wasn't familiar.

"Weissbard."

"Detective? This is Daniela. You interviewed me about Brian Sheridan."

A mental picture of the little brunette popped up. Hope soared that the killer had contacted her, that maybe he was on his way over to her house. Weissbard could have cops there in under five minutes. "Yes, I remember our conversation."

"You asked me about a bunch of dates and if I was with Brian on any of them. I think I was wrong on one."

Weissbard pulled out his notebook. "What do you mean?"

"Now I wasn't trying to lie or anything. I was just real nervous, and the dates all blended together. You know? I looked again at the calendar for something else and thought, 'Oh my

God!' But I'm fixing it all now, right?"

Why people can't just cut to the chase? he thought. "Which date is different?"

"The first date you asked about, two weeks ago? I was with him that night. I think. I mean I'm pretty sure. That was the last night we were together. He had this bad dream and I got fed up with him being off his meds, and left."

"And you're sure of that?"

"Well, sort of, no. Wait, yes, I'm sure. I'm really sorry. This isn't like perjury or something is it?"

"No, I'm just glad you called to set it straight. Sheridan hasn't been in contact with you, has he?"

"Ahh! No! That you would have known right away."

"Okay. I'll be in touch if I need anything else from you. Call me if he calls you."

The girl hung up. This little wrinkle was the wrong kind of development for this case. If the girl's second recollection was correct, Sheridan had an alibi for the night of the Karen Strong murder. And all the murders were certainly the work of the same person, so if he didn't do one, there was a good chance he didn't do any of them. Then everything Weissbard had put together would fall apart like a cheap suit.

He took a seat in his car and slammed the door. He used the insulated silence to sort his thoughts.

Okay, first. The girl might not be remembering things correctly. This was her second take on the same events. There were a half-dozen reasons she might change her story, both conscious and subconscious. Witnesses were only reliable when they could be corroborated.

Second, even if she was right, that was a weak alibi. She didn't leave in the morning, she left at night. Sheridan could have taken off from his apartment after she did, furious that his girlfriend dumped him, and taken it out on some other woman. Once he saw what a great substitute that was for a relationship, he stuck with it, and started his killing spree.

Weissbard jotted down all these thoughts in his notebook and snapped it closed. The awful sensation of having his case disintegrate before his eyes faded away. He tucked his misgivings back deep in his mind. He took a deep breath and walked into the station, all the while thinking of places Brian Sheridan, most certainly the Playing Card Killer, might be hiding.

CHAPTER FORTY-ONE

Weissbard stared at a satellite image of Derek and Camilla Sheridan's neighbourhood on the monitor at his desk. He zoomed in and out, panned left and right. There were only so many options Sheridan had when he escaped from his parents' house. He definitely hadn't passed through the security gate at the entrance, and without a ladder, there was no way he'd ever get over the spike-tipped, eight-foot iron rod fence that enclosed the other three sides of the enclave. Since a sweep of the fence line that night hadn't discovered any ladders, ropes, catapults, or trampolines, the swamp to the west was the only route he could have used to get away.

Highway 58 that bisected the natural area wouldn't be much help. It ran straight, true and uninhabited for thirty miles, two lanes of unlit asphalt without shoulders or cross streets. There'd be no witnesses to anything that happened out there. He envisioned an unwitting motorist giving a ride to a guy alone in the middle of the night on a desolate road, a guy with a good story about wandering away from his campsite. Hell, maybe an accomplice had just parked and waited to pick Sheridan up in the wee hours of the morning.

Weissbard countered both stupid ideas. Sheridan had no friends, certainly none that would stick their neck out for him after the publicity of his arrest. And with a serial killer in the news, no one was going to give a stranger a ride anywhere in the middle of the night. But Sheridan couldn't still be out there in the swamp. The alligators, cottonmouth snakes and mosquitoes would make even a tough guy volunteer for a jail cell instead. And Sheridan was no tough guy.

Weissbard's desk phone rang and displayed the number of Washburn from Forensics. He picked it up.

"This is Weissbard. Give me some good news."

"Say," Washburn said, "do you always answer your phone that way?"

"No. It would just make the disappointment more pointed when no one did give me good news."

"Well, I do have some for you, sort of. Why don't you come take a look at it?"

Weissbard didn't like the sound of that. A simple 'Sheridan's the killer' would have been better. "Be right there."

Minutes later, he opened the door to Washburn's tiny rat hole of an office. Washburn's indecipherable organisational system seemed to work for him, but to Weissbard it always looked like piles of folders, a dozen items open at once on his computer monitor and several machines on a long, cluttered countertop buzzing and whirring away, performing a host of incomprehensible analyses.

No one was certain if Washburn went out of his way to fit the forensics stereotype, or if being a geek came completely naturally to him. He had short, dark hair with a razor-sharp part on the left and wore an oversized pair of glasses with thick, black plastic frames devoid of any style. Every day he wore a lab coat, which he'd bought and had embroidered himself, since the police department didn't mandate, or even recommend, wearing one. He gave Weissbard an excited smile when he looked up and saw him in the doorway.

"Detective! Excellent! I've matched the thumbprint on the last playing card to the thumbprint on Brian Sheridan's booking records."

"How good a match?"

"A perfect one. And that's the rub. I tried to explain this to Francisco, but he either didn't understand what I was saying, or didn't want to. You were on the scene, so I figured maybe you'd get it."

Washburn turned his computer monitor so both he and Weissbard could see it. He clicked on the corner of one open file. It filled the screen with two side-by-side black thumbprints on white backgrounds.

"The playing card print is on the left. Sheridan's print is on the right." Washburn pressed a key on the keyboard and a bunch of red dots populated the two prints. Green lines connected a dot on one print to the dot on the other. "Twelve matching points will hold up in court. I've got over twenty."

There were times when Weissbard felt that pulling a quick answer out of Washburn was a frustrating chore. This was one of them. "And the problem?"

"Well, look at these two prints. Do they look the same to you?"

"Well, yeah. Even without the little red dots and green lines telling me so."

"And that's never true. When we take the booking print, the finger is rolled so we get the whole print. Real prints only get the contact surface, or some other partial impression. The one on the playing card is just as wide as the print on file. That means Sheridan had to roll his thumb across the card. I don't know about you, but that doesn't seem very natural to me."

Washburn had a point, one that resurrected that sinking feeling Weissbard had when Daniela updated her take on Sheridan's alibi.

"Then I checked the rest of the playing card. There wasn't anything as clear anywhere else, but I did get a partial on the back in the upper right-hand corner." Washburn clicked some keys and brought up a new fingerprint. Unlike the others, this one was crescent moon-shaped. "Now, on this one I have a seven-point match with Sheridan. Not good enough to use in court, but good enough in conjunction with the thumbprint."

"So that's good, right?"

"Except for this." Washburn ran the end of his pen along a jagged ridge near the centre. "This might be dirt, but it sure looks like scar tissue. The finger had some kind of trauma that damaged the skin deep, like a burn. The seven points match, but this scar doesn't."

"Unless Sheridan burned himself after he was printed."

"His prints are only days old. He'd have to burn himself between then and now. And have it heal. Miraculously."

"Or like you said, he had dirty hands. He *was* killing someone and stuffing the body in a barrel."

"Or," Washburn countered, "the thumbprint was a fake and

the other print doesn't match because it was from someone else."

Weissbard's sinking feeling sank even lower. "Is that what *you* think?"

Washburn pushed his glasses higher up on his nose with his middle finger and shrugged. "Not really, but a defence attorney sure would. He'd use it to cast doubt with a jury. Especially if Sheridan's finger isn't scarred. I'm just saying you need another layer of evidence on top of this print to keep the case tight."

"Jesus, man. You know your job is to make my life easier, not harder, right?"

"That's why you're getting the heads-up. You're welcome."

Weissbard went back to his desk. He shook his head in frustration at how seamless this case was a few days before, and yet now it seemed to have a lot of frayed edges. He stared at the map on his monitor, hoping that somehow it had changed for the better.

He switched over to the live feed from the tip line for Sheridan. Plenty had notes attached where they had been checked and dismissed. He scrolled past the completely unpromising entries where the Playing Card Killer was getting on a flight to Brazil or riding a coaster at Busch Gardens. He zipped past one entry, then backed up. Something in it looked familiar.

A convenience-store clerk thought Sheridan stopped at his station the night of his escape. The address was on Highway 58.

There were convenience stores along the highway at either end of the natural area. He typed in the address and the Wallaby Foods store popped up on the natural area's south side. Weissbard's heart skipped a beat.

But this tip was days old, and had already been dismissed as 'suspect did not match Sheridan' and signed off by Francisco himself. Of course he would personally latch on to a lead that looked this promising. He had to have been pissed when it didn't pan out.

Weissbard's gut wouldn't let him scroll past that entry. It wasn't just because he thought Francisco did sloppy police work, but that certainly opened the door of doubt. The location and timing were too perfect to ignore. With all the little puzzle pieces that didn't quite fit, this one fit perfectly.

It was a longshot, but maybe Francisco was wrong. Maybe Sheridan and whoever gave him a ride out of the woods stopped for gas. Or coffee. Or a piss. Anything that might get their faces on a surveillance video.

He could only hope. He headed out to his car.

CHAPTER FORTY-TWO

"I'm Detective Weissbard, Tampa PD." Weissbard flashed his badge at the man behind the counter at the Wallaby Foods convenience store. "You're Armand Kramer?"

"Now I get two cops," said the old man behind the counter. Bare wisps of white hair did little to cover the splotches of brown that peppered his scalp. His oversized glasses gave him a look like something out of a sci-fi movie. He wore a ratty brown cardigan against the store's over-amped air conditioning, despite the swelter going on outside. His voice carried the accent and world-weary tone of a displaced New Yorker. "But when criminals are loitering outside, what do I get? Bubkes."

Weissbard had long ago armoured his ego enough to let damn near every citizen barb bounce off without impact. "You called about seeing a homicide suspect here four nights ago?"

"Yeah, and some detective already came by and told me I was wrong. Even got mad that I called it in. Didn't he do a report?"

"I like to do my own investigations," Weissbard said. "Tell me about that night."

"The night-shift kid, Ricardo What's-His-Name," Armand said. "He thought he saw the kid on the news, that Playing Card Killer you people set free."

Barb #2. Weissbard was about to lay the blame for Sheridan's freedom at Judge Enger's feet, but instead opted to keep the conversation on track. "Do you have security footage?"

"Yeah, right over here. The other detective said it 'wasn't worth two shits', his exact words."

Weissbard prepped himself for disappointment. Unlike on television, where security footage was always crystal clear and the perp centre screen and full-faced, real-world video was usually grainy, incomplete and frequently useless. Armand opened the door behind the counter to reveal a room barely big enough for the desk inside it. A laptop sat amid piles of papers with a bouncing Wallaby Stores logo as a screen saver. Armand tapped a security code into the computer and up popped a desktop screen just as cluttered as its real-life counterpart. He tapped on an icon of a masked cartoon bandit with a red Ghostbusters' slashed circle over its face.

The screen switched over to a live feed of the empty gas pump island. A time scale at the bottom of the screen displayed the current time on the right and five days ago on the left.

The front door chime rang in the store. Armand sighed and stepped back to the doorway. He eyed with suspicion two teenagers who'd entered.

"Back it up to that night," he said to Weissbard. "You'll see him."

Armand stepped out. Weissbard dropped into the uncomfortable high-backed desk chair. He grabbed the mouse, clicked on the time scale, and slid it back four days.

The screen went black for a second, and then a night view of the island appeared. The background was completely dark, and the harsh floodlights gave the chrome edges on the vacant pumps a fuzzy glow.

A few seconds later, a car pulled up past the pumps at the edge of the camera's range. Only the passenger side stopped within the glow of the floodlights. Weissbard dared nurture a sprig of hope. A silver Toyota Camry. Ubiquitous, yes, but coincidentally the same car from Sheridan's description. He bit his lip as the plate details showed as nothing but lens flare at this distance.

On the darker driver's side, the front door opened. A figure got out and dashed around the hood of the car. His right foot dragged a bit, as if he'd injured it. He knelt by the fender well and scooped out a muddy wad of vegetation impaled with an oak branch. He tossed it aside in frustration and it splattered against the asphalt. He looked at his filthy hands, shook them, then uttered some curse the silent footage could not record. He spied the island's hand towel dispenser, sent a clearing glance toward the convenience store, then rose and dashed into the brighter lights under the pumps.

Weissbard's heart jumped and he hit the pause button. Right

height, right race, most importantly, right face. No question in his mind. That guy in the video was Sheridan. It looked like he'd put on an oversized shirt, probably one stolen from his father's closet, and he'd dyed his hair blond and spiked it, but even at the camera's downward angle, the face was unmistakably Sheridan's.

But that was to Weissbard, who'd spent a lot of time talking to Sheridan live. If all someone had seen was the kid's 2D, straight-on mug shot, like Francisco had, the harsh lighting, oblique angle, and the radically different hair could easily make an identification impossible.

Weissbard hit Play. Sheridan pulled two paper towels from the dispenser, wiped his hands and dropped the dirty towels in the trash can by the pumps. Then he jogged back to the Toyota and drove off.

Weissbard backed it up and played it one more time for the sake of certainty. Sheridan. No question about it. Admissible in court? Only if Sheridan still had the dye-job when Weissbard finally caught him. He'd need a little DNA to go with the video.

He ran out of the room, past Armand at the counter and straight across the lot to the trash can Sheridan had used. He looked inside. Empty. He jogged to the dumpster beside the store and lifted the heavy plastic lid. Also empty.

Damn it, he thought. *Of all the days for trash removal to be efficient.*

As he walked back to the store, he pulled out his phone and called Washburn to come out and download the security footage. He entered the store and noticed that Armand had his eyes locked on the two teenaged customers. The two boys were meth-head skinny and ungodly pale for residents of the Sunshine State. They both had the furtive look of stupid people about to commit a stupid act. A glance over his shoulder revealed the sun-scorched blue Ford beater they'd arrived in. Even if he hadn't been a cop, Weissbard could tell that this situation was headed someplace bad.

He walked down the aisle like he owned the place, and stopped a few feet short of the two teens. They managed an unconvincing look of defiance. He pulled his badge from his back pocket and flipped it open. Their mouths dropped open.

"You two are going to leave before this becomes your worst day ever, right?"

The two beat a hasty, silent retreat out the door. A grinding starter forced the ageing Ford back to life and it wheezed out of the parking lot. Weissbard turned to Armand. Armand's face displayed what, for him, probably passed for a smile.

"I got a guy who'll be here within the hour," Weissbard said. "Don't mess with that surveillance recording."

"You got it!"

Weissbard exited the store and walked over to where Sheridan had thrown the debris from his fender well. A number of cars had already compressed it into a pancake. But the oak branch was still intact. Sprigs of fern and moss dotted the mud.

He returned to his car. A pickup pulled in from the south with a trailered wave runner behind it. Sand sprayed the sides of the truck.

The truck's sandy coating came from the boat ramp to the bay, where the beach always blew over the ramp in places. The mud in Sheridan's wheel well had come from a freshwater swamp, like the one behind his house. There was the chance for one more clue after all.

He piloted his Charger down Route 58 between the sections of wildlife preserve. A narrow strip of grass was all that separated the road from the untouched reserve. He slowed when the GPS map indicated he was at the closest point to the Sheridans' backyard. He pulled over on the western side of the road, got out, and walked across to the strip of grass. It didn't take him long to find what he was looking for, a long tyre rut pulling out of the swamp. A car had struggled to make it back to the highway after pulling over. His educated guess was that the car was a Camry.

He called Washburn back and told him he had a stop before getting to the convenience store, and to bring his tyre-casting kit.

* * *

After showing Washburn the tyre track to preserve, Weissbard went to the Sheridans' house. He had to nail down a few more points.

Camilla answered the door. Weissbard gave the dark roots in the part of her blonde hair a long look. With an unnerved look on her face, she reached up and flicked at her hair as if something might be there. Weissbard smiled.

"Ms. Sheridan, I have a few more questions. May I come in?"

She gave her hair one more brush with her fingertips. "Yes, certainly."

He began as soon as she shut the door behind him. "The evening Brian escaped, had you noticed that he'd done anything to alter his appearance?"

"No. Don't you think we'd have mentioned that?"

"You'd be surprised what people forget to mention. Is any of your hair-colouring dye missing?"

"Hair colouring?"

She assumed a haughty air of being horribly offended. She stared down Weissbard to extract an apology. Weissbard just stared back. Her upper lip quivered. She looked away.

"I have a stylist."

"So there aren't any dyes in the house."

"Certainly not."

Unfortunately, Weissbard believed her. She'd think that covering her own grey to pass for blonde was well beneath her station in life since she could pay for someone else to do it.

"Mind if I check a few things out?" he said.

She stepped out of the way, as if granting permission for the indignity of a search was beneath her as well. Weissbard went upstairs. She didn't follow.

He went to the master bathroom first. A quick search of the cabinets turned up nothing from Clairol or any of its rivals. Brian Sheridan's room didn't have its own bathroom, so he went to the guest bathroom down the hall. The bath towel on the rack had been used, and a toilet paper core sat in the trash can, so it didn't look like the Sheridans had let the maid loose in here since Brian's escape.

But there wasn't any evidence Brian had done any midnight dye job in here. Weissbard bent and smelled the sink drain. Hair dye stank to high heaven, and all this smelled like was the same coconut-scented soap that sat in the dispenser on the counter.

While failing to find confirming evidence wasn't the same thing as finding contradicting evidence, Weissbard still had the sickening feeling of drilling a dry well. But there were a dozen other ways to explain Sheridan's hair colour shift, and there was no denying the video of him at the convenience store.

These little riddles could go unsolved for now. The important question to answer was where had Sheridan holed up after his drive south on Highway 58.

CHAPTER FORTY-THREE

Tyler skipped the chemical sleep aid he'd doused Brian with on the trip back from scouting Candy at the dollar store. Instead he just tied a T-shirt around Brian's head to keep the route secret. It worked just as well. The blasting stereo masked any outside noises and until the air conditioning finally made its way into the open trunk area, Brian was too worried about suffocating on his sweat-drenched gag to pay attention to anything else.

He did pick up one clue. Before they returned to the garage, Tyler slowed and then stopped the car. A metallic creak moaned from the direction of the hood, and then Tyler accelerated. Brian recognised that kind of sound, a security gate, like the one in his parents' neighbourhood. Tyler had stopped so a scanner could read a barcode decal, probably on a side window, and then the scanner sent a signal to open the gate. Most communities had one manned gate for deliveries and visitors, and the rest were automated. Brian knew Tyler wouldn't be taking chances dragging Brian through a manned gate where some security guard might ask questions about a guy blindfolded, gagged, and hog-tied in the open trunk space.

That gave Brian an idea. He'd spent way too many hours in the backseat of his parents' car, where the security pass decal partially blocked the side window view. The barcode was printed on the outside, but the name of the development had been printed on the inside. He stared at Sewanee Lakes, the name of his parents' subdivision, for hours on end, the way convicts read Department of Corrections on their work detail bus. There was a chance this decal was printed the same way.

The car passed into shade and stopped. A garage door ground and clunked closed and Brian knew they were back. He bit the edge of his lip.

The driver's door opened and closed, then the passenger door opened. Brian managed a muffled kind of whine and shook his head back and forth like a dog trying to dry itself.

"What's the matter, bro?" Tyler whipped the rag off Brian's head and pulled his gag down.

Brian spit to the side and flashed several exaggerated blinks. "Uh, thanks! The sweat, it was just stinging my eyes." He squinted as if the sunlight hurt, then turned his head toward the side window.

A white decal covered the window's lower left corner. He trained his eyes on it.

Tyler reached in and grabbed Brian by the shirt front and pulled him up. Brian let his head loll just enough to look a bit loopy, but his eyes never left the decal. A string of tiny words flashed by as Tyler pulled him out the door. But they passed just slow enough to register.

They read Palm Bay Preserve.

The name didn't ring a bell, but he doubted it would. There were probably hundreds of gated subdivisions all over the Tampa Bay area, and new ones popped up every year. It didn't matter that the name didn't help him know where he was. It mattered that it might help someone else find out where he was. If he ever got the chance to tell someone.

Tyler flicked out the cherrywood knife and cut the zip tie that bound Brian's hands to his feet. He left the other two ties that bound his hands and feet together, though. Tyler pulled him out of the car, onto his feet, and hopped him into the bathroom prison. With two savage cuts he sent the zip ties at Brian's feet and wrist sailing. He dropped Brian's pants to his ankles and shoved him down in the chair. Before Brian could even think of leveraging the escape opportunity, Tyler pulled four of the ever-present zip ties from a pants pocket and bound his wrists and calves to the chair.

"Now sit tight." Tyler's face was alight with genuine enthusiasm. "This idea is, like, a total winner. I don't know why I didn't do this from the start."

Tyler rushed out. His absence left a vacuum, but not a bad one. With the insanity in another room Brian could finally exhale, finally take a moment to steel himself against whatever Tyler was about to unleash on him.

Pots and pans banged in the kitchen. There was a silent pause, then a clang in the hall. The door opened and Tyler stepped in. He had a pair of rough, brown leather work boots in his hands. He started to speak without even looking Brian in the eye.

"See, I figured it out, brother. You don't understand the release. The rush of the kill is the release of the pain. It's like a dam breaks and it all flows out, at least for a while. See, you got no water behind that dam. You missed out on so much that I didn't in my life. All drugged up and shit. Dude, I really feel for you."

He knelt down between Brian's knees. He continued speaking as he pulled the sock off Brian's right foot.

"So you asked me about my foot, right? And I got all pissed. Sorry. I mean, that's not me at all, right? I was just stressed with our reunion plan and all. So here's the real story."

He tossed Brian's right sock aside.

"The Dunhams were really big on everyone doing their fair share on the farm. Kids gotta learn responsibility, they said. Yeah, well, it was more like work on the shitty patch of dust they owned to grow the food they sold. Slavery is outlawed, just not family slavery. So we all had chores."

He yanked off Brian's left sock.

"So Old Man Dunham is with me in the barn, and we're trying to get this DOA tractor running. I'm like six years old so all I can do is hand him tools and shit. So he asks for the sledgehammer. Now it's a small, handheld one, but, dude, I'm six and the thing weighs like a ton to me."

He threw Brian's left sock across the bathroom and against the wall. The air conditioning chilled Brian's sweat-soaked feet. Tyler took a deep breath before he continued.

"The hammer slips out of my hand and of course, it lands on the toe of the stupid cowboy boots he always wore. I mean, right on the pointy tip, where there's no foot or toes. I practically pissed myself I got so scared. I knew what was coming. He totally lost it."

Tyler put a work boot on Brian's right foot and snugged it up. He smiled. "Well look at that, surprise, a perfect fit. And I already broke it in for you."

His face went dark again as if the thundercloud of a memory

returned. "So Old Man Dunham scoops the hammer up off the floor. He points the thing in my face, screaming about how I thought dropping it on him was funny. Shit, funny was the last thing I thought it was. Then he screams, 'Let's see if this makes you laugh!'"

Tyler yanked the laces on the work boot so tight they practically cut off circulation. He whipped the ends into a knot and pulled again. He shoved the other boot on Brian's foot and jammed Brian's toes in the process.

"So then the son of a bitch raises the hammer like he's fucking Thor or something and brings it down on my foot. I had on boots like this, but it sure felt like I was barefoot. I could hear the bones crush through the leather. The pain…oh, shit."

Tyler finished lacing Brian's boot like he was trussing a straightjacket. Brian winced.

"But that wasn't the best part. I wasn't going to a doctor. Medical care wasn't the Dunham way. Not for the foster kids, anyway. Experiencing the pain was going to be part of my lesson. So the son of a bitch made me go out to work in the fields. All fucking day."

Tyler had finished with Brian's boots, but he didn't get up. He stayed kneeling, staring at some unseen thing about a hundred miles past the other side of the bathroom floor. His voice slowed and softened and his rant turned into a monotone remembrance.

"So by the end of the day, hell, way before that, my foot swelled up so big I couldn't get it out of the shoe. That cheap leather was probably the only thing that kept my foot together at that point. I slept with the shoe on. Shit, the next day I *showered* with that shoe on. The bastard farmer kept me out working until I just couldn't do it anymore, and I collapsed in the corn rows. Then his wife got real scared, scared that some child advocate would see I was hurt, step in and derail the gravy train by emancipating all their slaves."

Tyler slid back and looked up at Brian again. His chipper persona surfaced again and his salesman's smile returned.

"But hey," he continued, "by then, too little, too late, you know? Permanent nerve damage, bone splinters, all sorts of reasons I walk like this. It's a lasting reminder of the hellish path our mother sent me down, another of the flames under a pot of rage that gets up and boiling every now and then. A year after I escaped that hell, I went back and evened the score with the old man. It didn't satisfy. Then I found that nothing releases that steam like a little of the old velvet rope around a woman's neck." He patted Brian's knee. "Dude, that's why you don't get it. You've missed out on the physical rage. But big bro is gonna fix that."

Brian's stomach dropped. "No, Tyler. I see where you're coming from. I get it. You don't have to."

Tyler smiled his freaky kid-on-Christmas-morning smile, the one that only accompanied some evil act. "Little bro, this is for you. You need this."

Tyler stepped out of the bathroom. Brian struggled against his bindings to no avail. The chair rocked back and forth against the toilet's porcelain with a tattle of clanks. Tyler stepped back in. He held a big, black, cast-iron pan in one hand. He pumped it up and down a few times.

"The weight seems about right," he said as he stepped closer. "There's no sledgehammer in the house, but I think this will do just fine." He eyed Brian's right foot, then looked at the left. "You know, I was going to do the right, like mine, but the left would be more like a mirror image. I kind of like that inside joke, don't you?"

Adrenaline blasted through Brian's system. His muscles burned as they bulged against the ropes and zip ties. "Tyler, no! Don't! I'll help you without this. We can be a team."

Tyler's hand shot out, clamped around Brian's neck, and crushed his shout to a squeak. His arm locked and forced Brian and the chair still. He raised the pan to an inch from Brian's face. A snarl replaced Tyler's grin. "Don't make me make your face the target."

Malevolence radiated from Tyler, like heat from a sunlamp. It enveloped Brian, suffocating him even more than Tyler's iron grip around his throat. A bit of that horrific feeling crept in as well, that disgusting sharing of consciousness from his Tyler-point-of-view dreams. Between the evil Tyler displayed and sensing the cruelty that consumed him within, Brian feared for his own tenuous sanity. He froze and closed his eyes.

"That's a good boy," Tyler whispered.

Brian gritted his teeth. In his mind, he shouted for deliverance from this living hell.

The cooking pan whooshed by his ear. Milliseconds later a sickening crunch sounded at the left base of the chair, a chorus of snaps and grinds muffled by leather and flesh.

Then came pain. A debilitating blast of excruciating agony that raced up his left leg into his spine, and threatened to make his head explode. Brian shrieked. His eyes popped open, so filled with tears the whole room seemed to be swimming underwater.

"One finishing touch," Tyler said.

The black pan flew by again. Another sickening, mushy crunch. The second, stronger wave of pain this time was instantaneous, blinding, unbearable. Brian slipped from white-hot agony to a black unconsciousness he hoped would be eternal.

CHAPTER FORTY-FOUR

He's shopping. Pushing a cart through his neighbourhood supermarket, surrounded by shiny, fresh vegetables, bathed in over-amped fluorescent lights, chilled by the ultra-conditioned air interior Florida demands.

Relief floods through Brian, washing the last traces of panicked anxiety away in its soothing slipstream. He is free. The nightmare is over. He's awakened and returned to his real life, apparently still in progress. The kidnapping plotline, the twisted twin antagonist, the cast of victims, all the parts of the fiction his subconscious had spun are gone. A level of happiness Brian had thought forever gone infuses him at full strength. The urge to finish this restocking ritual and get back to his apartment swells.

The cart contains strange things he never buys. Corn dogs. Coffee-flavoured ice cream. Twinkies. He fears he's accidentally switched carts, left some woman and her kids with his cart full of far healthier fare. He tries to turn and scan the aisle.

He cannot. The cart continues on its way to the checkout. On the fly, he reaches out and pulls a carton of canned store-brand soda from a sale display. He realises where he is, and in this point of view, who he is. Anxiety winds up to deliver the opening pitch in another long game. His mind races in circles for an escape from experiencing his brother's world.

His left foot throbs, not here, but somewhere else, far away. A reminder that what waits for him awake is no respite, just a different shade of terror from the one he experiences now.

The groceries are scanned, sacked and returned to the cart. He trundles them out into the parking lot's thick, Florida heat. The cart stops at the familiar silver Camry with the rear windows covered in sunscreens. The trunk pops open and he loads the groceries into the space Brian had memorised as a passenger. To Brian's horror, another trip had preceded this quest for food. A new package of clear plastic drop cloth, a bag of zip ties, and a fresh roll of duct tape sit in a pile in the trunk. On top of them rests a small, bright red hatchet, cutting edge silver and sharp, barcode tag still affixed to the wooden handle. Tyler might as well have written Candy's name on each item with a big Magic Marker. The revulsion Brian feels at the sight is the opposite of the sickening giddiness that seeps in from the other side of this vision as his brother sees the same thing.

The trunk lid slams shut, and he takes the driver's seat. The urge to break the connection, to awaken and disassociate himself from the repulsive sense of glee at an upcoming murder grows.

He stays. Not because he wants to avoid the physical pain that awaits his return, but because he realises this is his chance. Somewhere there could be a clue to where he and the Palm Bay Preserve subdivision are in the state of Florida.

The distant pain in his left foot moves closer, grows stronger. Brian's vision of the world around him fades into darkness as the sharpening agony threatens to force him back awake. He tries and fails to will himself back to a deeper level of sleep.

He pulls the Camry out of the lot and onto a four-lane road. Strip-mall stores line the sides with a sameness photocopied from every other city in the state. The street signs are too distant to discern. A swelling, throbbing ache sends a ripple of black across the view.

His senses snap to high alert. A police car approaches in the rearview mirror, a thin bar of multicoloured lights reflected in the white roof. Again, emotions bounce in conflict, trepidation in the parallel consciousness and hopeful elation in his own.

He takes his foot off the gas, though he wishes he could stomp the car into speeding ticket territory. The Camry slows. The police cruiser looms larger in the mirror. He imagines the cop calling in the Camry's plate, the car coming back stolen, the blue lights firing up to signal the end of Brian's captivity.

The police car swings left out of the mirror's field of view. It accelerates and blasts past the Camry's left side. Brian's heart sinks as he senses his brother's jubilation. He realises the opportunity, and focuses on the retreating cruiser. Just in time he makes out 'Osceola

County' in green letters under the wide banner reading 'Sheriff'.

Pain like a shark bite slices through him. The connection to his brother goes black

* * *

His bathroom dungeon jumped into bright, unwelcome focus. Excruciating agony pulsed through his body with every beat of his heart. Tears streamed down his face and he whimpered. His foot felt like it weighed a hundred pounds, that it must have surely burst through the leather boot and torn it to shreds. He glanced down his left side. Somehow the shoe was in one piece. He was certain that the foot within it was not.

Despite the torment, he managed a grim attempt at a smile. 'Knowledge is power' people always say. Well, now he had some knowledge. Palm Bay Preserve in Osceola County, east of Tampa. He just had to figure out how to tell the police what he knew, and share with Weissbard the location of the real Playing Card Killer.

CHAPTER FORTY-FIVE

The rich smell of brewing coffee drew Weissbard upward from slumber into consciousness. Then his eyes snapped wide open. How late was it if Maryanne was already up making breakfast? He jerked up out of bed to check the red readout on the clock radio.

Ten after five in the morning. Darkness still filled the gaps between the window blinds. He stood down from internal panic mode. He threw back the covers, then shivered as Maryanne's Ice Station Zebra version of temperature control swept away the accumulated warmth of the bedding. He pulled on a bathrobe and padded into the kitchen.

White marble countertops amped up the glare of the kitchen's overhead lights and he squinted as his eyes struggled to adjust. Maryanne stood by the sink, long hair in a ponytail and already dressed in shorts and a T-shirt. He smiled at how he still thought her legs looked sexy. She saw him enter the room and sent two pieces of wheat bread on a dive into the toaster.

"What are you doing up so early?" he said.

"Partly because I want to weed the flower beds before the sun turns the yard into an outdoor sauna," she said. She placed a bowl of egg whites in the microwave and hit the Start key. "But mostly because someone needed to keep you from the fast-food drive-through on the way to work."

He sat at the kitchen table and sighed. "You're going to make me healthy, even if it kills me."

"Two birds, one stone." She set a cup of coffee in front of him. "You didn't sleep worth a crap."

"Sheridan's still in the wind, and he could be in Hawaii by now."

"Nope. That's the excuse you are going to tell everyone, but there's more to it than that."

"Like what?"

"I've seen you like this before. The, what was it, Malone case back home?"

"The couple killed walking home New Year's Eve about ten years ago?" It had been one of Weissbard's highest-profile cases.

"Yeah, that one. Everyone said robbery. The evidence said robbery. You dug up the vic's Mob connections and caught the contract-killer perp."

"Have I mentioned how hot you are when you talk cop?"

The microwave dinged. Maryanne pulled out a bowl of cooked eggs. She placed it in front of Weissbard, then dope-slapped him in the back of the head. "Don't be stupid. That look you had, your restless night routine, that was because you knew something didn't fit. A part of the puzzle was in the wrong place, no matter how much everyone else said it was all finished. Well, you're doing all the same things."

He tried to decide if he hated or marvelled at how she frequently knew him better than he knew himself.

The toaster slammed up two browned slabs of fibre for pickup. Maryanne dropped them on a plate, put them in front of Weissbard, and took a seat at an empty setting. Weissbard searched the table for the butter tub. He opened his mouth to ask, translated her 'Don't even waste time asking' look, and the question died in his throat.

"It bugs me that he escaped," Weissbard said. "But you're right, there are other inconsistencies. The logistics of his escape don't make sense, like why he'd cut the tracker in his bedroom, and apparently bring nothing with him when he bolted. Then, he looks different in the gas station video and I can't account for how he did that. And the last murder? It doesn't fit the M.O. because it isn't a woman, and the clues at the scene were clear, more like they were planted than they were the result of a sloppy murderer. The last thing Sheridan would be was rushed, killing someone in familiar territory, and somewhere he knew he wouldn't be interrupted."

"So why aren't you working that angle?"

That was a good question. One he should have asked himself days ago.

"Because I guess I wanted Sheridan to be the one," he said.

"Because he came to you and thought he could practically

confess to being the killer without you arresting him. And that insult really got under your skin."

"Yes. And the department brass, and the District Attorney, are all convinced he's the Playing Card Killer. Can that many people be wrong?"

"They were about the Malones."

And so they had been. Had he been that much hungrier ten years ago, or had the year-round Florida humidity just sapped all the fight out of him? He pushed himself away from the table.

"You're right," he said. "There's some missing piece I need to find."

Maryanne cupped a hand to her ear. "Say that first part again. It sounds so sweet."

"No time. I need to get to work."

She slid the plate of wheat toast closer. "After you eat, Columbo."

Weissbard gave her an exaggerated look of exasperation and slid back to the table. She smiled and went back to the sink. He bit into a slice of wheat bread. It tasted like stale particleboard. He didn't dwell on it. His mind was already searching for new solutions to the disappearance of Brian Sheridan.

★ ★ ★

Hours later, Weissbard sat at his desk scrutinising a list of phone records from the last week to and from the Sheridan house. His desk phone rang and Washburn's number lit up the ID. Weissbard answered.

"Detective, I finished analysing the tyre track casts from yesterday."

Weissbard waited for the rest of the news. Nothing. He sighed.

"And what did you find, Washburn?" he recited.

"The tyre casts are practically no help, at least for now. They're from Tourenza brand tyres that would fit on a Camry. Tens of thousands were sold in Florida last year."

Weissbard hadn't held out much hope they would be a breakthrough. "You said they were no help now, but…?"

"There's a definitive wear pattern along the inner edge because the car is out of alignment. People always align the front end, but forget about the rear. If you do find the car, I'll be able to confirm that it was the one at the scene."

"Well, that's something," Weissbard said. "Congrats. You earned half your pay today."

"That's almost a compliment coming from you. I'll take it."

Weissbard hung up and returned to the phone call listing. Most of the incoming were under sixty seconds long, with the Sheridans wisely letting them go to voicemail. The outgoing were to the same few numbers: work, lawyer, family.

The phone rang. It was Washburn again.

"Now what?" Weissbard said.

"I just got something to earn the other half of today's pay," Washburn said. "A partial DNA hit on Sheridan's sample. But you won't believe from where."

Again, Weissbard waited in vain for the punch line. "Damn it, I don't have time for guessing games. Just tell me."

"Virginia. About two years ago. An assault victim was beaten practically to death. The assailant's skin cells were found under the vic's fingernails. The DNA was probably degraded by time and the nasty condition of the vic's hands, but it's a partial match. Place Sheridan there and you establish a pattern of behaviour."

"Yeah, I kind of know how that works. Email me the files."

"Already on the way."

Washburn hung up and an email from him popped up on Weissbard's monitor. Weissbard clicked on it and opened up the file from the Culpepper, Virginia police.

Darrell Dunham. Forty-seven years old, but his picture looked a decade older, with the leathery skin of a life-long smoker and a swollen, rosy nose that said booze had accompanied those cancer sticks. The farmer and his wife managed a parade of foster kids. One look at the guy and Weissbard knew his motivation for hosting the kids was less likely to be altruism than the pursuit of free labour.

The second picture was Dunham after the assault. Holy Jesus. The guy's head looked like a purple beach ball with two swollen eyes and a pair of misshapen blackened lips. The ME's report also listed numerous puncture wounds in the midsection, likely from a large knife. Someone really hated this loser.

Dunham's story was he was jumped from behind out in the fields by several men in hooded sweatshirts with bandanas around their faces. He couldn't make out who they were. They left him for dead, but lucky for him his wife found him and called paramedics. Weissbard doubted that was particularly lucky for the wife or foster kids.

Local PD thought the story was bullshit, but couldn't shake him from it. DNA under the fingernails said the assailant was a white male, but didn't hit anyone in the system. Given Dunham's reputation as a general prick, the list of suspects included most of the town, but the foster kids in the house moved to first on that list when the cops got a good look at how they were treated. But none of them matched the DNA, and all were accounted for at the time of the attack. Child Services pulled them after checking out the farm and the Dunhams were out of the child-rearing business for good.

Weissbard searched for Dunham's current status. He didn't lament finding the scumbag had died less than a year later, from complications of his injuries.

None of this helped explain the weak DNA hit. At seventeen, Sheridan, with his mass of anxiety problems, wasn't going to be on a solo road trip to Virginia to murder a stranger. He'd have been a high school senior living at home that October. Weissbard could double-check that, but it would be a waste of time.

There was always that one-in-a-billion chance of duplicate DNA, the odds that the experts always allude to testifying in court. That was as likely as Sheridan running around Culpepper, Virginia last fall.

Then something clicked. Foster kids. Sheridan was adopted. Maybe the partial match wasn't because the DNA was degraded, but because it was from a relative. If Sheridan's birth mother gave him up, maybe a sibling was part of the package as well. How the hell that tied up a bunch of loose ends in Florida was a mystery, but his gut, the one he'd been ignoring lately, told him it was a straw worth reaching for.

Sheridan's birth and adoption records were sealed. His parents weren't about to unseal them and release more details about the adopted-son-turned-serial killer. That wasn't a problem. Weissbard was on a first-name basis with a law-and-order judge always ready to cut away the veils of secrecy the government seemed way too happy to drop. Weissbard looked up the judge's number and in his mind rehearsed his sales pitch for getting those adoption records unsealed.

CHAPTER FORTY-SIX

Day and night had lost all meaning in Brian's perpetually lit bathroom jail cell. But when a slamming door and the sound of something dragging through the house awakened him, his internal clock told him it was past midnight. That combination of revelations made his stomach turn. On the other side of the door, Tyler was no doubt making this whole situation worse.

Brian shifted in the torture seat and the boosted blood flow to his leg made his foot throb like someone was pounding it in time with his heartbeat. He moaned and tried not to move his damaged foot. It felt two sizes too large for the boot.

A few loud thuds came from the direction of the living room. Then came the rustle of heavy plastic, followed by the zip and rip of unrolling duct tape. Brian remembered the vision of Tyler's car trunk, the big tube of clear drop cloth, the roll of duct tape.

Oh, yeah. The situation was getting much worse.

A few minutes later, Tyler burst into the bathroom, his face flush with maniacal excitement. Brian's heart sank at the sight.

"Little bro! C'mon! Everything is really coming together. Totally major breakthrough time."

Tyler stepped in and tapped Brian's broken foot with his toe. Pain exploded up Brian's side and he yelped. He wished he could beat Tyler to death with his bare hands right now.

"Hurts like a son of a bitch, don't it?" Tyler said. "Trust me. Been there. I feel your pain. But it's just what you need. You'll see."

Tyler reached down between the legs of the wheeled chair and pulled it forward. Then he went behind him and rolled Brian out into the hallway. At this distance, Brian felt Tyler's consciousness again, a foetid, turbulent mess of negative emotions and irrational euphoria. It was like letting his mind touch sewage. They turned right and rolled into the living room.

Most of the furniture had been piled against the walls. Clear plastic sheeting draped everything else. Flat rectangles covered the floor, joined at the seams by slashes of silver duct tape. The recliner sat near the middle of the room, sloppily wrapped in plastic held together by a Frankenstein-calibre stitching of duct tape. The laptop he'd seen before still sat on a low table at the couch's far end, still making the psychedelic screen saver, still an impossible dream to use. The whole room smelled of fresh plastic, the scent of wild anticipation as a kid on Christmas morning, but now just fuel to stoke anxiety. Brian had the bad feeling that he might be the one who wasn't going to leave this well-protected killing room alive.

Tyler rolled him over and parked him a few feet across from the empty recliner. He plopped down in it and sighed with a smile.

"So, as you can see, big day. Got a whole lot done. Gonna have a major payoff, I can feel it."

"Tyler, just kill me and get it over with. Do me that favour, as your brother."

"Because you're my brother, I wouldn't even consider it. We're on the verge of some major bonding, of you opening your eyes to the wider, brighter, freer world I've known for years."

He gave Brian's broken foot a kick. Pain flared, new and bright. Brian screamed.

"Damn, that's gotta sting, eh?" Tyler said.

A satisfied, sadistic look crossed his face and he launched a far more savage kick at Brian's foot. On impact, the pain turned Brian's world white. With every ounce of his being, he wanted to tear his brother to pieces. He shrieked in fury.

"Good! Good!" Tyler said. "Now wait here and hold that thought."

He turned away, then turned back and looked at Brian's shorts down around his calves.

"Damn, sorry. That won't do."

He pulled Brian's shorts up, dragged the waistband across his ass and up to his waist. The crooked shorts pinched Brian's testes. Nothing compared to the pain in his foot, though.

"There we go. Much less humiliating." Tyler practically skipped out of the room.

Brian blinked his eyes back into focus as the pain retreated. He searched for anything that might help him get free, anything he might use as a weapon. Nothing.

He thought about that brush he'd had with Tyler's mind just then when the two of them were physically close. It was the same way he sensed his brother's feelings in their dream connection. But Brian was awake. Tyler didn't seem to notice his emotional bleed over. Perhaps it only went one way.

The door to the garage creaked open, followed by the click and moan of a car door or trunk. A minute later, Tyler returned with a woman slung over his shoulder in a fireman's carry. Zip ties bound her ankles together. The blackened, dirty soles of her bare feet faced Brian as his brother entered the room. Brian couldn't see her face but the black and red rayon shirt she wore took his breath away. Tyler slung her into the chair opposite him. He saw her face and it confirmed his worst fear.

It was Candy from the dollar store.

She looked dazed, as if whatever knockout drops Tyler used hadn't worn off quite yet. A blue, terrycloth hand towel parted her lips and tied behind her in a big knot. A barrette pulled half her short hair back from her face, but the other side hung down like a tangled, shredded veil. Her hands were bound behind her.

"Talk about a wide load," Tyler said. He stretched his back. "Damn near herniated myself with that one. From now on we stick to lighter victims."

Tyler leaned over and gave her a few little taps on the cheek. When that elicited no response, he smacked her hard. She shook her head and blinked her eyes.

"There you go, Candy. Rise and shine! Now I need to get something. You two get to know each other."

Tyler stepped out. Brian leaned as far forward as he could. Every muscle screamed from being immobile so long.

Candy's eyes met his. They filled with terror at the full realisation of her predicament. She started to struggle. Not tied in the chair, she flopped around like a beached walrus to no avail. With her bulk, and no arms or legs for leverage, Tyler must have figured tying her into the chair wasn't necessary.

She screamed into her gag. "It's you!"

Brian could barely understand her. But the next few words were unmistakable.

"The Playing Card Killer!"

"No, Candy. That's not me. It's him. He's the killer. We're both victims. We need to get out of here."

Panic had taken hold of her and wasn't about to let go. Her face turned beet red. She bucked in the chair. Sweat-soaked skin smacked against the plastic cover. Every person had a mental breaking point, and she looked on the verge of hers.

"He's coming back," Brian said. "You need to fight him. We'll both die if we don't get away."

Tyler reentered the room, hands behind his back. Brian jerked back upright in his chair. Candy's screams jumped up to a new level. Tears streamed from her eyes and her short hair scrubbed her flushed face as she snapped her head back and forth in a plea for mercy.

"And how are you two getting along? Hmm, no chemistry? Little bro, did your pleas to escape fall on deaf ears? She's fat and stupid, not a winning combination. But I do have something that can cure her of her ills."

Brian pulled his hands from behind his back. He held the velvet rope, the one Brian had so often seen in stark black and white before. The sight of it made him shiver. He'd seen it do its dirty work too many times.

Candy loosed a new round of terrified screams into her gag. Tyler's face filled with rage. He strode over and slapped her hard across the face.

"Just shut the hell up," Tyler said. "Or this will go way worse for you, bitch."

Her screaming dropped to a hopeless whimper. Brian guessed she was going into some kind of mental shock, some paralysis as her brain went into full denial about this horrific reality.

Tyler turned to Brian, his face near instantly serene and smiling again. "Now, I know you've seen this rope, felt its power through me. Haven't you wanted to feel that power yourself?"

"Hell no, you sick bastard."

"You can't lie to me, bro. I know we're the same inside."

Tyler stepped next to Brian. He wound the velvet rope a few times around his hand, then caressed Brian's cheek with it. "See how soft and comforting it is?"

The idea that this same rope had ended the life of so many repulsed Brian. He jerked his head away. "Get away from me."

"Oh, wait. Even better." He spun the rope off his hand, then whipped it around Brian's neck. He grabbed both ends and gave it a slight tug. "See how it feels around the neck? Soft, but firm. Like it had a job to kill you, and was going to do it, but would give you a little joy while it did."

Tyler rocked his hands back and forth. The rope slithered around Brian's neck, just a bit too tight for comfort. He swallowed hard.

"Catch the feel of it?" Tyler said. "Really amazing. That's why I only wore the tips of rubber gloves during kills. Enough protection to hold back fingerprints, but not so much barrier that I missed all that sweet sensation." He pulled it off from around Brian's neck, then wound it around his own. He pulled it back and forth, his eyes closed. He rocked side to side, as if the sensation of the rope drove some silent, irresistible beat he had to dance to. "Seriously, I do this all the time. Really lets you know what they're feeling when you snuff them."

He left the rope wrapped around his neck like a scarf. If Brian's hands had been free, he'd have grabbed both ends and really let Tyler know what it felt like to be a victim. Tyler dragged the easy chair around one hundred and eighty degrees, so the back faced Brian. Candy let out a terrified whimper.

Tyler kicked the side lever with his foot and the chair reclined enough that Brian could see the back and top of Candy's quivering head. Tyler flipped the velvet rope into a loop and then put it around Candy's neck. He let the two ends drape over the back of the chair.

Tyler pulled out the big knife and snapped it open. He slit the zip ties around Brian's wrists and they fell to the floor. With all his concentration, Brian tried to lunge upward and throttle Tyler, but he could barely move.

Tyler pulled Brian's arms forward. Brian screamed as his muscles stretched for the first time in hours. Tyler tied the ends of the velvet rope around Brian's wrists and laid the rope against Brian's palms. Brian's heart sank. Tyler was about to make him the instrument of Candy's death.

"I'm not going to do this," Brian said.

"Sure you are," Tyler said. "You're going to feel the release, see the beauty, understand the freedom."

Tyler kicked Brian's broken foot. Waves of pain pounded his leg and Brian yelped.

"That's the pain you've been missing. I've got to squeeze years of my torture into minutes for you." He kicked Brian's foot again. Harder.

Brian bit back another, louder scream, unwilling to give Tyler the satisfaction. Tyler's face screwed up in anger. He reached down and squeezed Brian's foot. He pressed pain all the way up Brian's spine and through the base of his skull. This time the scream came out loud and hard.

Tyler looked up at him with a grin. "Feel that, bro?"

Fury at his helplessness filled Brian.

"You asshole!" he panted. "You sick fucking bastard!"

"That's what we need, that anger. Work the pain and anger together."

Brian jerked one arm toward Tyler. Tyler squeezed again. The wallop of pain turned Brian limp.

Tyler moved to behind Brian. He reached around and grabbed Brian's wrists. He gave the rope a little tug. It tightened around Candy's neck.

The velvet constriction seemed to shatter her stupor. A fresh, unintelligible cry sounded from behind the terrycloth gag. Candy flopped so hard in the chair that it rocked side to side. The rope jerked Brian's arms back and forth.

"Whoa there, Nellie!" Tyler clamped his hands over Brian's hands and squeezed them against the ropes. He gave both sides a sharp yank. Candy choked and went still. She began to cry. "Now, see, bro. This is control. This is release. This is what you've been missing all your life."

Brian struggled against his brother's grip. But his jellied muscles were weak, his brother too strong. He felt like a kitten under a tiger's paw.

Tyler let off a little pressure. Candy sucked in a deep, jagged breath between sobs. The rope throbbed in Brian's hands. His stomach turned as he realised it was in time with Candy's pulse.

"Fuck you," Brian said. "You psycho piece of—"

A wave cut him off as Tyler jammed the toe of his boot into the side of Brian's broken foot and held it. Then he pulled Brian's wrists back. The makeshift noose cinched around Candy's neck. She jerked against the pressure.

"Now feel that?" Tyler said. His voice was calm, detached. "You got to play them, like setting the hook in a fish. Reel them in slowly, make them really appreciate that sweet release of death."

Tyler pulled Brian's hands back harder. The rope tightened. Candy gagged and pulled away. Tyler burrowed his toe deeper against Brian's foot. Bones ground and Brian yelped. Tyler's dark, evil cloud of emotions permeated Brian's entire consciousness. Physically, emotionally, he felt poisoned.

"And then it's finally time," Tyler announced. He pulled hard and snapped the velvet rope tight. Candy made one last, great spasm. Tyler pulled his foot from Brian's and the pain blessedly stopped. Relief washed through him just as the pressure against the rope in his hands evaporated. Candy's head sank back against the recliner headrest.

Brian shuddered at the horror of what he'd just done. Rationalising his forced role in it made no difference. The combination of relief from the pain and revulsion at killing made his stomach churn.

"You asshole," he managed to whisper.

Tyler dropped Brian's hands and said in his ear. "See, bro? See how much better you feel with one less witch in the global coven, and so much less pain in your life? It all comes together." Tyler stepped away so Brian could see him again. He was smiling. "Now, I need to drop her somewhere before she starts doing that bloated, rotting thing. Be right back. I'll give you a few moments here. You'll like to kind of savour the experience. I always do."

Tyler untied the rope from Brian's hands, draped it across his shoulder, and walked out of the room. The door to the garage opened and closed.

Savouring, or even acknowledging, this moment was the last thing Brian wanted to do. He closed his eyes, but the afterimage of Candy's lifeless head seemed burned into his eyelids and inescapable. It made his skin crawl.

He noticed something about the image and popped open his eyes. The black hair barrette on the side of her head secured a few locks of her hair away from her face, the kind of practical thing someone heading to work does without thinking. A detail the usually methodical Tyler hadn't noticed during the euphoria of her kidnapping, or he certainly would have removed it.

Something sharp, metal, strong.

Brian needed that barrette.

He reached up for it. His arms barely moved. He didn't have time to be slow. Tyler could return at any moment. He willed his arms forward. They responded like they were moving through syrup, but they did move. His fingers finally grazed Candy's hair. A shiver ran through him as he thought about touching a corpse. He fumbled at the barrette with clumsy fingers that seemed several sizes too large. He felt around to the back and released the clasp.

The barrette popped open and sailed out of his fingers.

He made a sloppy grab for it in midair. By some combination of luck and divine intervention, he swatted the flying accessory and trapped it against the recliner. He sighed in relief, closed his fingers around it and pulled it back to his chair. Brian wedged it under his leg, tucking it into the woven seat bottom.

The door to the garage opened and closed. Brian sat down hard in the chair and pushed himself back to what he approximated as his earlier position. Tyler walked in, smiling.

"All right, bro! The car is ready." He walked over to the recliner and flipped the sides of the drop cloth up and over Candy's corpse. "Have to drop her off somewhere. Outside the police station would really rub the cops' faces in it, but I'd really be happier if they found her later, after we've gone. I'll make sure they still give credit where credit is due. It just might be better if we got that credit later."

Brian bit back a wisecrack about how *he* was the killer in this situation, not *we*. But antagonising Tyler wouldn't help any now. He didn't say a word.

Tyler pulled Brian's chair back from the recliner and slipped two zip ties from his pocket. He knelt and bound Brian's left hand to the chair at the wrist and cinched it tight. He bent over Brian to do his right hand. Brian needed this one a bit looser, and didn't want Tyler to notice it. Tyler threaded the zip tie through the chair and around Brian's wrist. Tyler pushed the tip through the locking eye and then pulled it tight.

"What are you going to do with her?" Brian practically yelled it in Tyler's ear.

Tyler jerked back as he pulled the zip tie tight. Brian moved his wrist a bit up from the chair and gripped the edge of his shorts. The zip tie noose tightened and bit into his wrist, but he held fast to his shorts and managed to leave a quarter-inch gap between his wrist and the chair frame.

"Shit, bro! You seriously need to chill. I've got a spot." He stood up and patted Brian on the head. "Wish I could take you, but we're not quite there with the trust thing yet. But don't worry, you still get to be part of it."

Tyler took a deck of cards from his pocket. Brian recognised the design on the back from the news reports. Tyler spread them into a fan, one handed, like some card-trick impresario.

"Pick a card, any card," he said.

He ran the deck across the tip of Brian's nose and stopped midway. He separated the two halves of the deck a bit and pulled it back. Brian twisted his head away in disgust. Tyler pulled a card from the split in the deck and showed it to Brian. The two of hearts.

"Bro! Excellent choice. Two brothers use a two for their first strike against the gender who screwed them over. The hearts are a little sappy, but it's all good anyhow." He tucked the cards back in his pocket, went behind Brian and grabbed the back of the chair. "Now back to your bedroom while Candy and I go for one last sentimental drive."

Tyler wheeled him into the bathroom and backed him over

the toilet. He stood in front of him and grabbed the waist of Brian's shorts. "Don't want to come home to a mess here."

Brian panicked. A vision of his shorts catching the barrette and sending it cartwheeling through the air filled him with terror. Just as Tyler pulled, he managed to use his legs to lever his butt up from the seat a fraction of an inch. Brian's shorts shot to his knees without touching a thing. But the effort pivoted his crushed foot against the chair leg. He whimpered.

"Dude, sorry there. Be right back. Sit tight." He made that snorting laugh Brian found so damn annoying, then closed the bathroom door behind him as he left.

Brian sighed and slumped in the chair. He heard the rustle of plastic drop cloth and then the open and close of the garage door. He could sense Tyler's retreating presence, his brother's darkness receding from across his own soul.

The plastic edge of the barrette poked into his bare thigh. A flicker of hope made him smile.

CHAPTER FORTY-SEVEN

He had one shot at this. Tyler would be gone for a while, so Brian could work faster, unconcerned about making noise. And he'd need to work quickly. Tyler would be back here to gloat as soon as he performed on Candy whatever sick rituals his screwed-up psyche demanded. Plus, the longer Brian waited, the more his muscles would lock up in position. Now was the time to get out of these zip ties and escape.

He slid his leg back and forth against the barrette, trying to move it out of the weave of the seat bottom. It didn't budge. He'd gotten it in there, so he figured it had to come out.

A round of anxiety made an unwelcome return. His hands and feet started to tingle, which restarted the throbbing pain in his left foot. The last thing he needed now was an unwelcome visit from Mr. Jitters. What he did need was to get this done.

He rubbed against the barrette harder, faster. Still no movement. Friction heated up the plastic. Then the clip's edge ripped a scratch in his thigh. He cursed and paused.

He took several deep breaths to try and calm his pounding pulse. He imagined blood dripping on the barrette, then drying and glueing it into place. Until Tyler lifted him off the seat at some point and noticed it there. Tyler would have no problem removing it. Brian cringed at the thought of the punishment the discovery of his deceit might bring on.

Brian recalled how he'd slid it in place, tried to estimate how much pressure he'd used. It hadn't been much. He shifted his weight left, raised his right thigh a bit. A flash of pain skittered up from his smashed foot and he winced. Then he brushed his thigh up along the barrette.

It seemed to move. He hoped like hell that wasn't just his wishful thinking. He executed another soft, painful caress with his thigh. This time the hair clasp definitely moved. Back and forth, he inched the barrette up and nearly out of the wicker weave.

He paused. If he botched this, and set the barrette free the wrong way, it might slip sideways and drop through the hole in the seat and into the toilet. The sound of that splash would be the sound of his freedom sinking.

He slid his right hand around in its zip-tie noose. He reached for the barrette and came up short. He tried again, this time pulling as hard as he could against the tie. He still felt nothing but woven wicker. Without seeing, he couldn't tell exactly how far away it was, but it seemed close. As if it mattered. A millimetre or a mile, he'd still be trapped.

He reached as far as he could, and dug his fingers into the holes in the wicker. Then he contracted his fingers and pulled. His hand inched forward. The zip tie dug into his wrist. One finger at a time, he popped them from the wicker gaps, and then inserted them into the next set of holes. He pulled again.

Wicker rubbed against his palm as his hand moved forward. The zip tie's rough edge crushed muscle against bone. The pain screamed for him to stop. He still couldn't feel the barrette.

He pulled his middle finger from the seat-bottom weave. He strained and reached for the next set of holes. His finger came up short. A fingernail barely gripped the rim of the hole. He took a deep breath and pulled.

The zip tie hacked through his skin like a dull knife. His fingernail bent and threatened to snap. A shrill chorus of agony sang from his fingertips to his shoulder. His hand moved millimetres closer.

His pinky and ring fingers gripped new holes. He reached forward with his middle finger and prayed. The tip bumped over ribs of wicker....

...and touched hard plastic.

Brian's heart jumped. The zip tie sawed a deeper groove in his flesh. He gritted his teeth and struggled not to flinch, not to recoil to relieve the pain. He nudged the barrette toward his waiting palm. Progress seemed infinitesimal. The barrette slipped past one finger, than the next. He grabbed it, and then pulled his hand back out of the zip tie's bite.

His fingers ached. His wrist felt like it had finished a date with a guillotine. The anxiety-driven part of him shouted to start using the metal half of the hair clip, to saw through the zip tie that just tried to saw through him. The rational side of him took control with warnings that his numbed fingers weren't up to the task, and might fumble away the key to his escape.

Brian took a deep breath and, with his palm firmly on the barrette, began to stretch his fingers for the next phase. Each contraction sent more blood seeping from the slash on his wrist. He didn't worry. In no time, he'd be free.

CHAPTER FORTY-EIGHT

When his dexterity returned, Brian flipped the barrette open and reversed it in his hand. The point of the steel clip faced his wrist. He slid it under the zip tie and began to saw.

Twenty minutes later, hand nearly cramped from the odd angle he forced it into, he paused. He tucked the barrette between two fingers, then slid his hand down so his index finger could inspect his progress against his plastic captor.

He ran a fingertip across the tie. He couldn't find a groove. He looked down. He couldn't even find a mark. He cursed. The barrette wasn't sharp enough, or the zip tie was too tough. Or both.

It didn't matter. What mattered was that he'd failed.

Brian let rip a howling, inhuman scream, a throaty release of frustration and fury at the pain that now ravaged his right hand, right wrist, and his mangled left foot. He thrashed against his bindings, consciously aware of the futility but subconsciously needing the physical release. The chair clanged hollowly against the toilet but barely moved. Pounding pain in his foot and the searing agony of the zip tie against his gouged wrist sent him a message to calm down. He listened.

He was about to toss the useless barrette into the toilet and hope to bury it in shit before his brother returned. He paused.

He couldn't cut his way out. The barrette was certainly no saw, but it might be a key. The tail of the zip tie ran through a square eye where a tiny plastic clip held it in place. He'd used small screwdrivers to pry that clip back and release zip ties without cutting them. He might be able to do the same thing with the tip of the barrette.

He flipped the hair clip around and pinched it between his thumb and two fingers. He bent his wrist to an unholy angle until his entire hand resembled a question mark. The slash across his wrist opened anew, and fresh blood ran warm and wet down his arm. He manoeuvred the metal tip into the zip tie's square eyelet. A perfect fit. He smiled at the win after so many losses.

Then he lost again. He couldn't pry the clip open. He had no leverage at the awkward angle, not enough grip to make the metal push and pry the way he needed to. He couldn't fail now, not after getting so close.

Inspiration struck. He didn't need to pry the clip open, he just needed to make the ribbed tail slide by it. He pressed the barrette straight down, as far and as hard as he could. It wedged into the eyelet and stuck. He prayed it had gone deep enough.

Keeping the pressure on the barrette, he raised his arm. The zip-tie loop held fast. He raised it again. Same thing. He took a deep breath, clenched his jaw, and this time yanked his arm up hard.

The zip tie dug into his slashed skin and sent a shaft of pain straight to his elbow. But the force pressed the metal tip in deeper. It separated the clip from the zip tie's tail. The tail slid unrestricted through the eyelet, and his arm flew up past his ear, free.

"Yeah!" His joyous scream shattered the house's silence. It was practically unbelievable. After fearing his captivity inescapable, he was about to make it possible. He shivered with happiness, then reached over to release his left arm.

Outside the bathroom, the garage door rumbled open.

"Son of a bitch!" Brian made a quick estimate. Undoing three more zip ties and getting out of the bathroom and house before Tyler got inside wasn't going to happen. And if Tyler came into the bathroom and saw Brian had one hand free, there'd be a beating and a new set of bindings that would ensure a similar opportunity would be impossible in the future.

He'd have to cover his tracks. He'd opened the zip tie once, he could do it again. He'd make the barrette a lot easier to get to next time.

He extended his hand down to pick the zip tie up off the floor. He couldn't reach it. He stretched further, until the zip tie on his left wrist dug in hard and threatened an impromptu amputation.

Still an inch short.

The door between the garage and the house opened and

slammed shut. Brian's racing pulse thudded in his ears. A level of panic that would have incapacitated him months ago surged through his body. He kept thinking, searching for a solution.

The barrette!

He plucked it out of the wicker chair. With his thumb and two fingers, he held it like a pair of tweezers. He stretched again and clamped the barrette around the zip tie. He lifted, but the slick plastic popped out of the barrette's grip. It dropped back to the floor.

"Dearest brother!" Tyler sang from somewhere near the kitchen. "What an event I had with Candy. You won't believe the fun!"

Brian stabbed at the zip tie again, this time lower, where his congealing blood coated the glossy black surface. He pressed the barrette pieces together and raised the zip tie slowly off the floor. It stuck to the barrette.

"I didn't warn you," Tyler called again, "but vengeance builds an appetite. I'm always starving after a kill. I'll bet you are, too." Cabinets banged in the kitchen.

"Damn it, the son of a bitch is about to deliver room service," Brian whispered to himself. He'd go to free Brian's hands to eat, and the last few hours of agony and anxiety would have been for nothing.

He laid the zip tie on the chair beside him, then tucked the barrette under his thigh. It jabbed the raw spot he'd made earlier, but panic overrode any pain at this point. He threaded the zip tie through the arm of the chair and tucked the tail through the eyelet.

It didn't catch.

"Oh, shit." He'd damaged the clip when he jammed the barrette into it. That's why it was so easy to pull free. Now it wouldn't close. He was screwed.

"Brother, the two of hearts was a perfect choice." Tyler was right outside the door. "Looked so good sticking out of her mouth."

Brian tucked the tail of the zip tie under his thigh and jammed his hand through the loop. It was much bigger than before. Way too big to fool Tyler.

The door opened. A beaming Tyler stepped in, carrying a bag

of corn chips and two frosty bottles of soda. "We are definitely picking skinnier ones next time, my back is—"

"Get out of here!" Brian screamed. "I don't want to eat, I don't want to see you, you murderous bastard!"

The outburst caught Tyler off guard. He recoiled in the doorway. "Hey, bro. What the hell?"

"I don't want to even see you, sick son of a bitch. Get the hell out of here!"

The confusion in Tyler's eyes snapped over to rage. Exactly as Brian knew it would. Brian gripped the side of the chair with both hands.

Tyler charged into the bathroom, face red, lips pulled back in a snarl. He backhanded Brian across the face, then hit him again in the opposite direction. Then he grabbed him at his shirt collar.

"I'm helping you! You'll be better, stronger, when I'm finished. You don't see it now, but you will. And until you do, you need to act with respect. I'd hate to think you're a lost cause." He shoved Brian back against the chair. "Well, you just smart-assed yourself out of dinner, and ruined my mood and our celebration. See how the rest of the night in the dark works for you."

Tyler stormed out of the room. On the way he slapped the light switch off. Then he slammed the door.

Brian sighed with relief in the dark, and relaxed. His face felt like it had been beaten with a two-by-four on both sides. He could taste warm copper and a molar in his left jaw was definitely loose.

But he was alone. And his right hand was free.

CHAPTER FORTY-NINE

Brian waited. Water drips in the sink were four seconds apart. He counted a thousand after he heard the last noises from outside the bathroom. Enough time for Tyler to fall asleep. He hoped.

He slid his right hand out of the loose zip-tie loop, picked up the barrette, and went to work on the binding around his left wrist. Even in the dark, doing it by feel alone, the task was much easier with a free hand. The tie was off in a second. He bent over to undo his right foot. His long-immobile back screamed as muscles stretched for the first time in days. It took several rounds of slow, forward bobbing before he could reach his ankle. He removed the zip tie.

One remained, and then he'd be out the door to freedom. He shifted right and released the final zip tie. His left foot slid to the floor. As soon as it touched the tile, a lightning bolt of pain surged up to his hip.

"Son of a bitch," he whispered. It took all his self-control and fear of discovery to keep from screaming.

He gave it another try. Even the lightest touch set loose a wave of agony. He wasn't getting anywhere on this foot. This would be one ridiculous, screwed-up escape, him hopping through the subdivision like a human pogo stick.

Then he played out the rest of the scenario in his head. What if he just crawled to a neighbour's house and banged on the door? Whoever answered would see the face of the most wanted man in Tampa Bay, the Playing Card Killer. If that didn't get Brian shot on sight, it would earn a nine-one-one call and a phalanx of screaming police cars. That would tip off Tyler, he'd escape, and Brian would be back in jail, with Sidney's murder, and probably Candy's, added to his list of crimes. Any evidence in this house could more easily be interpreted as left by Brian than by an unknown, long-lost brother.

Being back in jail would be better than being a tortured prisoner, but not by much.

His stomach sank as an even worse scenario came to mind. If Tyler was asleep, he'd be able to see through Brian's eyes. Once Tyler got a glimpse of anything but this bathroom, he'd bolt out of bed and drag Brian back inside before he even got his hand around the front door knob.

Damn it! Tyler could be doing it right now. But wait. There was nothing to see in the bathroom darkness. Thank God.

But as soon as he hit daylight, and it had to be daylight out there by now, his point of view might blaze into Tyler's subconscious full-force. He'd gone to all this effort for nothing. He had been trapped here by far more than four plastic zip ties since the moment Tyler dragged him through the garage door. He just didn't know it.

Mr. Jitters came knocking. Hard and long. The tingle of an anxiety attack began to stir. Brian pushed it back. He couldn't quit now, couldn't give up after he'd gotten this far. A plan formed in his head. A long shot. But it beat waiting for Tyler to waltz into the bathroom and see that Brian had freed himself.

Brian closed his eyes tight. His connections to Tyler were video only, and he hoped that worked the same both ways. He pulled his shorts up to his waist. Grabbing the edge of the sink, he raised himself up on his right foot. Leg muscles threatened to shred at the unaccustomed motion. Blood surged down to his left foot and it felt like someone was pounding it with a mallet in time with his thudding heart.

He stagger-hopped to the bathroom door, felt for the knob and turned it slowly. He pulled the door open without a sound. Even with his eyes closed, he could sense the outside world was brighter. That worked into his plan.

He stood in the doorway and listened. Silence. Another good sign.

Now he had to get to the laptop computer he saw yesterday in the living room, assuming it was still there. Tyler wouldn't have had time to move it, nor a need to, as far as Brian could tell. Brian couldn't risk opening his eyes to find out. He'd just have to pray it was still there.

He dropped to his hands and knees. He crossed his left ankle over his right to cradle his pounding, smashed foot, then began a slow, awkward crawl across the living-room carpet.

He drew a mental picture of the furniture as he remembered it. The couch, the repositioned recliner, the end tables, including the one with the laptop. He aimed himself in the direction of the couch and crawled. Each pull of his arms opened the gash on his wrist a bit wider. The carpet ignited friction burns on his knees with each skidding inch across the rough fibres.

His shoulder grazed the couch. The vinyl sheet was still in place, an unwelcome reminder that Tyler probably planned for the two of them to deal a few more playing cards together here. He inched along the perimeter of the couch, found the corner, then the end table where he'd last seen the laptop. He raised himself up, took a deep breath, and ran a hand across the tabletop. Disappointment mounted as he found nothing there. Then his fingers touched something hard and thin. They ran across a keyboard. Brian smiled.

He swept the laptop off and into one hand. It felt cold. He prayed that just meant it was off, not dead.

He crawled back across the carpet, aiming for the hallway. His hands hit tile and he edged to the right. He touched the hall closet door. He reached up, turned the handle, and crawled inside. He dragged his throbbing left foot in after him and shut the door.

Back in near total darkness, he dared open his eyes. The closet smelled musty. The sleeves of a few windbreakers brushed his head. A collection of shoes dug into his butt. The bones in his left foot felt like a collection of darning needles jabbing into each other. He positioned his foot across a pair of boots so it could stay suspended. That felt a little better. He pushed the laptop's On button, and hoped for a charged battery.

The machine hummed and began to boot up. He closed his eyes again. Until he was ready to put his plan in motion, he didn't want any visions interrupting Tyler's slumber. He couldn't risk more than a split-second of an image every now and then.

The hard drive stopped humming. He took a quick peek at the screen and then shut his eyes again. No log-on code, just a message saying 'Hi, Benjamin!' This must have been the homeowner's laptop and Tyler had appropriated it along with the rest of the house. Good news for Brian.

He glanced long enough at the screen to find an internet browser icon and clicked on it. He waited a few seconds for the page to spool up. Then he blind-typed in www.planetearthview.com, knowing the address would end up in the search box. He hit Enter.

He'd used this site for years. Planet Earth View had used a fleet of VW Beetles with bulbous rooftop cameras to do street views of damn near everywhere. There was one place he knew for sure was in the database, because he'd checked it out before moving last year.

Still without opening his eyes, he typed in the address of his apartment complex and hit Enter. He moved closer to the laptop screen. He counted to ten and opened his eyes.

His apartment complex dazzled on the screen, high definition and lit in beautiful Florida sunshine. He made sure that no edge of the laptop screen was in his field of view. Then he tapped the left arrow key and began a slow virtual stroll through his neighbourhood. With the minimal pixelisation, and filtered into black and white, and with his view in motion, the scene might not look as static as it really was. Now he just needed Tyler to take the bait.

Brian started a second lap around his block and began to think of REM cycles and what combination of sleep patterns enabled his connection with his brother. He started to worry about how much battery old Benjamin had left in the laptop, but wasn't about to break his neighbourhood view to find out.

"Goddamn it!" Tyler shouted from the bedroom. A door slammed. Bare feet slapped the hallway tile. Another door opened with a crash against a wall. "Goddamn fucking shit!"

Tyler had bought it. He'd tapped into Brian's point of view, and recognised the apartment complex. Brian imagined him bolting out of the bedroom and the fury in his face when he saw the bathroom prison empty. He wished he could have seen it.

Muffled profanity continued to spew from the other side of the door. Several items crashed, no doubt thrown in frustration. Then the door to the garage opened and slammed closed. The exterior rollup door began its muffled, slow, groaning climb. The Camry fired up and screeched out of the garage before the door even stopped moving.

Brian sighed with relief and popped open the door. Fuzzy sunlight filled the closet. He took a deep breath and for the first time in days, relaxed.

Now he had to get out of here.

Walking was out of the question. Calling the cops would leave him in jail and Tyler in the wind. Calling his parents would be the same thing as calling the cops. His mother probably had Detective Weissbard's number on speed dial. Only one person might listen to him long enough to agree to get him out of here, and give him a chance to contact the police on his own terms.

He didn't have a phone, but he had the next best thing, the internet. He called up SnappyWords, the instant messaging service Daniela always had active on her phone. He searched her name, then typed a message.

ITS BRIAN. NEED YOUR HELP. IM INNOCENT, SETUP. KIDNAPPED.

He waited. Would she answer? Was she showing her phone screen to a cop right now?

A reply popped up. *WHERE ARE YOU?*

He pumped a fist in joy and typed in *PALM BAY PRESERVE IN OSCEOLA COUNTY* and hit Send.

That wouldn't be enough. The complex was huge. He needed an address, at least a house number. He put the laptop on the floor, grabbed the door knob and pulled himself up. He hopped over to the long window next to the front door. There'd be a house number here, or across the street. If he was at a corner, maybe even a street sign. Wouldn't that be great! He leaned against the glass and looked outside. His heart stopped.

The silver Camry was in the driveway.

"Hey, brother," Tyler said from behind him.

Brian whirled around. Tyler swung a fist and it crashed into Brian's jaw. Brian fell on his broken foot, screamed and collapsed on the ground in unbearable pain. Tyler pounced on him, pinned his arms to the ground with his knees and wrapped his hands around Brian's throat. He squeezed and Brian choked. He tried in vain to buck Tyler off, but searing pain rendered his left foot and leg useless. Tyler squeezed harder and Brian stopped struggling. Tyler relaxed his grip and Brian took a breath.

"Seconds down the road," Tyler said, "and I figured, hey, wait, there's no way you could get so far away with that foot I gave you. Then I realised it was cloudy, and in the dream vision, it was sunny. I didn't know how, but somehow you'd tricked me. Nothing fit. Back I came to find you still here. The question is, how in the hell...."

Tyler looked around the hallway and into the open closet. He left one hand clamped on Brian's throat. He reached over with the other and batted out the laptop. Planet Earth View and SnappyWords were still open. Tyler focused on the bright picture of Brian's apartment complex. "Ah, clever, little bro. Almost clever enough."

Tyler's gaze shifted down to the SnappyWords window. "And what the hell is this?" He scrutinised the window. Wrath filled his face as he realised what it was. "Motherfucker! A message? To...." He searched for the name. "Shit! Daniela! Well, you've done your best to fuck this all to hell, haven't you?"

At the sound of her name, Brian went numb. He'd just put her in Tyler's crosshairs.

Tyler squeezed harder. Brian gagged and his lungs screamed for air. The edges of Brian's vision turned black. He felt his body going numb.

"No worries, bro," Tyler said from somewhere that seemed really far away. "I'm going to set all this straight. And you just inspired me how."

Then everything went dark and quiet.

CHAPTER FIFTY

Tampa Bay's morning had dawned lousy. The thick, pregnant kind of raindrops that only the tropics could deliver pounded the ground, and a sky full of black clouds promised a full day of it. Some low-pressure mess had settled off the coast and the forecast guaranteed a full day of wet.

Weissbard's mood matched the weather. No good news awaited him when he arrived at work. No one on the task force had dug up any promising leads. Calls to the tip line had dropped to near zero, and the ones who did call were obvious crackpots. Sheridan's unsealed birth records weren't waiting in his email inbox, either. His police-friendly judge had issued the order, but who knew how long it would take the state of Virginia to comply? Even then, the records might add up to nothing.

Detective Sergeant Francisco rushed in from the hallway. He looked worse for the wear from the Playing Card Killer case. The supposed quick victory he'd snatched from Weissbard had morphed into a quagmire and his usual big smiles and glib comments couldn't extract him this time. Every shining hair on his head was still in perfect place, but dark circles shadowed his eyes, and his face appeared pallid and drawn. The last few days he'd snapped at every question anyone asked, barked every order he'd given. Weissbard guessed he'd just returned from giving the chain of command a briefing on the manhunt for Sheridan. He also guessed that it hadn't gone well.

Francisco eyed Weissbard and grimaced. This whole event had done nothing to make their working relationship any better. Out of all the other detectives, Francisco made a beeline for Weissbard.

"Tell me you're working some productive angle, Swissbard?"

"Double-checked the ex-girlfriend, didn't pan out. Neither did a tip-line sighting report."

Francisco didn't seem in the mood to hear Weissbard's theory that Sheridan might not be their man. Weissbard wasn't in the mood to share it with the prick anyway.

"Well, why don't you work on something that does pan out?" Francisco said. "This isn't up north. We solve cases here."

He stormed off. More than ever, Weissbard wanted to split this case wide open. His phone rang and displayed an unfamiliar number. He picked up.

"This is Detective Weissbard."

"Hi, this is Daniela Schiavetta. You left me your card when we talked about Brian Sheridan."

Weissbard perked up. She wouldn't be calling just to say hello.

"Of course, Daniela. Has something come up?"

"Brian might have texted me. Now I'm scared to death."

"Daniela, there's a uniformed officer parked across from your apartment. I've had someone watching over you for days. You have nothing to be afraid of. Are you sure it was Brian contacting you?" Calling Sheridan anything but Sheridan really stuck in Weissbard's throat, but he wanted a softer tone with Daniela.

"I'm not sure," she said. "I didn't recognise the SnappyWords account. I messaged him back, but then he didn't answer. His message was strange, some craziness about being kidnapped in Osceola county. Come here and I'll even give you my phone so maybe some CSI kind of guy can track down where the message came from."

Hell, yeah! Weissbard thought. "Of course."

"I'm at home. I need to leave for work soon and can't be late. Can you make it over before I go?"

"I'm on my way. Don't leave before I get there."

Weissbard hung up, flush with adrenaline. Sheridan had shown his hand. Guilty or not, it would all be easier to sort out once he was back in custody.

CHAPTER FIFTY-ONE

Pain summoned Brian to consciousness. Breathing hurt like hell. Tyler had crushed his neck and it felt bruised from the inside out. His attempted escape had sent his mangled foot into an even deeper circle of trauma-induced Hell. He was sure that bones were floating around in a soup of shredded muscle under his skin. His right wrist felt like it was on fire, so an infection had no doubt set in where the zip tie had sliced him.

He opened his eyes. The light, muted as it was, still felt like needles through his retinas. He wondered if he'd gotten a concussion when he hit the hall floor.

He was sitting up. He tried to move and looked down. He was zip-tied back in a chair, a different one, heavy, very high backed, made of solid wood, like from a dining room table. And this time with a half-dozen zip ties on each arm and leg. He couldn't even flex a muscle.

He squinted against the light. He was in the kitchen. The table and chairs were gone and he sat alone in the middle of the tile floor, facing the door to the garage. Closed blinds kept him from seeing out through the French doors. But rain pattered against the glass and the dull illumination that oozed through the blinds conjured a dreary outside world. He tried to twist his head around to see a clock, but the pain in his swollen, damaged neck made it impossible.

"Tyler," Brian managed to croak. Whatever sick shit his brother had in mind probably included ending Brian's life. Given the pain he was in, he might as well get it over with. "Tyler!" This time it came out a whisper.

No answer. The house was silent. He thought the bastard might just be playing with him, then figured that Tyler couldn't resist taunting and torturing Brian if he'd been there.

Yesterday he'd have used this alone time to devise an escape, to investigate what he might make use of in the kitchen. Today, he didn't care. His body was broken a half-dozen ways. Escape from this chair would be impossible, let alone getting out of the house. His only getaway would be as a corpse in the trunk of the Camry.

This should certainly have been Mr. Jitters' cue to come on stage. If minor events brought a swell of anxiety, this situation should have summoned a tsunami. But he felt nothing of the kind. Was he over the drug withdrawal, or just over the idea of living? He couldn't tell.

The garage door grumbled open. Brian's head sagged in defeat, then the pain of bending his battered neck made him jerk it back upright. The sound of the Camry's engine grew louder as it drove into the garage. The transmission thunked into park, and the engine cut off. Brian thought how odd it was to know that the rest his life was measurable in seconds, and that he didn't care. The garage door growled shut.

A car door opened and closed, then the door to the garage opened to reveal Tyler. He was soaking wet, his spiky blond hair all matted to his head. His red-rimmed eyes focused on Brian as soon as he passed through the doorway. Water dripped from his sodden clothing and puddled on the floor. He left the door open behind him. He'd backed the Camry into the garage, with just feet to spare before hitting the home gym. A surge of rain lashed the glass doors to Brian's left. Distant thunder rumbled.

"Brother, brother, brother," Tyler said. His voice was harp-string tense. "Look at what you've put me through, put us through. When I think of it...." His turned a deep red, his lips curled back in fury. He shook like he was about to explode.

Subconscious waves of Tyler's unmitigated anger washed through Brian's mind. The sensation was stronger now than it had been any time before. He could practically read Tyler's desire to strike him. Tyler jumped forward and backhanded Brian across the face.

Brian's head snapped sideways and his neck felt like it was about to tear in half. He could barely manage a groan.

"Dude," Tyler said, the flush draining from his face. "That's what you drive me to, hitting my own brother. How much lower could I sink?"

Brian wanted to say *murderer*, but he couldn't summon the strength.

Tyler began to pace the kitchen, hands clasped before him, fingers flexing back and forth like a seething ball of tiny snakes. He looked at his shoes as he spoke.

"I really had it all set up. I had a great plan. So much to show you, so much to teach you, to make you as strong, as adapted as me. And you just threw it all away. No, worse, you threw it back in my face. You're just a weak, drugged version of me, but you act like you're somehow better than me."

"I *am* better," Brian managed to whisper.

Tyler didn't react. He probably wouldn't have reacted if Brian had been able to shout it. He seemed deep in his own reality.

"Then you tried to leave, to abandon your only real family, and tried to bring the cops down on me in the bargain. Wouldn't be enough to maybe say, 'Hey, Ty, this isn't my thing' and we go separate ways, no harm, no foul. You want to be only half a fucking man the rest of your life, that's your issue. But you're jealous of my strength, of my passion, so you had to try and destroy me. Dude, that's not what brothers do."

In his incessant pacing, he'd dripped a stripe of water along the tiles. His shoes made little slapping noises with each step. The slaps kept getting closer together.

"So, here's another story from my childhood, another experience that made me the bigger, better you. The Dunhams had a dog. A black-and-white mutt with floppy ears. Called him Chipper because he slept in the pile of woodchips.

"It showed up uninvited a few weeks after they got me. The thing must have eaten out of the trash because I never saw anyone feed it, or do anything else to take care of it. Anyhow, me and that dog, we got real close, because you know, no one really gave a shit about either of us. We were both just tolerated.

"So one day, I'm throwing rocks at this old rusty windmill over the well, and to my own shock, I hit the fucking thing. The rock ricochets into the windshield of Dunham's shitbox Ford and cracks it. The old man hits the roof, pounds the shit out of me right there in the yard, and then drags me back to the porch.

"He starts shouting about how I need to know what it feels like to lose something. He beats me hard enough to make me stay down, then he drags over Chipper by the collar. The dog is scrambling to break free, but Old Man Dunham is one big bastard. He stops, towering over me, and whips out a knife."

Tyler pulled out his big cherry-handled knife from his pocket and flipped it open. His eyes still never left the floor. His pacing never stopped.

"Then he holds that dog right next to my face. Chipper's eyes are so wide they look like cue balls with pupils. I can feel his breath on my face. Hot, fast, and scared. Then that asshole takes that knife and cuts that dog's throat."

Tyler made a savage slashing motion through the air with the knife.

"Goddamn dog soaks me in blood. Then Old Man Dunham throws the carcass on top of me and jabs the knife into it, leaves nothing but the handle sticking out. He twists it and snaps off the blade. He throws the handle on my chest, tells me I need to keep it with me every goddamn minute of the day. That he'd check, and it better be on me, reminding me of what real loss felt like.

"And I kept it." He rolled the open knife in his palm. "Until I had a new blade put in and gave him a little something back with it years later, long after I'd aged out of that hellhole."

Tyler stopped and looked Brian straight on. "So see, I know loss. You don't. But you're about to. Not only gonna know it, you're gonna cause it, gonna breathe it. And you directed me right to the target."

Anxiety came charging into him and gave Brian an energy boost. He hoped Tyler wasn't talking about....

Tyler reached past him and grabbed the laptop off the kitchen counter. He gave it a pat. "Yes, bro, you and your pathetic plea for help led me right to her."

CHAPTER FIFTY-TWO

As soon as Weissbard pulled up in front of Daniela's apartment, he was pissed. Between clearing swipes of the car's wipers, the uniformed cop on duty and his car were nowhere to be seen through the windshield. He raised dispatch on the radio to get the officer's location.

"Detective, there's no one assigned at that location," dispatch answered.

"I assigned a detail myself a few days ago."

Pause. "Sorry, Detective. Detective Sergeant Francisco reassigned that unit yesterday."

Weissbard nearly tore the mount off the car's dash as he slammed the mic back into place. That prick had probably cancelled the security just to irritate him, to assert some of his new-found authority. Dumbass.

Weissbard left his car and made a crouched dash through the rain to the cover over Daniela's apartment door. He knocked and got no answer. She wouldn't have left for work anyway, not after she called for him to come over. Besides, her car was still here. He tried the doorknob. It rotated unlocked.

No woman who lived alone ever left her front door unlocked. He drew his pistol and eased the door open.

The place looked like hell. The coffee table was in pieces. Broken glass littered the carpet. Daniela's phone lay on the floor, half under the couch.

"This is the Tampa Police," Weissbard shouted.

He entered, pistol raised. He swept the one-bedroom apartment and confirmed it empty. He cursed and holstered his weapon. From his cell phone he called to get a uniformed officer to guard the new crime scene. A crime scene that wouldn't have happened if Francisco hadn't countermanded his detail.

His first thought was that Sheridan had beat him here, and then kidnapped the girl. He'd asked for her help, she wisely refused, and that sent him off the deep end. First Sidney, now Daniela. From the looks of the place she put up a fight.

He realised that wasn't the answer his gut wanted to give. On the surface it fit perfectly, but now Weissbard second-guessed every perfect fit when it came to Sheridan. First, this was not Sheridan's style. He wasn't easily angered. Even if he was the Playing Card Killer, those murders weren't acts of fury, they were cold and calculated. Second, Daniela was the closest thing he had to a human relationship. She said he'd never been threatening. Her call said Sheridan reached out to her for help. If he had the means to get here, and get her out of here without taking her car, what kind of help could he need that a poor vet tech could provide?

He grabbed her phone from where it poked out from under the couch. He gave it a tap and it powered up. It asked for a password. He took out his notebook and flipped to his interview with Daniela. He tried the month and day of her birth, then the address of her apartment, then the year of her birth. Nothing. If he was going to have to take this in for Washburn to crack, he was going to lose some precious time. His wife had this same phone. The default password when she got it new was 1234. He tapped in the numbers.

A screen full of apps appeared.

"Lazy people make this job much easier," he said to himself.

He tried to remember the app she mentioned to him, but drew a blank. Those things came and went all the time. Snippy… snappy…something like that.

He brushed through the apps. The title SnappyWords appeared superimposed over an icon of a hand snapping its fingers. That sounded familiar. He tapped it open and hit pay dirt. The last message was from Sheridan. Or at least the person identified himself as Sheridan.

ITS BRIAN. NEED YOUR HELP. IM INNOCENT, SETUP. KIDNAPPED.

WHERE ARE YOU?
PALM BAY PRESERVE IN OSCEOLA COUNTY.

That was it. She hadn't sent another response. Weissbard gritted his teeth when he noticed she also didn't call Weissbard for hours after she got the text. If she'd called right away, he'd have been here before whatever-the-hell-happened-here happened.

A uniformed officer arrived at the open front door. Raindrops bounced off the shoulders of her yellow police slicker. "Detective?" she asked. "You called for backup?"

Weissbard slipped the phone in his pocket and approached her. She looked like she was sixteen years old. Her new raincoat still had the creases from where the factory folded it into its cellophane wrapper. She looked just as untested, and nervous. *Fantastic.*

"No, I called for you to secure this crime scene. I'm sending CSI in to pull this place apart. Everyone stays out, including you."

"Yes, sir."

He called in the suspected kidnapping and put out an APB for Daniela. He arranged for CSI to sweep the scene. He jogged back to his car through the rain.

Inside, he pulled out his laptop. The storm beat a staccato rhythm against the car's roof and glazed the windows with sheeted water. He ran the records for silver Camrys registered in Osceola County. That gave him a healthy list, but he narrowed it down to Placid Springs, the town that contained Palm Bay Preserve. That pared the list down to four.

His email beeped that he had a new message. The sender was the State of Virginia. He clicked to it immediately and opened the attached PDF without even reading the cover letter. Up popped Brian Sheridan's birth certificate, or actually the birth certificate of Brian Tracy. But the date was the same as Sheridan's, so he was willing to take this one on faith and his gut concurred. Unmarried mother, age seventeen, father unknown. Hell of an uphill start. Then he noticed the box checked on the right side of the form. Twin birth.

He slammed a palm against the car's steering wheel in celebration. Now he was getting somewhere. He swiped to the next page, which was the Child Services Record. He and his twin brother Tyler had to be weaned off prenatal narcotics at the hospital before going into foster care. The mother signed them away with no option for getting them back, or even having contact if they requested it. What a sweet kid she was. The record showed Brian getting adopted by the Sheridans, and that's where his brother Tyler's record diverged from his, and disappeared.

He used his police ID to access the foster care records in Virginia. Tyler's case rolled up. Bounced between half a dozen families before he aged out of the system. But one of them was in Culpepper, Virginia, a couple with the last name of Dunham.

"Holy shit." The state of Virginia never found Darrell Dunham's killer, but the police only checked the crime scene DNA against the current foster kids. They'd skipped the previous kids, including the one who'd been gone for about a year. Dear brother Tyler, sibling of Weissbard's partial DNA hit.

Sheridan wasn't the Playing Card Killer, his twin brother was. After getting his rocks off killing Dunham, Tyler probably came down here for some twisted family reunion, one celebrated with a deck of playing cards. When Sheridan didn't buy in, Tyler set him up as the killer as punishment. Sheridan either escaped his parents' house or Tyler got him out, but one way or another Tyler ended up taking control. And Sheridan probably still wasn't amenable, so Tyler came back and took Daniela for leverage.

But Sheridan knew details around the killings. Did he really have some psychic connection with Tyler? Weissbard doubted it. The 'seen it in a dream' excuse was probably just Sheridan's clumsy way of trying to share with Weissbard things his brother had shared with him.

That scenario filled in a lot of spaces between facts with supposition. Way more than he'd be able to convince Francisco of. No way would Francisco reassign task force members to fan out over rural Osceola County. That was if the jackass even let Weissbard start explaining. But the one person who needed no convincing was his gut. His gut said he'd nailed it.

And if he was right, Sheridan had sure been screwed over.

Innocent, but jailed, abandoned by his family, assumed guilty by everyone, Weissbard included. Poor bastard.

He fired up his car, snapped the wipers on high, and peeled out of the apartment complex. He had four houses to check for a silver Camry and a missing vet tech.

CHAPTER FIFTY-THREE

As soon as Tyler picked up the laptop, Brian's spirit broke. He'd dropped the computer in the closet. He hadn't closed out the chat window yet. Tyler would have seen that he was talking with Daniela.

But he wouldn't know where she lived. Brian corrected himself. Of course Tyler would. He'd been seeing through Brian's eyes. He knew everything. For his own sanity's sake, Brian clung to the fading hope that might not be true.

Tyler marched behind Brian and slammed the laptop back on the kitchen counter. He grabbed the top of Brian's chair and yanked it back until the chair balanced on the rear two legs. Brian's head slammed against the chair back and his neck screamed at the unwelcome twist. Tyler spun the chair around, and dragged him backwards out the garage door. The chair legs bumped the threshold and the jolt triggered another shockwave of agony.

Tyler dragged him around the tail of the Camry, and past the stack of weights at one end of the home gym. Tyler lugged the chair sideways and sat him facing the gym's bench. A cord dangled from the overhead bar a few feet in front of him. Past it, Brian could see the open door to the kitchen and wished like hell he was still on that other side.

"So brother, time to move up to the emotional big leagues." Tyler's rage had cooled. His voice was back to its enthusiastic frat-boy tenor, but with a brittle edge, like he was troweling it over the fury that still boiled within. "And you won't believe the present I brought for you."

Tyler reached in his pocket, pulled the Camry's keys out, and tapped the trunk release. The lid popped open. Tyler walked back to the trunk. Brian prayed there was something, anything else in the trunk but what, or really who, he knew was in there.

Tyler reached in and pulled Daniela up from under her shoulders.

She wore her white veterinary scrubs with kittens on it. Her hair stuck out at odd angles from under a silver duct tape blindfold.

"Ta da!" Tyler said. "My first thought was your parents, but hey, you might enjoy that."

She didn't move. Brian's eyes went wide in panic. The stomach churn of anxiety charged in, but brought with it a rejuvenating adrenaline rush.

"You asshole," Brian wheezed.

"Fear not, bro! She's not dead. She's just a lightweight for sedatives. I used a Candy-sized dose and this one hasn't got Candy's gross weight by a long shot. But better safe than having her banging around in the trunk on the way here. And I didn't want her awake enough that I had to chase her around in here."

Tyler propped her up against the edge of the trunk.

"The bitch put up a fight. I was tempted to snuff her just to save time and energy. But the goal is to have you feel loss, and bringing her here dead wouldn't have the impact of seeing her die. Old Man Dunham taught me that lesson."

Brian looked around for the velvet rope, but didn't see it anywhere.

"But good old foster dad, he missed one thing. It would have hurt more if he'd made me kill the dog. That would have really screwed me up in the head." Tyler snort-laughed, frowned, then reapplied his sales-pitch smile. "So what I'm going to do, is have you kill her."

"No way in hell," Brian said. "I'll die first."

"No, you'll die second, unless I decide to just cut you free afterwards and leave you here for the cops. Still up in the air on that one. As a good citizen, how could I not call in the whereabouts of an escaped serial killer and his murdered girlfriend?"

Tyler gave Daniela a disapproving look. "But this won't do at all. We need her awake for this. Can't miss your own murder, right?"

Tyler slapped Daniela in the face. Twice. Hard. "Wake up, bitch!"

She rose to consciousness. She reached for her blindfold, but her wrists were tied together and secured at her waist. Terror spread across her face as she seemed to remember what had happened to her.

"No, Brian!" she slurred. "Stop!"

Tyler turned to Brian and mouthed 'She thinks I'm you!' He covered his mouth and pantomimed stifling a laugh.

Brian tried to call to Daniela and tell her he wasn't her kidnapper. But his words came out as painful, unintelligible rasps.

"Just get out of the goddamn trunk," Tyler said. He dragged her out of the trunk and plopped her down on the concrete floor. She made a wobbly attempt to sit up, but failed, still under the effects of the sedatives.

Tyler grabbed the cord that hung from the gym's pull bar. With a yank, he raised a set of black, iron weights from the stack at the other end of the gym. He tied the cord off to the bench support.

"You know what impresses me?" Tyler said to Brian. "How quickly I came up with this plan. I was furious with you and then like.... Pow! This whole plan came together at once. Dude, it was like an inspiration."

He went back to Daniela and dragged her to the other end of the gym.

"Brian, no!" Daniela said. Her words were fuzzy, but fast, and filled with fear. "Don't do this! Whatever you want, I'll do whatever you want!"

"Whatever I want?" Tyler said. He made a faux thoughtful face. "Tempting, but work before pleasure."

He placed her head on the remaining stack of weights, between the two guide cables, and right over the hole the centre pin used. The raised weights hung five feet over her head, centre pin pointed at her forehead like the sword of Damocles. She moaned and her head rolled between the cables.

Brian hoped she was too out of it to really understand what was happening. Tyler walked back to Brian.

"Just thirty pounds up there," he said, "but between the drop and the big pin, heavy enough to kill her, but light enough to make it interesting."

Brian wasn't going to play. Tyler had no leverage to make him do anything. He'd be dead soon anyway. Maybe if he didn't kill Daniela, she might survive.

"I won't do it," Brian muttered. His voice was weak, but his tone strong as steel.

"Sure you will," Tyler said. He smiled that evil smile of his. "Eventually."

He untied the cord from the bench support. The weights dropped a few inches and Brian caught his breath. Then Tyler yanked the cord and ran the weights back to the top. He shoved the end of the cord in Brian's mouth and pressed his jaw closed. "Now bite!"

Brian saw what was about to happen and clamped down on the cord. Tyler let go and the pressure of the weights jerked Brian's head forward and to the side. His manhandled neck bent and he screamed through clenched teeth.

"Wait, I need to ice the cake," Tyler said. He stepped back beside Daniela and pulled a playing card from his pocket. He showed it to Brian. The Queen of Hearts. "What else would the spurned lover use on his ex-girlfriend?" He dropped it on her chest.

Saliva slicked the cord and it slipped between Brian's teeth. He bit down harder. The nylon tasted like dirt and gasoline. His neck felt like it was ready to tear in two.

"Trouble, bro?" Tyler said. "You look stressed. Now for the cherry on this cake. Off with the blindfold so she can see who's actually ending her life. The look on her face will be priceless."

Tyler pulled his knife from his pocket, the dog-killing, foster-father-slaying special, and flipped it open. He knelt and tucked the tip under Daniela's tape blindfold.

CHAPTER FIFTY-FOUR

Two houses down in his search, and panic metastasised in Weissbard like a cancer. Both had been busts. That only left him two to go. The girl's life expectancy dropped exponentially with every second he wasted. And if, God forbid, all four were dry wells…the girl would be dead and he'd have a lot of trouble explaining following his gut and not staying at the kidnap scene and reporting it to Francisco. He didn't even want to think about that.

He pulled up to the third house, got out and walked up the driveway through the rain, too wet and too worried to even pay attention to the downpour. A subtle variation on every ranch house he'd stopped at, every home in the neighbourhood in fact. One of the bushes by the front stoop was just a blackened, leafless skeleton. Odd. Neighbourhoods like this had homeowners' associations that harped on residents to get things like that back up to code. Unless they were part-time residents and weren't home to fix it. He approached the garage door. The four windows were covered in newspaper. People often did that to keep the sun from fading things in the garage. But this was a north-facing door, out of indirect sunlight. And a date along one edge of the paper read that it was yesterday's paper. He drew his weapon and flicked off the safety.

A muffled shout came from the other side of the door. Then, softer, a female voice. Something clanked.

The cop in him said this didn't rise to probable cause. His gut screamed that it didn't give a shit, and get in there.

He ran to the front door. He reared back and kicked it. The doorjamb splintered into a dozen pieces. He charged in, pistol levelled. He ran down the hall to the kitchen, then turned right in the direction of the garage.

The door stood open. Decades of skill doing flash-scene assessments jumped into action and he soaked up the picture in a millisecond. On the other side sat Brian Sheridan, near naked except for work boots and shorts, bound in a chair next to a home-fitness machine. He had a cord stuck in his mouth that held a brace of weights suspended over the head of a bound and blindfolded Daniela.

Sheridan's eye were wide, his neck craned forward, his face beet red. Tears streamed down his cheeks. His terrified look telegraphed that he was about to lose control of that cord.

Weissbard charged in.

★ ★ ★

The instant the smash at the front door had rolled through the kitchen and into the garage, Tyler had reacted. He leapt like a cat to the far side of the doorway, knife at the ready for whoever came through.

Brian's psychic connection to his brother had grown stronger still. At this distance, he could feel Tyler's emotional state, and it wasn't one of fear. It was sheer predatory glee.

Weissbard appeared in the doorway, soaked to the skin, weapon drawn. Brian first felt relief, then panicked dread. As soon as he stepped through the threshold, Tyler would slice him in two.

Weissbard. Tyler. Daniela about to die as soon as his tenuous grip on the cord in his mouth gave way. It was all too much. Anxiety exploded from every nerve ending. His mind reeled as he involuntarily shook within the bindings. It took all his concentration to keep his mouth clamped shut and Daniela alive. He tried to warn Weissbard with his eyes, with a look, that death awaited inches away.

Weissbard missed the message, his eyes more focused on the girl in peril. He lowered his gun and sprang for the doorway.

His brother would have Weissbard's throat slashed before the cop knew what hit him. Seconds later, he'd kill Daniela. His complete powerlessness amplified Brian's anxiety.

Brian grabbed for a straw. He could feel Tyler's emotions stronger and stronger each day since Brian had abandoned his medications. Now they ran so powerful Brian could almost taste them. The transient link that once only sputtered when his conscious mind was at rest now crackled live all the time. Tyler made no mention of it, and God knows he would have gloated about any deeper insight into Brian's mind. If Brian could now receive so clearly, perhaps he could send.

Brian bit so hard on the cord it flattened between his teeth. Then he dropped his mental defences and let the anxiety flood in. The incapacitating, overwhelming sense of impending apocalypse took over. He looked in his brother's murderous eyes and psychically shouted "Tyler!"

Brian sent a blast of his roiling anxiety out across the room.

Weissbard crossed the threshold. Tyler coiled to lunge. Then his jaw dropped. His face paled. All his confidence, all his bravado seemed to drain away. His knife hand, seconds ago poised for the kill, shook like he had Parkinson's.

Brian's mouth twitched. The cord slipped. He bit down harder. Molars rolled in his jaw. An image of Daniela, smiling at him outside his apartment, appeared in his head. A tendon in his neck snapped like a stretched rubber band. The cord slipped free. It scorched a burn across his tongue and slid through his mouth. The steel cable zinged through the home gym's pulleys.

Weissbard sprang from the kitchen threshold. With more grace than a guy that big should have, Weissbard dove for the gym. One hand grabbed a support cable. The hand holding his gun shot out under the falling weights. The impact drove his arm down. He dropped to one knee, and cocked his arm straight up under the weights. Thirty accelerating pounds of iron slammed his elbow into the stack below. Bone cracked like dropped china.

But Weissbard held up the weight. The centre pin stopped a half inch from Daniela's duct-taped eyes. Brian nearly passed out with the rush of relief.

Tyler slithered over the Camry's rain-slicked hood and landed beside the red Honda. His eyes darted everywhere, driven by panic and confusion from his first full-blown encounter with Brian-level anxiety. He jumped into the Honda's driver's seat. Weissbard's head jerked in Tyler's direction at the slam of the Honda's door.

"Shit!" Weissbard said. He reached with his left hand to lever his right hand and his gun from under the weights.

The Honda roared to life with a belch of black smoke against the garage door. Tyres squealed and the car jumped into reverse. It crashed into the flimsy garage door and swept it out of its tracks and through the opening. The car barreled onto the driveway. A blast of the deluge outdoors blew into the garage.

The Honda rocketed down to the street, pushing the detached door like an eight-foot-tall plow. Then the door flew up and over the car's hood to land half-blocking the garage opening. The Honda sideswiped Weissbard's Charger in a crash of shattered side-view mirrors. The little car hit the rain-swept street in a lateral slide, skidded to a stop, then raced forward and out of sight.

In that moment, though Tyler was free, Brian didn't care. He was alive. More importantly, Daniela was alive.

Or so he hoped.

Weissbard winced, raised the weights, and placed his gun on the floor. He slid Daniela clear of the gym and lowered the weights. She didn't move. Brian held his breath.

"Is she okay?" he croaked.

Weissbard placed his fingers against Daniela's neck. He smiled, then gave her a quick inspection. "She's got a pulse. Strong, but slow. She may be drugged, have fainted, or both. She's out of it, but she seems okay."

"He drugged her."

Weissbard glanced at all the zip ties holding Brian in place. He looked around the garage and his eyes rested on a pair of hand pruners. He retrieved them and snipped Brian free.

"Now do you believe me?" Brian rasped. He started to stretch his arms and his right leg.

"I've believed you for a while, just couldn't find you."

Brian nodded toward where the Honda had made its exit. "That was my twin brother."

"Yeah, I put all that together. Better late than never. How badly are you hurt?"

"Bruised, mostly. But my left foot's broken."

"I'll call in an ambulance and we'll get you and Daniela to a hospital."

"I don't have to go back to jail now, right?"

Weissbard thought about it. "Uh, yeah, you are an escaped prisoner on bond. You'll need to go back to jail until the District Attorney agrees to drop the charges. Which he'll do as soon as he sees all the evidence about what really happened."

"You can help make that happen?"

Weissbard smiled, as if stoked by more than just job satisfaction. "Oh, yeah. I'll take this right to my sergeant and all the way up to the mayor. Trust me."

CHAPTER FIFTY-FIVE

Weissbard's call from the garage actually brought two sets of EMTs. One went straight to Daniela. The tension on their faces and the urgency in their acts dissipated as soon as they'd checked her vitals. Brian relaxed as well.

The second set approached Weissbard as he cradled his injured arm. He waved them off and over to Brian. They gave Brian a quick line of questions, then eased him from his chair and onto a gurney. As he lost sight of Daniela behind the tail of the Camry, he wondered if he'd ever see her again.

Between the lack of sleep, the beatings, and the anxiety relief, the rest of the ride to the hospital turned into a blur. As he passed in and out of various levels of consciousness, he experienced a swirling mix of anger, frustration and fear. But the emotions weren't his. All carried the bitter aftertaste of his brother. He could sense Tyler on the run.

★ ★ ★

As his hospital stay progressed, Brian was able to make some uncomfortable comparisons to his Palm Bay Preserve confinement. Bad food, long days alone, and his throbbing left foot in a sling that kept him damn near immobilised. But adding insult to literal injury, he had an ankle monitor on his right leg. He was, after all, still on bond from the Florida state penal system. The truth hadn't set him free as rapidly as Weissbard had promised. A uniformed police officer guarded the door to his room around the clock in case Tyler returned.

The doctors had reassembled his foot and said that with the right therapy he'd be up and about in a few weeks. When they were a bit evasive about any permanent damage, Brian flashed back to Tyler's signature foot drag, and hoped he'd end up nowhere near that bad off.

On his sixth day, while Brian was forcing down a lunch of limp vegetables and unknown meat, someone knocked against his open door. He looked over to see Daniela, wearing pink scrubs that had a pattern of tiny puppies. She gave a tentative wave.

"Hey, Bri."

She hadn't been to see him since their rescue. He wasn't sure that she would ever visit, given everything that had happened. Seeing her engendered a sense of relief, tinged with sadness. "Daniela, come in."

She came as close as the end of his bed, as if a communicable disease afflicted him, not traumatic injuries. She didn't say a word.

"The police said Tyler didn't hurt you," Brian said to break the awkward silence.

"No. A few bruises from the struggle but that's all. I don't remember anything clearly after that, until I was in the ambulance on the way to the hospital."

Brian thought that was a very good thing.

"You look good," she offered.

He knew that he was a bruised, swollen mess, but he appreciated the lie. "Thanks. See, no harm done at all getting off my meds."

Daniela managed a weak smile.

"I guess you know the truth. My twin brother and all."

"Yes, Detective Weissbard explained it all to me, and the whole story's blown up all over the internet. Totally bizarre, right?"

"To say the least."

Silence hung in the air like a guillotine.

"Look, Bri. . . ." Daniela started.

"Don't worry," Brian said. "I know that everything that's happened the last two weeks has ruined whatever we might have had."

Relief spread over Daniela's face. "Oh, good. I mean, you're a good dude, Bri. But when Tyler kidnapped me, I really thought it was you with a dye job. He *was* your twin and all. I just don't know if I can get past that image."

"Hey, I appreciate you coming to clear the air about it," Brian said.

Daniela stepped back from the bed. "Okay, great. I'm glad you've gotten through this. I really hope everything works out for you."

"Same for you."

She flashed the same timid wave she made when she'd entered the room, and then backed out the door.

Brian hadn't really expected anything more from her. In fact, he wouldn't have been surprised by far less. What she'd been through would likely kill a strong relationship, and theirs had been far from that to begin with. It was nice of her, and a bit brave, to not leave the whole thing hanging.

Two deep voices began a low, professional-level conversation in the hall. Then there was a second knock on his door. Brian had been practically alone for six days, now he was the most popular guy in the hospital.

Detective Weissbard walked in, beaming. One arm was in a sling. Brian hadn't seen him since making a statement that first day he'd been admitted. He didn't think he'd ever seen him smiling.

"Brian, looks like the hospital is about to release you and make you a free man."

Brian glanced at his ankle monitor. "Freer, at least."

"I can take care of the rest." Weissbard pulled the unlock device for the monitor out of his back pocket. "The DA has officially withdrawn all the charges related to the Playing Card killings and bail violations. He's even expunged your record so the arrests won't come up in background checks."

That solved about half of Brian's problems. As Weissbard bent over Brian's leg and began to unlock the monitor, Brian asked the question he wished Weissbard had already answered. The fact that the detective hadn't meant Brian wasn't going to like what he was about to hear.

"Has Tyler been caught?" Brian said.

Weissbard's smile dwindled to nothing. "Still in the wind, but likely far away. His car was found abandoned at a Wal-Mart in Valdosta, Georgia three days ago. Two cars were stolen in town that day. He might have taken one of them, he might have hitched a ride, he might have stowed away on a freight train for all we know. He's got no credit cards and no cell phone, so he'd going to be tough to find. But we'll find him. He'll surface somewhere. But trust me, it will be a long way from here. The whole state of Florida is on the lookout for him."

"I'm sure you're right," Brian said.

Weissbard zipped the monitor's band into two and pulled it off Brian's leg. "There you go. You had a crazy story from the start. But you understand why I thought you were the killer?"

Brian definitely understood that was as close as he was going to get to a Weissbard apology. "The evidence was stacked in that direction. I'm just glad that you changed your mind and got to that house in time."

A commotion echoed in the hallway. Then in strode Chance Monroe, resplendent in a light grey suit and bright yellow tie. He pushed an empty hospital wheelchair in front of him. His artificial broad smile seemed glued in place. Brian swore he'd whitened his teeth for today.

"Detective! Good to see you've removed that unconstitutional monitor. Brian, time to get you home, a free man."

Weissbard's eyes narrowed. "Monroe, let the kid go home in peace. He doesn't need to be one of your media spectacles."

"Oh, yes he does. Son, a media spectacle is exactly what you need. If you don't publicise the shit out of your exoneration, the rest of the world is going to keep looking at you as the Playing Card Killer. Everyone remembers your arrest. I'll make certain everyone remembers your vindication from the Tampa Bay PD's witch hunt."

Weissbard balled his fists. Brian touched the cop's arm with his fingertips.

"No, it's fine," Brian said. "He's right."

Thinking about how this whole event was going to impact the rest of his life had hatched a few spells of anxiety the last two days. The falsely accused often carried the undeserved mark of the guilty in the public's eye. What appeared to be Chance Monroe's uncharacteristic altruism was likely just a reach for more publicity. But Brian was still going to take advantage of it.

A pretty young woman in a sharp, dark blue pants suit and heels walked in carrying a new men's suit on a hanger.

"My assistant coincidentally has appropriate clothes in just your size. Now get yourself dressed to impress."

CHAPTER FIFTY-SIX

Twenty minutes later, Chance checked his hair one last time in the reflection of the glass doors, then wheeled Brian out of the hospital exit. A wall of local and national media greeted them. Still cameras clicked and flashed white strobes. Red lights lit up on video cameras. An unintelligible tangle of shouted questions arose from the crowd.

Chance rolled Brian up beside a set of microphones on the hospital sidewalk. He held up a hand and the crowd went quiet.

"Today you see the righting of another miscarriage of the justice system as Brian Sheridan goes home a free and vindicated man."

Seemingly from out of nowhere, Derek and Camilla suddenly appeared behind Brian's wheelchair. It appeared that Camilla had her teeth whitened for the day as well, and perhaps endured a few shots of Botox.

"After all my years practising law," Chance continued, "I pride myself on being able to immediately identify an innocent man. I represent no other. This case once again proves me correct."

Brian stifled a moan. Chance had conveniently forgotten that just after he'd been released on bail, he'd told his parents that Brian was most likely guilty.

"So the family wants to put this all behind them, and hopes that you'll respect their privacy as they come to grips with all they have had to endure."

The family? Brian thought.

"And remember," Chance said. "When you step into my office, it's the only time you'll win leaving everything to Chance."

Questions exploded from the crowd. Chance waved them away with a plastic smile and wheeled Brian down to the second of two white limousines waiting at the curb. His parents got into the first. Chance made a big demonstration about helping Brian in the rear door. Inside, a pair of used crutches lay against the far door. Brian scooted across as best he could with his bulky foot cast. Chance followed him in and took the rearward facing seat opposite Brian. He slammed the door and the limo leapt from the curb. All the simulated warmth left Chance's face and he loosened his tie. His cell phone rang. He answered it and began to harangue someone on the other end about a DUI case.

Brian stared out the window, even though the black tint made it almost impenetrable. At first he wasn't certain, but a landmark later he knew the car wasn't heading in the direction of his parents' house. He looked ahead out the windshield and the other white limo was gone.

Chance hung up his phone and uttered a whispered curse to himself.

"We're not going to my parents' house?" Brian asked.

Chance looked over like he just realised Brian was there. "Are you kidding? Of course not. The court says you are innocent. It's the perfect time for them to get some distance from any future legal issues you might cause. I even convinced your therapist to release you from your last few months of treatment, certified cured. He sold out cheap, trust me. When I told you that you'd be free once you got out of the hospital, I wasn't kidding."

"This whole show today at the hospital entrance was about covering my parents' asses. It wasn't for me at all, was it?"

Chance punched open the door to the liquor cabinet. "Kid, you aren't the one paying the bill."

* * *

Twenty minutes later, Brian exited the limo and started his on-the-job crutch training. The pounds of bulky extra weight at the end of his foot made it even more of a challenge. Chance shouted to him that his assistant would be by in an hour to pick up the suit Brian had on. Brian managed to hobble his way to his front door, unlock it, and hop inside. The suitcase and backpack he'd taken to his parents' house sat right inside the doorway.

Aw, how thoughtful of Derek and Camilla, Brian thought with bitter sarcasm.

The place felt like a brick pizza oven. He went to check the air-conditioning controls. Off. His landlord must have cut off the air, figuring Brian wasn't coming back. If the landlord was going to be stuck with an unpaid electric bill, he wanted to minimise his losses. Brian turned the air-conditioning back on. A gust of hot, then cooling, air puffed from the vent over his head.

In the quiet of his apartment, he realised how alone he was. No girlfriend, no family. Even the only person he worked with, if Brian even still had a job, was dead. This was going to take some getting used to.

He shuddered when he realised he wasn't completely alone. Somewhere out there he did have a brother.

Completely alone would have felt much better.

CHAPTER FIFTY-SEVEN

Weissbard rolled his Charger into a parking spot at the police station and killed the engine. Releasing Sheridan's ankle monitor likely would be the high point of his day. What waited for him inside wasn't going to be anywhere near as warm and fuzzy.

He passed several uniformed officers on the way to the building. His old problem of having the average cop not know him was officially a thing of the past. Each officer he saw now knew who he was. He might have saved two lives, but he was still the detective who let the Playing Card Killer get away. Most looked away as soon as they recognised him. The rest gave him a pointed look of disgust.

No one knew all the details. No one asked. All everyone cared to know was that the supposed superstar detective from the NYPD had the Playing Card Killer cornered, and didn't take him down. In what most considered a shoot-first-justify-later situation, Weissbard hadn't shot at all.

And while his reception outside the precinct was ice cold, the one that awaited him inside was going to be hot as hell.

He'd filed all his reports about the incident at the house with Tyler. Francisco hadn't commented. Dying of anticipation the next day, Weissbard even asked if Francisco had any questions about it. The sergeant said no, and they'd discuss it later.

That kind of response was worse than bad. Francisco wasn't going to be content to underhand toss him a ball of bad feedback about his performance. He was winding up for a full-blown pitch, a fastball of condemnation with enough heat to burn his career to the ground. Weissbard knew he was about to step into the batter's box. Francisco had scheduled a meeting with him for five minutes from now.

Weissbard entered the precinct. As he stepped into the detective squad room, the office went silent. The detectives knew more of the story, knew the choice Weissbard had made between killing a murderer and saving the life of an innocent woman. But they also knew the half-dozen protocols he'd skipped that got him into the position in the first place. They knew the daily decisions a detective made about when to stay behind the line drawn by departmental policy, and when to step over it. Sympathy tainted their silence. That only made Weissbard more certain that what awaited him with Francisco was worse than he'd expected.

Weissbard made only fleeting eye contact with any of the others as he walked to Francisco's office. He knocked on the door. Francisco called him to come in.

Weissbard stepped in and his heart sank to somewhere below his knees. Francisco sat beside his desk. Lieutenant Liz Hanley of Internal Affairs sat behind it. The short African American woman was built practically square and had her hair shorn short enough that she could be described as bald. She had a reputation for being tough as hell. Everyone hated IA. Something had to be really screwed up for her to jump into the fray. Weissbard was sure he qualified as a 'really screwed-up' event. For Francisco to be smiling at her side meant he'd invited her in to investigate. That asshole.

"Close the door and have a seat, Detective." Lieutenant Hanley's voice was naturally deep and authoritative. The weight of it pressed Weissbard down into the chair opposite the desk.

Francisco tried to stifle a grin and look professional. He failed.

"Sergeant Francisco and I have been discussing your performance on the Tyler Tracy case." Hanley wasn't the type to use the media nickname for the serial killer. "I thought we'd have a private discussion before anything escalated to a disciplinary hearing."

Disciplinary hearing? His pal Francisco had been working overtime to sink him if a disciplinary hearing was the next step on the ladder.

Lt. Hanley looked down at the top page of a sheaf of papers. "Brian Sheridan came into the station early in the investigation. Sergeant Francisco sent this promising lead to you."

Weissbard's spine stiffened. That prick Francisco had done nothing of the kind, or at best had done it indirectly by having Weissbard clean up nuisance tips. Outnumbered two-to-one in the room, he opted to stick with what he knew were facts. "I was the first to speak with Sheridan."

"And the last for a while. You didn't believe him when he told you things he couldn't possibly have known about the killings."

"Well, no. I did believe him. Dr. Kent Williams spoke with him and said he wasn't credible."

"Weissbard," Francisco said. "If I sent him to you, that should have counted more than what some doctor says."

Weissbard was about to snap back that Francisco hadn't even known about Sheridan until much later, but Lt. Hanley cut him off.

"Now, you were convinced that Mr. Sheridan was the killer for a while."

Weissbard knew he had to start mounting a defence, because this witch hunt was just getting started. "Yes, as did the rest of the department and the District Attorney."

"Mostly based on your investigation, it seems. An investigation that came to the completely wrong conclusion. But let's talk about the last few days. Sergeant Francisco investigated and discounted a surveillance video supposedly of Mr. Sheridan at a Wallaby convenience store on the night he escaped from his parents' house. You went back there to cast doubt on his investigation?"

"No, I didn't know Sergeant Francisco had been there at all. I was just driving by and it seemed like a place Sheridan might have been seen."

"That's a hell of a coincidence," Francisco said.

"The video did show Tyler in the stolen Camry that night," Weissbard shot back.

"The DA disagrees," Lieutenant Hanley said. "The images won't be used be used at trial. He believes they are inconclusive."

"Which is exactly what I determined when I saw them," Francisco said.

"Then there is the kidnapping of Ms. Schiavetta," Lieutenant Hanley said.

Dread swept away some of Weissbard's righteous indignation. Everything up to now had been Francisco's bullshit spin on the facts. Lieutenant Hanley was about to flip over a rock covering an actual screw-up.

"You discovered her abduction when you arrived at her apartment," she continued.

Which would have been guarded if Francisco hadn't called off the surveillance, he wanted to say. But he knew it would just sound petulant. "And I called for backup right away."

"But instead of continuing the investigation there, you left Officer Beatriz Allen, six weeks out of the academy, in charge of the crime scene."

Six weeks? Shit! "Time was of the essence. I knew that Tyler was planning on killing her. I had a potential location where she might be held. Officer Allen could secure the scene by just closing the door and standing in front of it. Once I found Ms. Schiavetta, any evidence at the kidnap scene would simply be corroborative."

"So you called for backup to secure the apartment, but not to rescue Ms. Schiavetta?"

"In the time it would take to explain everything, Ms. Schiavetta might have already been murdered. Sergeant Francisco would have to redirect a lot of officers to four potential sites. I thought I could get the job done faster."

"Faster than the whole Tampa PD?" Francisco said, voice dripping with sarcasm.

Weissbard had enough of the smug bastard. He looked straight at Lt. Hanley. "Honestly, I doubted, in the time available, or *any* amount of time, that Sergeant Francisco would listen to any suggestions I had."

"And that's the real problem here," Lieutenant Hanley said. "By all accounts, you haven't gotten along with your sergeant since you started here. And while a little social friction is no big deal, now a serial killer is still on the loose because you think a former NYPD cop knows better than the veterans in the Tampa PD."

"Now wait a minute," Weissbard said. "If I'd gotten there any later, that woman would have been dead, Tyler would have still escaped, but now he'd have had Sheridan with him. And all of you would have still been chasing Sheridan, because I was the only one who even knew Tyler existed."

"Another example of not sharing information with everyone else," Francisco said.

"I'd just found out about Tyler," Weissbard said.

Francisco shook his head in a fine display of mock disappointment.

"This discussion just confirmed everything Sergeant Francisco relayed in his report," Lieutenant Hanley said. "There will be a disciplinary hearing tomorrow at 10:00 a.m. You should call your union rep. You have the day free to go home and prepare."

Weissbard shook with frustration. He wanted to rail against Francisco and this back-channel kangaroo court. But he knew adding anything here was a waste of time. Lt. Hanley was just here to check his neck size so that she could have the proper noose ready tomorrow. Events had been twisted around one hundred and eighty degrees. Francisco wanted him out of the Tampa PD. Lieutenant Hanley wanted to serve up a scapegoat for this investigation's shortcomings. It was the perfect storm and he was at the centre of it. He wondered what his union rep's phone number was.

He stood without a word and left Francisco's office. He ran right into Chief of Police Everett Stamp.

Stamp was a crew-cut, barrel-chested bulldog of a guy, a cop's cop, or so everyone had told Weissbard. Weissbard had never met the man, and, with so many layers of command between them, Weissbard hadn't ever thought he would. These certainly weren't the circumstances he wanted to foster the unlikely get-together.

Stamp sized him up. "You're Detective Weissbard?"

"Yes, sir."

Stamp broke into a wide smile and shook his hand. "Good work on the Tracy case."

Stamp spun the two of them around and presented Weissbard to the rest of the room. The detectives were silent, mouths open. They'd already been riveted on Francisco's doorway, watching for Weissbard's exit from the office. The Chief of Police had just turned that sideshow into a spectacle.

"Gentlemen," Stamp announced. "This man has done some great police work. A lot of old-fashioned investigation and a lot of trusting his instincts, I'll guess. Even when most of the evidence pointed one way, he still checked the leads pointing in the opposite direction, never let conventional wisdom colour his assessment. If it wasn't for his initiative, a woman would be dead right now.

When the choice was saving a life or cuffing the perp, he made the right choice. That's because Tyler Tracy will still see justice. All of you will make that happen." He turned to Weissbard and clamped him on the shoulder. "You were NYPD, right?"

"Yes, sir."

"I grew up in Brooklyn. Moved down here before high school and lost the accent. Good to have another New Yorker on the force."

Stamp turned and looked into Francisco's office. By now, Francisco and Lieutenant Hanley were both standing by the threshold. "Francisco, good man you have here. Hanley? What are you doing here? I wasn't aware of any IA investigation going on."

Weissbard stifled a smile. She and Francisco must have been targeting him under the radar, hoping for a big splash when they shot him down. Looks like they were about to make their own splash.

"No, Chief," Lieutenant Hanley said. "Just dropping by to congratulate the detective."

Stamp nodded and left the squad room. Lieutenant Hanley followed two steps behind, red-faced. Stunned conversations broke out between the detectives in the squad room. Francisco stepped up beside Weissbard and whispered through clenched teeth.

"This isn't over by a long shot."

Weissbard was certain it wasn't. "No, Sergeant. We've still got a killer to catch."

He headed for his desk and wondered how the hell he was going to make that happen.

CHAPTER FIFTY-EIGHT

Low-wattage bulbs barely light the motel room. But that may be a good thing. Mismatched, dated lamps sit on chipped particleboard furniture. Rumpled sheets more grey than white lay tangled with a thin bedspread at the foot of a lumpy queen mattress. A louvered closet door hangs crooked in its frame. Split seams in the rough, worn carpet open around the room like tiny mouths in the floor, ready to bite feet careless enough to tread upon them. Black mould speckles the lower, curling edges of the room's wallpaper. Brian is glad he's spared the view of whatever bathroom would accompany such a dismal room.

Tyler's emotions are easy to sense. Depression. Failure. Anger. The three twist and turn around each other, trading places back and forth from dominant to secondary moods. So vibrant is his filial connection that Brian believes with time he could actually read Tyler's clear thoughts.

He moves to a sagging desk in front of a window. Thin drapes are pulled tight, but the glow of blue and red neon bleeds through from the outside world. He pulls an older model black laptop from the drawer, opens it, and turns on the power. The machine boots up and he summons Planet Earth View. He types in a search for Moultrie, Tennessee. A map of a small rural town south of Nashville fills the screen. He begins to scroll through street views with one hand.

The other hand rummages in his pocket, finds something hard and rectangular, and extracts it. He places a box of playing cards on the desk beside the laptop. Brian cringes at the familiar red pattern of two inverted women over spring and winter trees.

Tyler's three emotions beat a hasty retreat, replaced by one new one, stronger and more focused than all three combined.

The thrill of predation.

* * *

Brian's eyes snapped open. The red alarm clock face and the glow from his cell-phone charger were all that lit his bedroom. He turned on the light. Days ago, as soon as he stopped taking the painkillers for his mending foot, he'd put a notebook and pen on his nightstand. He grabbed both and finally put them to use.

With hurried strokes, he transcribed everything he could remember from his vision. The hotel-room décor, the colour of the outside sign, Moultrie, the name of the town Tyler was in, or just the town about to become his hunting ground.

Brian would find out which. One night at a time, one clue at a time. He'd do what he knew the police likely couldn't. Track down Tyler's location.

The throbbing pain in Brian's left foot amped itself up. He leaned back into bed and elevated his foot on top of a pillow. The pain eased.

Once he found Tyler, then what? Call the Tampa cops? Call the local cops? The FBI? If they caught him, then there'd be days of extraditing him back to Florida, a year before bringing him to trial. Then Brian would have to move back into the spotlight, with hours of public testimony and a cross-examination on the stand by some jerk like Chance Monroe, if not Chance himself, the soulless media whore. Assuming Tyler was convicted, and not allowed to skate on some psychological loophole, then what? Florida had the death penalty, but Brian didn't remember anyone being executed without spending decades dragging out the process with baseless appeals. When the blessed event of Tyler's lethal injection finally did occur, the media would be dragging Brian back centre stage again for his reaction to it.

That scenario meant thirty more years of Tyler languishing in prison. But his brother would only be there half the time. He'd be paroled to see the world through Brian's eyes whenever Tyler slept. Even worse, there'd be thirty years of Brian forced to live the hell-on-Earth experience of Tyler's incarceration every time Brian went to sleep. Decades of nightly punishment for his brother's crimes.

Unless Brian went back on his medication schedule, and let

the pharma break the link to his brother. But he'd come too far, experienced too much, felt too free, to snap those shackles back on.

No. His brother had spawned too much evil already, ruined too many lives. The legal system would only slow the rate at which Tyler poisoned the world. Instead, that flow just needed to end.

Brian decided he'd solve this problem on his own.

CHAPTER FIFTY-NINE

Two months later.

Tracking his brother had been easier than he'd thought, and it made Brian realise what a helpless target he'd been in Tyler's psychic sights.

But before Brian had even started, he'd taken steps to protect himself. A move to day shift at Orange Star Trucking meant Brian could adjust his sleep schedule to the opposite of the one Tyler favoured. He awoke when Tyler went to sleep, usually about 2:00 a.m., so any connections Tyler might have would be the boring routine of Brian puttering in his apartment in the wee hours, or his repetitive morning routine at the start of the workday. Brian double-checked everything he did during those hours to ensure that Tyler, if he was tuning in, would see nothing suspicious.

Going to bed ridiculously early meant that he slept through Tyler's prime waking hours, the evening and night. When he awoke, he'd write down all that he'd seen, every street sign, every person, every activity. A comprehensive understanding of his brother's life soon took shape. Tyler lived in the Lamplighter Motel, a one-storey, L-shaped dive so old its original name included the words 'motor court'. It sat on Highway 41 north of the little burg of Moultrie, and near several other small towns. Tyler made ends meet through a combination of low-end burglary and an ascetic lifestyle. The good news was, he hadn't killed again.

The bad news was, he wanted to. During each mental connection, Brian felt Tyler's sickening desire, his rising hunger for the rush of the hunt and the orgasmic release of the kill. When Brian tuned in one night to Tyler staking out a women's gym from the front seat of his car, he knew he'd run out of time. He had to act.

Brian headed to Moultrie that Friday night after work, a long drive he made during Tyler's usual waking hours. Once he arrived at the Lamplighter, he parked a bit down the road at a convenience store. A large coffee combined with a mix of over-the-counter stimulants pumped him up. For the next day or two, he might not sleep, but afterwards, he was certain he'd spend the rest of his life sleeping like a baby.

He caught his first sight of Tyler midday as his brother left his rented room for the Lamplighter's weed-choked parking lot. Tyler had shaved his head and grew a moustache and goatee. He sported dark glasses, though the day didn't demand it. He wore jeans, boots, and a faded T-shirt, an ensemble apparently designed for blending into a relatively redneck crowd. Tyler made his familiar right-foot-drag-walk across the lot to an older model pickup with Georgia tags.

Brian's heart pounded. His left foot throbbed, as if it were shrieking at the bastard that had permanently damaged it. Anger surged through him, and he gripped the steering wheel until his knuckles turned white.

He could finish this now. Fire up the car, blast across the street and catch Tyler before he made it to the truck. Brian imagined the shocked, horrified look on Tyler's face as he stared through the approaching windshield and recognised Brian at the wheel. Brian relished the potential surge of satisfaction of plowing Tyler under the front bumper of his car, then the gratifying crunch of Tyler's rib cage after backing the rear tyres over the killer to finish him off.

But that would be too quick, it would be too messy, and it would lack the kind of justice Brian's true plan would deliver.

Hours later, after night fell, Brian pulled on a pair of latex gloves. They made a sharp snap when he released the ends, gave his skin a tingle. Anxiety's familiar upwell began to swirl in the pit of his stomach. In the next few hours, a hundred, no, a thousand things could go wrong. Random police patrols, stray dogs, the desk clerk might actually look out a window and see Brian approaching.

But his worst fear was that he'd lose his nerve. That somewhere between his first step out of the car and the last milliseconds of his brother's poisoned existence, Brian would quit. Sweat beaded between his palm and the glove. His right leg began to jiggle.

He punched his dashboard in frustration. He forced back the

anxiety like swallowing bad food. His emotional reactions would have their place later. Now it was time to finish what he'd started. More accurately, to finish what his brother had started.

It was time for revenge.

Brian turned his brother's meticulous planning for worst-case scenarios against him. Tyler had prepped the bathroom window in his room for a quick escape, removing the latch, oiling the runners, and placing a crate outside underneath as a step during a potential emergency exit. Brian's plan was to reverse the path, and use the exit for egress.

He left the car and snuck around to the rear of the hotel in the darkness. He crept under the bathroom window to Tyler's unit and waited. Silence reigned inside, as it did from the rooms on either side. He stepped onto the crate, slid the window up, and slipped inside.

A light at the base of a cheap wall-mounted hair dryer gave the bathroom more illumination than Brian needed, or wanted. The stained, rusting collection of shopworn ceramic lived down to all his expectations. He wondered if someone would actually be cleaner after washing there. He stepped into Tyler's room.

The view of the room flashed Brian back to his first post-captivity connection with Tyler. The dingy room looked no better in colour than in his first black-and-white vision. Same curling wallpaper. Same threadbare bedding. But now he had the added pleasure of sampling the room's stale, mildew-tinged scent. There was something to be said for his visions restricting themselves to a limited visual medium.

He had his plan. He had everything he needed stuffed in the cargo pockets of his pants. He stepped inside the closet and closed the door. The view through the louvered slats perfectly framed the desk, chair and window.

Brian leaned back against the wall and waited.

CHAPTER SIXTY

Seconds before Tyler entered the room, Brian felt him. That familiar, churning mix of anger and frustration was practically Tyler's emotional fingerprint. Brian had experienced it first-hand for days, then remotely for months. While a prisoner in the Palm Bay Preserve bathroom, sensing Tyler's impending arrival had stoked debilitating fear. Now, it spurred joyful anticipation.

Tyler entered the room and turned on the lights. They were dim, but after waiting in the dark, even the low light passing through the closet door louvers made Brian squint. His eyes soon adjusted. Tyler crossed the room with his signature right-foot drag, a bit more pronounced than Brian remembered.

A bit worse for the wear, Brian thought. *Tough break, asshole.*

Tyler tossed a wrinkled paper shopping bag on the bed. It landed sideways and an assortment of smartphones and jewellery skidded out across the ratty bedspread. Tyler plopped down at the desk, back to Brian, and opened his laptop.

Tyler began to flip through screens as he surfed the internet. Brian couldn't see what he was doing, but whatever it was didn't matter. It was time to get the show started.

Brian pulled his phone out of his pocket. He scrolled down to a waiting message, pressed Send, and returned the phone to his pocket. With two fingers, he eased the closet door open.

A few seconds later, Tyler's phone beeped. He gave it a confused look, as if he hadn't heard the noise before. Brian thought that could indeed be true. Tyler probably hadn't gotten a text message until now. Who would he be texting with?

Tyler checked the message. His spine snapped straight. He dropped the phone back on the desk.

Now Tyler radiated one overwhelming emotion. Distress. Brian smiled as he thought about the text message replaying through Tyler's mind.

Prepare to see life from both sides. Receive instead of giving with the Better Relationship Institute.

"B. R. I.," Brian whispered to himself. "Bri. I see you get it, jackass."

Tyler nearly sent his laptop flying as he jumped to his feet, leaned over the desk and yanked the curtains apart. His eyes swept the dark, vacant parking lot and the empty street beyond. Tyler's surging paranoia now flowed to Brian through the empathic connection.

Then Brian summoned his anxiety, the debilitating, nerve-frying, mind-scrambling panic he'd fought all his life. The unwelcome friend he'd fought back as he left his car for this encounter now had an engraved invitation. He remembered multiple childhood incidents where the emotion had swelled to fill his whole world. His pulse soared. His nerves tingled. Sweat formed on his gloved palms.

He took all that passionate panic and did what brothers are supposed to do.

He shared.

Months ago in the garage, Brian had been able to imprint Tyler with a hint of his own psychological issues, little more than the spray from the waves of angst that pounded Brian's mental shores. Now Brian was stronger, his mind clearer, his resolve focused by months of plotting this revenge. Brian pushed back along their psychic connection, and sent Tyler a crushing tsunami of anxiety.

Tyler shuddered under the impact. With shaking hands, he gripped the window frame for support. His legs buckled and he collapsed back into the desk chair.

Brian summoned the second wave in Tyler's mental demise. He painted himself a vision of his mental fabrication, dear Mr. Jitters, with his long, spindly, spider-like limbs, his carnival-coloured clothes, and his death-white face with the painted skeleton's smile. He added the screeching maniacal laugh. Reliving it sent the hairs twitching on the back of Brian's neck. Then he sent Mr. Jitters for a call on Tyler.

Brian couldn't see what Tyler saw in his mind's eye, but he could feel the impact of it. Sheer, knife-edged terror swept his brother. He backpedalled the chair away from the desk and in Brian's direction.

"What in the fuck are you?" Tyler shrieked. "Get the hell away from me!"

Brian's moment arrived. He pulled a short length of white, nylon rope from his pocket, gripped it in both gloved hands, and snapped it into a loop. He rushed from the closet. He had to favour his healing left foot, reminding him of Tyler's torture. The memory added a last load of fuel to his burning vengeance. He flipped the rope loop over Tyler's head and yanked it tight.

Tyler choked. He clawed at the rope with both hands, but could get no grip. Brian pulled harder and Tyler's hands dropped back to his sides.

Brian bent his head to Tyler's ear. "This is how the other end really feels, Ty. Is it everything you imagined? Ready for that sweet release you forced on all those others? Meredith, Carla, Keisha, Sidney, Candy? All of them are just waiting for you to die like this."

With the drapes pulled back and the desk light illuminating them, Tyler and Brian cast a sharp reflection in the window against the night's black background. In the reflection, Brian's face hovered just above and behind Tyler's, two white masks against a dark abyss. Tyler's wide, terrified eyes made Brian smile.

The differences in hair couldn't distract Brian from the inescapable similarities. Eyes. Nose. Mouth. He and Tyler were two mirror images, reflections in a reflection.

The fear drained from Tyler's eyes. The corners of his lips turned up.

"See," he barely wheezed out. "You finally feel it."

The realisation came like a flash of lightning. The fixation. The hunt. The lust for revenge. The pleasure at the edge of this kill. In seconds he'd become what he thought he was about to destroy.

If he didn't stop it. Now.

He pulled the rope tighter. Tyler gagged. His eyes bulged and his face turned blue. Then his body went limp.

Brian dropped the rope and lowered his brother to the floor. He checked for a pulse under the swelling ligature mark around Tyler's neck. Still there. He sighed with relief. In that last moment, he'd only wanted his brother unconscious. He had succeeded. He rolled Tyler over and bound his hands together behind him with the nylon rope. He pulled his phone from his pocket and dialled.

"Moultrie County Nine-One-One. What is your emergency?"

"Tyler Tracy, a dangerous fugitive, is in Room 122 at the Lamplighter Motel on Highway 41. You need to send someone to pick him up."

AFTERWORD

There is something a bit disconcerting about identical twins.

Sorry, all you twins out there. Nothing personal. But we are hardwired to see everyone around us as a unique individual. The wide range of facial features people have are likely there to make the thousands of different combinations we need to quickly and automatically assign a different identity to each person we meet. So when we see two people next to each other who we can't tell apart, it naturally inspires a double-take. I mean, that's the whole gimmick behind the old Doublemint Chewing Gum Twins ad campaign, right?

A number of studies, especially the landmark, long-running Minnesota Family Twin Study, show that when separated early, the genetic make-up of the twins has more of an effect on their likes and personalities than different environments do. The Minnesota study assigned seventy percent of IQ level to genetics and only thirty percent to environment. The studies also cite multiple examples of twins raised apart, unaware of each other, who end up with eerily parallel lives.

So that gave me the spark to start the blaze that became this book. What if there were twins born with some serious psychological damage who were separated at birth? They would both teeter on sanity's razor's edge, with that environmental thirty percent being the breeze that could push them to the side of good or evil. And while we don't want to admit it, what if Darwinian processes meant that tipping to the side of evil, to prioritising self-preservation, made that person stronger? Now there's some conflict to wrap the story around.

And what kind of reaction would Brian have when meeting his evil alter ego? One study found that eighty percent or reunited twins instantly feel closer to their twin than to the families who raised them. So poor Brian, longing for family his whole life, would finally feel the intimacy of it, and be repulsed by it at the same time. Kind of like finding out you love the taste of raw squid. This story idea now had real traction.

But what about this psychic connection Brian and Tyler have? Lame plot device? I mean, Dumas used it in 1844 in *The Corsican Brothers*.

Well, twenty percent of twins claim to feel a psychic connection with their sibling. Many say they somehow felt that there was someone else out there that matched them, even though they were unaware of a lost twin or even of their own adoption. As with all things psychic, the stories are anecdotal and impossible to prove using the scientific method. But in the way of anecdotes, one set of twins I know do seem to possess a special connection. And it is far more than just finishing each other's sentences.

When asked if he is hungry, one of the twins I know may respond that he isn't, but his brother is. When his brother enters the room minutes later, he asks what's around to snack on. One twin in the classroom will stop work and tell the teacher his brother needs help, at the same moment his brother has fallen during recess. The two will get dressed separately, and often select the same or similar clothes, commenting that it will match his brother's.

How far can a connection like that stretch? Well, halfway up the east coast of the United States in my fictitious world. And that gave me another way to make the story of Tyler and Brian even creepier.

In this story, I painted Detective Sergeant Francisco as a real jerk. In the real world, I doubt that anyone like that could ever rise to a position of authority in the Tampa Bay Police Department. Ditto the corrupt system portrayed in the Polk County jail scenes. Just plot devices. Law enforcement has a tough, thankless job, and I'm glad they are there keeping society from unravelling every day.

Special thanks to nurse and fellow author Rita Brandon for again stepping up with medical advice on describing Tyler's improperly healed foot. You'll make me medically competent yet.

And thanks to amazing Beta readers and supporters Paul Siluch, Teresa Robeson, Janet Guy and Belinda Whitney. You folks are amazing companions on this writing odyssey.

Above all, thank you to my wife, Christy, who puts up with all the nonsense that being married to a writer entails. Without you, there is no me.

Russell James
September 14, 2018